Vamp
Until
Ready

JAMES MAGRUDER

RATTLING GOOD YARNS
PRESS

Rattling Good Yarns Press
33490 Date Palm Drive 3065
Cathedral City CA 92235
USA
www.rattlinggoodyarns.com

Cover Design: Rattling Good Yarns Press

Library of Congress Control Number: 2021940429
ISBN: 978-1-955826-00-6

First Edition

Also by James Magruder

Fiction

Sugarless

Let Me See It

Love Slaves of Helen Hadley Hall

Worth Our Breath (a chapbook)

Theater

Three French Comedies

for *Kennie Pressman* & *Robert Moss,*
who set me on a proper course
once upon a time

Part One

Cary Dunkler

1980

"Aunt Polly, it ain't fair. Somebody's got to be glad to see Huck."

~ *The Adventures of Tom Sawyer*

On my first audition for a professional theater, I chose not to sing something upbeat and youthful like "Corner of the Sky" from *Pippin* or "Something's Comin'" from *West Side Story*. Prepped by my best friend, Robin Tascher, I sang "The Ballad of Immoral Earnings" from *The Threepenny Opera*. In *German*. I kid you not. *Auf Deutsch*. "In einer Zeit, die nun vergangen ist, lebten wir schon zusammen, sie und ich…" und etcetera. It's a great song— for Mack the Knife. Not for a twenty-year-old with a big nose, freckles, and pitch problems. As I sang, my wide-armed gusto, a must for musicals, momentarily stilled the flies in the windows of Lincoln Hall, the Cornell theater arts building. My auditors were just as frozen.

Then I read for the role of Randy Hastings in *Gemini,* the season opener for the Hangar Summer Theatre. Randy is a college sophomore from Connecticut—I knew knew knew that—so why, and at the last possible second, had my brain decided to tell my mouth to talk like an Englishwoman whose hearing aid had just dropped into her lap? When that loud badness reached my own ears, I downshifted and began shading my Randy Hastings with Milwaukee colorations courtesy of *Laverne and Shirley…*

I'll stop there. But the thing is, folks, *I had been on stage before.*

I finished to the sound of rustling papers at the far side of the room. No one asked for an adjustment, or for me to read for other parts, or to sing scales. No one mentioned a dance call. I was going to work at Harold's Army-Navy—"Your Everyday Fashion People"—on the Ithaca Commons for the rest of my natural life.

"Thank you for coming in today, Cary," said Gavin Steeg, the new Artistic Director of the Hangar.

I nodded, face on fire, gave the script pages to the stage manager, then opened the door. The wannabes stretched to the other end of the gloomy corridor; the oldest ones were mumbling lines on wooden folding chairs. The most limber dancers all seemed to be smoothing their bangs with the balls of their feet.

I turned and called out to Gavin, "Give Dave my best.'"

Gavin smiled. Just past forty, he knew things. Since my foster brother, Dave, and I talked all the time, he knew my greeting was unnecessary, but he also knew that, after stinking up the room with my audition, I had to broadcast this tiny personal advantage in front of the competition.

"I will, Cary. And thanks again."

Singing Brecht and Weill to get a part as a baseball player in *Damn Yankees* was overcompensation on my part. I'm a townie. Dave had been a townie too, until he got an off-the-charts IQ score in the sixth grade. A childless sociology professor named Leigh Bailey snapped him up, put him into private school, and then got him a completely free ride to Cornell at Telluride House, the special college-within-the-college for brainiacs. I stayed on with my foster parents, Hugh and Mary Gabelson, and their real daughter, Judy. I left their house after getting my diploma from Ithaca High and before they had a chance to tell me to leave. Dave embarked on a double major in economics and the history of science; I took a few community college courses, including German (to impress Robin), and did musicals at the Strand Theatre for fun. I'm not stupid by any stretch, but I must have decided somewhere along the line that we couldn't both be geniuses. Dave claims that he envies me my solo apartment on East State Street, but he doesn't pretend that selling Belgian knapsacks and the world's scratchiest socks is anything but a dead end. He graduates with honors in two weeks. If I keep my nose clean, I could be assistant floor manager by Thanksgiving.

But it doesn't have to be this way, Dave's been insisting ever since his boyfriend Gavin Steeg took over the Hangar. A paid job in summer stock would give me experience and direction for the future. Basically, I auditioned to get Dave off my case. Gavin lives in Manhattan, and they've been using my queen-size bed on his visits, because, despite its sophistication, Telluride House would appear to have a "No Man Boy Love" policy, even though the two met there in December. (Part of Telluride enrichment is its "Artists & Experts Series." I suspect Gavin made an expert presentation.) When the season finishes in August, Dave is going to move in with Gavin and figure out what kind of grad school to apply to.

That both Dave and I turned out queer is less interesting to people when they discover we're not actual blood brothers. On the other hand, they seem to expect incest in foster kids. Dave had left the Gabelsons before puberty, and though we'd spent time hanging out together, the subject of girls versus boys never came up. I don't know who was more surprised the night I saw him walk into the Common Ground, Ithaca's only gay bar, with a crowd of jittery preppies and a fake ID. He's a year older than I am and American handsome. He claims he's envious of my mustache too, but I know better.

I haven't told Dave I have no interest in being an actual actor, though I do like to hang out with entertainer types. When I was in *Annie Get Your Gun* last November, I had an affair with a milkman from Trumansburg, also in the chorus, whose wife was pregnant. We'd make deliveries along the east side of Cayuga Lake right after dawn, then screw in his truck at the entrance to Taughannock Park. All these months later, the dairy section at the Hi-Lo can still get me going. That sounds so townie, doesn't it?

It was a nice day out, a little chilly for May. I thought about finding a campus payphone and calling Robin to tell her I'd tanked with the Brecht/Weill song, thank you very much, but I was out of quarters. The ground was soppy, yet, predictably, there were Big Red bozos in shorts and sandals all over the Arts Quad trying to catch some rays. I had an hour to kill before my shift, so, delaying the trek downhill to the Commons, I headed north to the College of Human Ecology. In the basement of Martha Van Rensselaer Hall, they have this research unit called the Family Life Development Center. Its chief feature is a model kindergarten where professors and education majors take notes on the way children interact. It's where, after watching for weeks, the Gabelsons picked Dave and me out in 1964. It's a pet store without the shavings and the chew toys.

I used to think they held a Foster Child Farmer's Market every semester, like mid-terms, but Dave said no, that wasn't the case, New York State had stopped donating kids to Cornell a decade ago. I'm a foundling, and I've never been able to shake the fantasy that my mother still works someplace in Martha Van Ren Hall. She had me late one night after grading exams, dropped me in the well of an interoffice mail cart, and wheeled me down to the kindergarten with the first name of her favorite movie star pinned to my swaddling blanket. My last name is Dunkler, the German word for "darker," as it turns out, but how that came to be is another mystery of my universe.

The person to answer my questions is Dr. Joyce Brothers, the Hume Ec School's most famous graduate, but I don't have her phone number.

I cross an interior court, which acts like a wind tunnel. Shivering in my blue button-down, I double-check the pocket for the Army-Navy badge I'd stowed there for the audition. The sun makes it hard to see into the windows of the model kindergarten, but a couple of the hardier boys have chased a girl outside and are whipping alphabet blocks at her. She's crouched in the doorway of a log cabin, fists cocked. Their screams are pitched too high for the students or for me to decode, and I wonder, like I do every time I come here, whether I had ever napped or played house or fought off Indians in that little cabin. Today I almost ask the maintenance guy sweeping leaves out of a concrete gulley how long it's been there. But then I see he's not much older than me and would have no clue.

After Dave graduates, I suppose I could apply for a Cornell job— bookkeeping, office machines, the like. The benefits are excellent, and they say once you're in the university system, they can never kick you out. I could be Chief Butter Churner at the Cornell Dairy. The miracle of cream plus elbow grease equals butter knocked me out as a kid. The Ag School provides the entire campus with homemade ice cream. It's a selling point in the brochures. Townies go to Purity Ice Cream on Cascadilla Street. They have a great product too.

┣━━━━━━━●━━━━━━━┫

I was near the end of my shift, racking construction boots along the store's back wall, when I heard "Cary Dunkler, please come to the register" over the intercom. I took my time and finished the 9½s. Only Dave ever had me paged, and that only when my boss, Kristy, was night managing. Making Dave wait a bit would give her a thrill. He claimed to be allergic to the packing peanut smell of the place, but I think he was afraid that if he came looking for me, an avalanche of Italian Army sweaters would fall from the ceiling and mess his hair. It was weird for him to visit me on a school night. His history of science thesis wasn't finished, and though he plays fast with the truth when he has to, Dave never fibs about academic stuff.

At any rate, Kristy Schroyer, mother of three, was batting her eyelashes and maximizing her chestal area at the checkout counter. Queer or no, Dave Bailey, brainiac charmer with a face like Dudley Do-Right, made her splash. The tilt of his dimpled chin on my approach meant he thought he'd done me a big favor. He did do me favors, but that sly look of his always made me tense up.

He dove right in. "You made a big impression at the Hangar auditions."

Boredom has its positives. Seven hours of stocking military surplus had made me forget my earlier humiliation. "Not possible, Dave. I sang in German. Loud and bad."

"Gavin said it was a bold, albeit less than optimal choice for the situation."

(Dave got away with words like "albeit" when he talked. Telluride talk. He had used "preclude" so often his freshman year, I had to give him shit about it. Then he moved on to "evince." It sounds as if I hate my brother. I don't. Not at all.)

"Am I in *Damn Yankees?*"

"It's too soon to know."

"So what's—"

"The big impression you made was on Larry Brownstein."

I didn't bite.

"He's Gavin's best friend from day one and the playwright of the last show in the season. The new play. He was in the room too."

After *Gemini* and the musical, I wasn't sure what else was going up at the Hangar. Out of the corner of my eye, I saw Kristy check her hair in the shoplifter mirror. She also waitressed across the Commons at Simeon's. Her nurse shoes for that job had to be black. Here they were white. Her mom watched her daughters. Sometimes I didn't know how they kept it together.

Dave was so revved up, I couldn't help but smile. "I didn't audition for any new play," I said.

"That's not the kind of impression you made, Cary."

The long and the short of it was that Larry Brownstein, professional New York playwright, wanted to meet me in that very special way. Gavin was suggesting an immediate double date—the next night—while they were still in town. Dave was suggesting I make dinner for "the boys" at my apartment. I liked to cook and bake. The Gabelsons had given me a copy of *The*

Moosewood Cookbook and I'd worked through most of it, even the eggplant recipes. I probably don't need to tell you that the Moosewood Restaurant is a two-minute walk from the Commons. Make it at home is my advice. Everything they serve there—water to chili—arrives at the same lukewarm temperature. The Cabbagetown Café on Stewart Avenue has better food.

"Are you seeing anybody right now?" Dave asked.

"Nah. I'm just screwing the President of Telluride."

Dave rolled right with it. "My sloppy seconds? How did he taste?"

Why did I go along with the plan? Partly because I didn't get to hang out with Dave enough, and he'd be leaving Ithaca before I knew it. We had been hilarious, bunk bed brothers, Goofus and Gallant, Tom Sawyer and Huck Finn, Heckel and Jeckel, until Professor Bailey took him away. I wasn't seeing anybody, and other than Gavin, I had never met a New Yorker. Or a writer. And every time I hear Harry Nilsson's "I Guess the Lord Must Be in New York City" I tear up. No other song can do that to me. Another mystery for Dr. Joyce Brothers. Part of it's the banjo, which sounds like water rushing through a paddlewheel. Sometimes I play it on my stereo to test its hold over me.

⊢————•————⊣

"The boys'" ages, added together, came to eighty. My symbol for Gavin Steeg would be his spiky ball of black, brush-cut hair. He took up room the way a big-time director would, telling me where to arrange the veggie lasagna, the bowls of vichyssoise, where to seat ourselves, and making me hold the spinach salad until after we'd finished the main course. Orders from anybody could set Dave off, but being more laid-back, I didn't need to run the show, even if it was my space.

My apartment was my favorite and probably queerest thing about me. After a couple of bad roommate situations, I asked Kristy for more hours at Harold's, took the financial leap, and went solo. I have the whole first floor of an 1896 Queen Anne, five rooms, with a wraparound gingerbread porch and a tin ceiling in the kitchen. I cut the grass, weed, shovel snow, and salt the driveway for a break on the rent. I'd been there since last September, walking to work, cashing my checks, and hitting the junk stores on lower Seneca Street to kit it out. I was definitely more excited to have brought a filigreed iron bed back to life than to invite another person into it with me. I had two Hoosiers in the kitchen, one with a built-in flour sifter, and a blanket chest full of trousseau linens. If the shop owner is a woman, the easiest way

6

to get discounts on *everything* is to gush over the needlework on an old tablecloth or pillowcase. It reminds them of their grandmothers and aunts, or if they're long in the tooth themselves, they take you down Memory Lane with them. I happen to like handmade items and make sure to rotate my purchases. That way everything gets used. I don't mind the ironing.

Larry Brownstein was younger than Gavin but, balding, but looked older. He had graduated from high school the year I was born. He had this way of sidling up—to the table, to questions, to me, as if things were liable to change any minute, and he wanted to take them down before they did. Talking or listening, he tilted his head forward, turtle-like. Maybe being that kind of listener was a sign of a writer. He was shorter than I was and had a round face, a reedy voice, and slender fingers. He said he wrote longhand on yellow legal pads and paid someone to type up the drafts of his plays. Dave shot me a look. I could do ninety words a minute.

"The boys" were outrageous with the compliments. I couldn't decide if it was the age difference, or their being Jewish, or New Yorkers, or out and proud, that gave them—well, more so Gavin—the confidence to praise everything. The pie safe in the dining room; the irises in the cut glass trumpet vase on top of the pie safe; the fresh chives I'd clipped directly from my herb pot into their bowls; the way my jaw met my neck was like a Bernini. It wasn't the wine talking. They'd barely touched their glasses. At one point, Gavin stretched upturned fingertips to his "little David" (taller too) and said to Larry that while the Jews were responsible for many of the most staggering achievements of the ages, they could never make a face like that.

My own face was still red from the Bernini remark, whatever that was, but Dave didn't blush or bolt from the table to hear this. He beamed. He glowed. He kissed Gavin's fingers. I'd seen him work people over all my life, but I realized that I'd never seen him with someone he said he was in love with. When he and Gavin used my apartment, I made sure to crash at Robin's. Dave having sex in the next room wasn't something I would ever need to hear.

My brother was no more of an actor than I was, but his non-stop chatter about all the Ithaca things we'd show the boys, and his smartypants references, and his constant handwork on Gavin made it seem like he was playing to a camera. Or it was like the way they bring in a stud to turn on all the broodmares. (Or is that the other way around?) He was drinking, and as dinner went on, he shot me more and more encouraging looks—he types, he refinishes, he irons!—like maybe next I was supposed to do a backbend for Larry Brownstein, or recite a poem. I wanted to tell him to settle down. He'd already landed the job of Gavin's boyfriend, and I'd made a four-course meal, wasn't that enough for a first date?

As for *my* job opportunity, Larry wanted to know where I had managed to find the German lyrics to "The Ballad of Immoral Earnings." He had brought the salad plates into the kitchen while I whipped cream for the blueberry apple crisp.

Robin had seen *Cabaret* eleven times, and her father, Dr. Tascher, was Chair of the German Department. I'd memorized Macheath's first verse by singing along to a record at her house. She coached me on my accent. Robin is a great mimic. We once slept together, but that had gone about as well as my audition. We never referred to it.

"I have a friend who's nuts about *The Threepenny Opera*. She thought it would make me stand out."

"She was right," Larry said over the electric mixer.

"She's going to be in *Mame* at the Strand. I might try out for that too."

He cupped his hand to an ear, meaning I should talk louder. I held up a finger to say wait until I was done whipping. He handed me the bottles of vanilla and rum extract when I pointed to them in the green Hoosier.

Finished, I rapped the beaters against the bowl and held one out. "How does that taste?" I asked, in all innocence. His hand lingered on mine as he took it. Fair enough.

"Heavenly," he said. I smiled to myself. Lovely, fine, or good would have worked too.

Blueberry apple crisp should be served warm. Too hot and the cream melts and disappears, so while we waited for a proper cool-down, I asked Larry about his play. He was adapting a Mark Twain novel called *Pudd'nhead Wilson,* about a small-town lawyer and a runaway mulatto slave. Had I ever read it? Only *Tom Sawyer,* I said, in high school English. I also mentioned that growing up, Dave was Tom, and I was Huck in our foster family. He'd get the ideas, and I'd get the world of trouble. The Frankenstein mask he shoplifted from Woolworth's in second grade and put under *my* ski jacket was only the beginning. I got caught but didn't rat him out to the store manager, or to Hugh Gabelson.

Larry surprised me by saying said *Huck Finn* was a much finer book. It was the fountainhead of American literature, in fact. Like salad after the entrée, I'd never heard that before. Larry didn't announce it like a teacher, or like Dave referring to "motifs" for bonus points. He claimed it like a personal belief.

I thought of him later, Huck Fountainhead Finn that is, as we all drove in Gavin's two-seated convertible to see the Hangar lit by moonlight along the lake. (The theatre had started life as a small-plane hangar in the thirties.) Larry and I were wedged in the non-existent back seat, top down, me in his lap, his legs cradling mine. It felt tighter to me than Huck's hogshead in *Tom Sawyer*. (I loved that Huck lived in a barrel.) It felt weird too, given our size difference, but the older one is the cradler. Dave, his hand on Gavin's thigh, looked back at us. Although the rushing air made it impossible to talk, it was clear he thought we were going to have a stupendous summer for four.

A few days later, I got a postcard from Larry of the skating rink at Rockefeller Center. He spilled the beans that Gavin had cast me in *Damn Yankees* and said that he looked forward to seeing more of me. Robin pounced on that double meaning. Which parts did he want most to see? I tend to be the pursued one, but not because I'm a catch. Robin claims I'm too laid back, if not downright lazy, on the romance front. I find it helps if I keep a time frame going in my head. A boyfriend is a shift. Mike the Milkman had been an ideal shift because I knew going in that we'd be through when his wife's water broke. If things worked out between Larry and me while he was in Ithaca, I could make myself as available or as scarce as the situation required, but his shift would end when *Pudd'nhead Wilson* opened. Dave's move to New York to live on love with Gavin all day every day struck me as Grade-A insanity.

Here's the other thing. A postcard helps because I'm dense when it comes to people flirting with me. Robin, and Kristy at work, marvel at the chances they say pass me by. I literally don't see it—or them.

To get ready, I bought the *Damn Yankees* LP, and I read *Pudd'nhead Wilson*. It's not very long. There's a pair of boys in it who get switched at birth. Chambers is $\frac{1}{32}$ part Black but, fearing that he will be sold down the river, his slave mother, Roxy, switches him with Thomas à Becket Driscoll, the white heir to the plantation she works on. Chambers grows up to become the spoiled rotten drunk Tom Driscoll, while the real Tom becomes the house servant Chambers. It ends with a murder trial solved by fingerprints, which were the latest advance in criminal evidence for the time.

I have to say that the plot put me off. Real people and events inspired writers. Did Larry Brownstein want to see more of me in order to find out what it felt like to be a foundling, then picked out of a litter at the age of four, then have a semi-brother raised to greatness because of a random IQ test? Listen to me. Not-so-random IQ test. An IQ test is the opposite of random. I took that test the following year in sixth grade, but I don't remember it; I can remember Dave's miracle score (168), but not mine; I remember Professor Leigh Bailey bringing me a model airplane kit in a swap for Dave; I remember taking apart our bunk beds, and Mary and Hugh Gabelson wondering if I'd like a puppy. Technically, I wasn't switched at birth like Chambers and Tom in *Pudd'nhead,* but I couldn't help but be sensitive to the theme as Dave prepared to graduate Phi Beta Kappa *summa cum laude* and I sorted a mountain of Chinese flip-flops next to a one-speed table fan.

My semi-sister Judy Gabelson also put me off when she asked on the phone whether I was attending Dave's commencement exercises. I shouldn't have barked at her that I'd turned down double overtime to go, because that gave her the opportunity to remind me that she had put up half my security deposit, helped load the van, given me her cherry wood bureau, and I had yet to invite her or her parents to my State Street apartment for any kind of a housewarming.

I'd been a bad foster child, but she was easy to sidetrack. "I promise to have you all over once the musical opens," I said. I teased her with a pause. Judy was stagestruck but had never chased the dream; she spent her surplus on bus trips to New York to see Broadway shows. "*Damn Yankees.*" I paused again. "At the Hangar."

It worked. "The *Hangar?*" she cried. "Oh Cary, that's fantastic. That's a big step up!"

"It's still chorus."

"Doesn't matter. It's *professional.* You'll get paid."

"I don't know about that," I said truthfully.

"They have actors there who come from New York."

Directors too, I thought, with apartments in Greenwich Village. The Gabelsons didn't know that Cary and I were queer. I sometimes wondered about Judy's sexuality, but lesbians, regular-looking ones, weren't a big presence at the Common Ground. We assumed they held their pussy potlucks up in the woods.

"The piano was just tuned," she said. "When can you come over?" Judy had a Music Ed degree from SUNY Albany and taught high school in Slaterville Springs. Whenever I was in a show, she helped me with the second tenor lines. She'd plunk them out over and over, then record them on a cassette tape. Saved my butt. Harmony is hardest for me.

"Soon as I get the sheet music."

"Deal. See you Saturday. Need a ride?"

"Nope. I can walk."

"It could be steaming out. Or pouring."

"Nope."

Ithacans are either rah-rah about Cornell graduation or they pretend it isn't happening. With all the parents in town, a four-day tidal wave of cash washes through the Commons and forget being able to park. Given its smaller student population, Ithaca College nets us less, but Harold's staples discount fliers on both campuses.

Judy called it. It was high in the upper eighties on Commencement Day. I regretted not packing roll-on and a spare undershirt in with Dave's graduation gift. Except for the lack of horses and centurions, it might have been the chariot race scene in *Ben Hur*—brass bands, giant vertical banners, the reviewing stand at the forty-yard line, not to mention thousands of people crammed into Schoellkopf Field roaring on cue. From my nosebleed spot, Dave was one indistinct scale in the skin of an endless green snake ribboning into the stands. With her pull Professor Bailey had arranged seats for us while she baked far below with the rest of the faculty. We'd all be meeting up at Telluride House after the conferral of degrees. And after that, David Prescott Bailey, Cornell B.A. 1980, was staying up late with Gavin Steeg in my apartment. Larry Brownstein was due in three days.

Given that the six of us had never occupied the same space before, the Telluride banquet felt herky-jerky at first. When conversation stalled, or when Dave was off hugging classmates and meeting their folks, there would be an odd "You must be so proud of him" ricochet among Mary, Hugh, and Leigh. Even Judy, who had taught him piano, got in on that. But then the champagne started, and Hugh remembered the camera around his neck. We took a boatload of pictures. There's even one of me with Leigh Bailey and two feet of air between us. Ten years later, she still gets thrown when I show up for Dave. She overdid the enthusiasm for my *Damn Yankees* gig. "I love how creative you're turning out to be, Cary," she said, as if I'd handed her a finger painting for her refrigerator.

Dave's flushed face signaled that he was close to bawling the entire time. (I got the mustache; he got the tear ducts.) This I understood. The day he'd worked toward for so long had come and was nearly gone. It was like the last performance of a show, though there's no comparison between his lifetime of overachievement and my clowning around on stage in a face coat of Tan Blush #2. He had a catch in his throat when he accepted, during the dinner, a summer research fellowship given "to the graduating senior who most represents the ethical and intellectual values of Telluride." The money was his to use however he liked. I wasn't surprised. I used to think Dave got all the luck because he had started out life with two parents, with real names, and who had wanted him. They'd died in a car accident before he could crawl. If they were watching him from above, or beyond, they'd be proud too.

My gift was another awkward moment. There's a used bookstore, The Bookery, in the Dewitt Mall on Cayuga Street. A lot of dead professors' libraries wind up there, so they have important items along with racks of paperback thrillers out on the sidewalk. I browse it on my Thursday lunch hours because that's the day Café Dewitt does its amazing dill carrot soup. Anyway, The Bookery had an early edition of Darwin's *The Origin of Species*, in two volumes. I talked the owner, Jack Goldman, into letting me have them for three hundred and forty dollars, down from four eighty. A lot of shifts either way. I'd held it and studied it for weeks before I approached Jack about a better price and paying for it in installments. It wasn't as easy as getting a crewel tablecloth out of an old lady, but booksellers want their treasures to go to good homes too.

I fretted about when to give Dave the Darwins and wound up waiting until dessert was being cleared, so there wasn't anything else for us to do but watch it happen in slow motion. Dave freed the books from their sailboat wrapping paper, looked, gasped, counted one, two—one, two. Then, during a tiny instant, after his face had lit up, I watched him wonder how I had pulled off this caper. Had I stolen them? I looked at him and said right back with my eyes—I paid for them, mo-fo, and you know I did. He understood. He also knew that I knew that that's what he would have done if he had wanted them that much and didn't have the dough. In the end, isn't Tom more devious than Huck? Then Leigh Bailey leaned over her teacup and said, "*The Origin of Species?*" in a tone worth the price of admission.

I pushed back my chair. "Darwin was part of your thesis, right?"

Dave nodded. His eyes were definitely teary now. Mary Gabelson's too. He shoots, he scores. Even with two payments to go.

After the banquet, borrowing a T-shirt in Dave's room—I was heading out to the bar with Robin while he and Gavin busted my bedsprings—I rerouted the subject away from this latest example of what he called my historic, "unstinting" generosity. I re-folded my sleeve cuffs and watched him from the mirror on his closet door. He was sitting on his bed, mouth open, hair heading off in the wrong direction, dazed and weepy from the weight of the day. The Darwins were balanced, one on each thigh, like the etching of Moses with his broken tablets that hangs above the magazine rack in the Tompkins County Library.

It turned out I wasn't as masculine as I had previously assumed, a ruling that hadn't much affected my day-to-day existence until *Damn Yankees*. I mean, no one had ever beaten me up for how I walked or talked or acted. Rednecks don't pick off the men leaving the Common Ground after last call, like they do up in Syracuse. Ithaca is live and let live, always has been. Some come for college and never leave.

Rehearsals were held in the game room of a senior center just off the Commons, a spot I'd passed my whole life without noticing. That anybody out on Albany Street could watch us dance through the windows made me feel like I had a theatre *job*. Thirty dollars a week, nothing to quit the Army-Navy over, but a good feeling. After the first read-through, Gavin dismissed everybody except the Senators, aka the ball team, aka the nine-member male chorus. (I won't tax you with the plot of *Damn Yankees*, except to say that it's about baseball, not the Civil War, and that the Devil is a major player. The songs are fun.) During a ten-minute break, the stage managers braced giant mirrored rectangles along one wall. The chorus boys from "The City" marked their territory by tossing their dance bags on a table in the corner bearing a milk crate of bingo cards.

Gavin, sitting in front of the mirrors, had us line up at the other end of the room. There was one other townie besides me, Clark, who I remembered seeing as Cornelius in a so-so *Hello, Dolly!* that Robin had also been in. There was an Ithaca College theater major wearing horn-rimmed glasses, a rising Cornell senior, and the five New Yorkers, two of whom had changed during the break into tights and leotards. Watching them stretch, I prayed I wouldn't be the worst chorus boy, given a pass because the director was screwing my foster brother.

Gavin made a speech about how, say what you will about the Faust story, it was the ballplayers who were the genuine heart of *Damn Yankees*. If the audience didn't fall in love with us as individuals, then there was no *Damn Yankees*. He let that sink in. Some of the guys were taking notes on their scripts. He said that the schedule was too tight for us to play a real ballgame together, as that would help us meld as an ensemble. Short of that, in order to become these individual teammates that the audience must grow to love, we would start with names and walks.

"Who wants to lead off?" Gavin said, cocking an eyebrow to see who got the batting reference.

I didn't have a dance bag and I didn't take notes, and the assignment confused me, so I drifted to the back of the group. Gavin wouldn't treat me any different, even with my Bernini neck-jaw double play. (I'd looked it up at Robin's house.)

"You just want us to walk across the room?" someone asked.

"No. I want you to think about your *character*, a baseball player who is not you. He walks differently from you, and he has a first name that you're going to tell me."

There was some uneasy shifting and muttering, then a New Yorker, with Superman's chest and arms, named Jon Camilleri squealed, "I'm Chauncey!" and began to prance down the room like a runway model.

Gavin met him halfway. "That's exactly *not* the point," he said, laughing with the rest of us.

"So, are you saying you want us to butch it up?" said Jon.

"I am indeed."

"Why didn't you say so?"

"I was trying to be sensitive, Jon. We aren't in the Ice Capades"—he gestured with the classic wrist drop—"and we aren't"—eyes now on the leotard duo—"the Ballets Russes. We're all men here." That got another laugh.

Jon began again. He spread his legs, bowed his knees slightly, and very slowly placed one foot in front of the other. "I'm Petey," he grunted.

"What's the matter with you, Petey?"

"I'd walk faster, Coach, but my balls get in the way."

Class clown, but it broke the ice.

After Petey came Smokey, Vince, Stretch, Poindexter (Ithaca College horn-rims), spitting, scratching, squinting, loping, peg-legging. Gavin nixed the names Zorro, Ringo, and Terence.

Dead last was too much pressure, so I slipped in as number seven. "I'm Lud," I announced to the group. For my walk, I imitated Robin's father, the German professor. I turned out my left foot some, dragged it slightly, then hitched it up a tiny bit on every third stride.

"Is there something wrong with your leg, Lud?" asked Gavin.

I flashed on Robin's father's standard response to "How are you, Dr. Tascher?" Slowly shaking my head, I said, "I have the sciatic pain from a herniated lumbar disc. Numbers three and four, if you must know."

The laugh was a nice surprise.

After the last two passed muster, Gavin set us all walking at once, then jogging, then he made us sprint. Then, using our character names, we threw an imaginary baseball around. I had never done stuff like this during rehearsals for Strand shows, but I tried to get into it. I caught whatever was thrown to Lud but got rid of it fast, always keeping the mirrors to my back. I did think some of the guys were hotdogging it—slides, basket catches, one-hops, miraculous saves. But no, Gavin explained that night at Simeon's, where we were having dinner with Dave and Larry Brownstein, that was the actor's imagination at play. And weren't all athletes hotdogs by nature? He said he was happy with how the day had gone, especially since the nine of us had begun the day looking like a bouquet of daylilies. And those two gazelles in tights…. Gavin slid down his reading glasses to peer at the wine list.

I flushed. I hoped I hadn't been as faggy as them. Or was still. Or as Dave—all over Gavin like an octopus again—was currently being. I could practically hear Kristy mouth breathing at the waiters' station. Catching her eye as she worked other tables, I saw that the ages of "the boys" shocked her silly.

For all his supposed interest in me, Larry was shy. He mostly let Gavin talk *Pudd'nhead*. I chipped in names from the Twain a couple of times to show them I had read the book, but it didn't register. While Gavin drew ideas for the set on the napkins, Larry dissected his fish and chips, as if he thought a ruby might roll out of a filet. And Dave—well, he wasn't accustomed to not being top of the agenda, and he hadn't read *Pudd'nhead Wilson*. This wasn't a date, I wanted to tell him once I'd figured it out; we were sitting in on a creative meeting, like in advertising or Hollywood. At one point, I motioned Kristy to come over, but she twisted her head away like a rearing horse, then made the "call me" sign with her thumb and pinkie. Gavin and Larry weren't *that* old. Kristy's deadbeat, almost ex-husband Wayne, had ten years on her.

I had decided over dinner that I would sleep with Larry, but out front after dessert, he nixed Dave's idea of going dancing at the Common Ground. He couldn't lose momentum on a crucial rewrite. He was so apologetic, I gave him a quick hug goodbye. I refused a lift. Gavin's and Larry's apartments were in the opposite direction, closer to the Hangar. Dave had yet to tell Leigh Bailey that he'd be rooming "with a friend" in a lake house for the summer. That would make an interesting conversation.

"See you tomorrow, Lud," said Gavin.

"Wait," said Larry. He stopped and looked up at me in that interested way he'd had at my place. "Is Lud short for Luddite, Cary?"

I shrugged. Let him guess in bed, all on his lonesome.

Early summer nights in Ithaca are so sweet, you forget the endless, defeating winters. It's not humid yet; the air is soft, alive with the rustle of new leaves and the chitter of insects. Breathing in the lilacs, I practiced my Lud walk up State Street until it got too steep.

Lud was not short for Luddite, a term that was going to require a second trip to the Taschers' encyclopedia. Jon Camilleri had gotten what Lud meant. He'd come over to me at the end of rehearsal. Imaginary baseball was hard work, so he was blotting his impressive, and impressively hairy, chest with a Rutgers T-shirt. A clown, yes, but no daylily.

"How's the cake, Lud?" he asked.

"Oh like always I guess," I said automatically.

"It couldn't be like always," he said. "I never got this kind of cake before."

"Hmmph," I said. "I thought something was different."

Then, not wanting to mess up a line in a routine that Jon clearly knew by heart, I bent over to tighten a shoelace, amazed that anyone else would love Lily Tomlin's "Lud and Marie Meet Dracula's Daughter" enough to memorize it like I had. It's a routine about her parents she does on her *Appearing Nitely* album, and it was another favorite thing of mine.

"Lud's a good name for you," said Jon.

"I could say the same, Petey."

He zipped up his dance bag. "See you tomorrow, *Margaret Ann*."

I was dumbfounded. He'd memorized "Tell Miss Sweeney Goodbye" too. He knew all of *Appearing Nitely*.

Jon had been the biggest hotdog in the room, but at the same time, his intense focus—wherever the ball went, he followed it with his eyes, played back-up to the other guys when it came close—made him the most believable Senator. When I got home, I sat up on my porch glider with a beer and wondered what it would be like to do something that captured my full attention.

———————

My peonies were bending over from the weight of their beauty. They had a week left at best. I cut a mix of white and pink and wrapped them in wet paper towels to take to Judy. She can't get them to grow at her place. She's tried cuttings, and she's tried from scratch, but nothing comes up. Could be the creek across the street has made the ground too soggy, or maybe her yard gets too much sun. I use eggshells and bone meal. She's tried that too.

Back when she bought her house on Titus Street, Judy Gabelson was said to be the youngest mortgage-holder in Ithaca. Whether being that sensible then makes her a catch now is another thing. She's twenty-eight, and not fat or flat-chested or bucktoothed. She had been self-conscious about her scoliosis at one time, but that's not the same as having a port-wine stain cover half your face, like her friend Emily, and she'd never had to wear a brace to school. She'd be classified as "plain," but you just know that the right person will make her beautiful one day. Like I said, I don't know what flips her switch, besides theatre trips to New York.

I really like her house. It dates from the 1920s, and except for a small front porch, it's this perfect two-story cube. Everything fits and flows together, with no wasted space, like a nautilus shell. I spot vintage items at the junk stores I feel belong there, but Judy's taste is Scandinavian—huge, trippy throw pillows, blond wood, square dinner plates, pebbled glass candlesticks, the stuff you can buy at Contemporary Trends, just off the Commons.

No such thing as a Scandinavian piano, though. Judy played the same walnut upright she'd taught Dave on when we were kids. I'd helped move it from her parents' house into her living room; it stood in the middle of the bright sectional pieces like a harassed chaperone guarding the punch. I have a Deco table runner embroidered with poppies that I would love to slip over its top like a comforting headscarf.

The first week of *Damn Yankees* was almost through, and I was there to learn my harmonies. Judy made much of the peonies. We lamented, like we did every summer, their criminally short growing season. She arranged them with scientific precision while I scarfed a wedge of her crustless quiche, a cooking technology I can't figure out. Why didn't it burn? Hot or cold, it's an amazing three-cheese brick. I wouldn't need another meal for days.

She plied me with questions about working with professionals, so I told her about our team improvs, and that there was a shorthand the New Yorkers used with each other, and that the men would be dancing a soft-shoe reprise of "Heart" with baseball bats as canes. I was one of three cast members who couldn't sight-read. My own music education had been a year of enforced trumpet. Scanning the contact sheet I'd brought along, Judy thought that the name of the actress playing Lola, Suzy Skurnik, sounded familiar. I was to ask her whether she had been in *They're Playing Our Song* on Broadway. I told her that my teammate (too early to say friend, though we did a lot of Lily Tomlin for each other during breaks) Jon Camilleri had just gotten off a bus and truck tour of *Shenandoah*.

Jon's gig had impressed me until Larry Brownstein said that *Shenandoah* was a terrible musical. Or so, he retracted politely, *he* believed. Our third date, the night before, had ended in Larry's apartment, where he kept me laughing with descriptions of all the horrible numbers he had seen over the years on Broadway, tops being a harvest ballet in a musical version of *East of Eden* where the dancers had thrown plastic vegetables to one another for a full ten minutes. I reached over and kissed him mid-laugh to get it over with. Or started. He really was a shy guy. We slept in his double bed. In fact, I had had to wake up, trek home for my sheet music, and come back down to Judy's for my lesson.

It was fun; Larry went overboard with the compliments again, but the dark covered my blushes. Although he was the oldest man I'd slept with by fifteen years, his body didn't jiggle. He did have back hair, but not so much that you could grab a handful. The nicest thing, besides our rocks getting off with no hitches, was his helping me put on my T-shirt in the morning. Trying to skedaddle, I had put it on backwards. Larry freed my arms, twisted the label side to the back, and kissed my neck before letting me finish the job myself.

At the door, he apologized for the lack of food in the kitchen; he was used to bagels out in the a.m. Saying goodbye, he sidled up to me just behind the screen door and bumped me with his hip, also very nice. He didn't mention a next rendezvous, unlike Gavin, who so instantly wanted all of Dave that he had gotten out his datebook and began scheduling months of Ithaca trips on their first morning-after.

Judy took me through my music. She would have me sing the second tenor part, first with piano, then without, again and again. She'd try to trip me up by cutting out on the piano or singing the baritone or soprano line along with. Finally, warning me, like always, that the orchestra wouldn't sound anything like the piano-vocal score, she played just the chords. That was toughest because sometimes my note wasn't in the chord, and I'd have to search my head memory to find and produce it. Judy was so patient with me, and so, I don't know, *jazzed* by the process, that I asked her whether she'd like to be the rehearsal pianist for *Damn Yankees,* join our stupendous summer and all.

She circled her wrist with her thumb and middle finger, one of her "settle down now" teacher gestures. "I couldn't possibly, Cary."

"But you love this, and you're great at it. They're going to need a back-up pianist once the orchestra starts practicing."

"I have school."

"School's out next week, Judy."

"I have grading."

"I can give your name to the director."

"Absolutely not."

"I won't even tell him how I know you."

"No, Cary!"

As per usual, when I pushed her to think about herself, she changed the subject to Dave: what he was up to and what he was going to do with this latest bucket of Telluride cash. I said I figured he'd bank it for his move and how great it would be that she could visit him in New York in the fall and see all the latest shows together. She made a tiny face and began the intro to "Heart," the hit song from *Damn Yankees.* She'd never say so, but I think Dave makes her feel like a townie too.

Whatever he'd be up to, it occurred to me that the three of us should have lunch at least once, just ourselves, before August was up. I would finally make Judy choose between us. That's a joke. Gabelson legend goes that twelve-year-old Judy had cast the deciding vote to take *both* of us from the Family Life Development Center, because at five and four, Dave and I absolutely would not be separated. We did everything together, shared every toy, even synchronized our naps and potty breaks. For all I knew, we'd been the subject of dozens of term papers—"The Boys Who Would be Twins." Whether it was Hugh or Mary who had only wanted one of us would never be revealed—three guesses which boy—but Judy broke her parents' tie, and they got two for the price of one. Eventually, I was able to work out my anger at the Gabelsons for taking foster money from the state instead of adopting us outright. If they had, Professor Bailey couldn't have stepped in and stolen Dave.

Listen to me. Why stuff like this used to bother me I can't say, especially when Dave and I were still tight. I was looking forward to a catch-up later with him about sex with older guys. We could start with back-hair comparisons. That's when it hit me that screwing "the boys" was another way to keep us tight. Gavin and Larry were the latest type of toy to share. Standing at the piano, I felt my stomach turn over with the feeling that Dave, brilliant as he was, might not be aware that our Manhattan Daddies were part of a pattern. I cut off an eight count. "Judy, what's the musical term for something you play over and over?"

"Leitmotif."

"Not that one." I racked my brain, trying to remember the classical album titles in the Gabelson's hi-fi cabinet. "I mean the same basic music but done in a different style."

"'Theme and variation'?"

"That's it."

She began playing "Old McDonald Had a Farm" six different ways. Funniest was the Bach. My nerves went away, and I was about to bring up the rehearsal piano job again when Judy asked me how my girlfriend was doing.

"Girlfriend?"

"Robin Tascher."

"She's not a girlfriend."

"Okay, but how is she?"

Robin was going to need a catch-up too. She was being over-sensitive, I thought, to my having moved on up to the Hangar Theatre, not to mention my involvement with a playwright, so I would have to downplay my enthusiasm when we got together. She hoped that Gavin or Larry knew a hotshot theatre dyke who could come sweep her off to New York. This didn't make strict sense, since Robin was so not gay. Her type was Jon Camilleri. She had ditched Cornell her junior year for Mitch Pingus, a ponytailed dude whose years unloading rail cars at a paper mill had given him forearms like a caveman's club. After five months of growing pot in Mitch's basement in Janesville, she'd moved back home, but didn't re-enroll; her vagueness ever since about "future plans" terrorized Dr. and Mrs. Tascher. Ithaca has its share of faculty brats on permanent drift. It really is a fantastic spot for hanging, hiding, or flopping out in.

"She's jealous of my gig, but she's happy for me too."

"Tell her she could have auditioned for *Damn Yankees*."

"I say that every single time. She wants me to go to Europe with her this fall."

Judy closed the lid on the keyboard and swiveled around like I'd smashed a violin in her class. "*Europe*? What on earth for?"

"For all the things Europe is famous for. To see the Berninis in the Borghese Gardens."

"The who?"

I shrugged.

"What makes you think you can just pick up and go to Europe, Cary?"

"Last I heard, there's no law saying I can't." What was her problem?

"You should finish college first."

"Finish? How about start?"

"Yes, how *about* starting, Cary?" If anyone was my mother now, it was Judy Gabelson. "Maybe with Dave gone...."

"Maybe with Dave gone what?" I asked.

She bit a fingernail. "Maybe when Dave leaves town, you'll have room to blossom in."

I flared against this assessment. "Hey, I work. I support myself; I have my own apartment; I read books. I look up words I don't know in the dictionary. I'm doing great."

"There's more to you, Cary. I know you know that."

I ducked that and moved to the window, on the lookout for raccoons, even though it was too early in the day. Judy said that a raccoon mother brought her babies to the creek bank most evenings. I like to think they kept house under her porch.

"There's no law saying only college graduates can cross the Atlantic," I said.

"I *know* that." She rose from the bench. "I haven't been to Europe," she said and sort of stomped upstairs to get the tape recorder.

Of course it was a harebrained scheme. Robin and I batted it around whenever we flipped through the foreign fashion magazines at Meyer's Smoke Shop. I'd have to rob a bank to get there; we all knew that. I just couldn't understand why it would piss her off. Nothing was keeping Judy here.

❘▬▬▬▬▬▬ ◆ ▬▬▬▬▬▬❘

Being his idea from the start, Dave put it into words first, but in such a fake-casual way, it was hilarious. Especially since he was wearing an apron and attempting to cut flour and butter together on the kitchen counter. Over the years, the most I'd ever seen Dave cook was a grilled cheese, and now, never one for baby steps, he'd jumped right to piecrust.

"Have you given notice at the Army-Navy yet?" he asked.

"Ha," I answered. "You need to throw some more ice water on that." I moved to the refrigerator to help him out.

When I had explained it to him, Dave had intellectually grasped the "theme and variations" angle of our time with "the boys," but he had yet to figure out that Gavin and Larry were as different one to the other as he and I were. I won't say I wasn't flattered that Dave would want me around in New York. It's just that there was no view, postcard or otherwise, of the city that I could imagine slipping into. Taking the simplest angle possible, I would ask myself what would I do with my hands? What would they take hold of there?

"I'm not moving to a place I've never even visited," I said.

I flicked water on his dough and slid a French door open for some breeze. The chief perk for the new Artistic Director of the Hangar was this summer cottage built on a lakeside bluff. If you sat real still, you could hear the slurp of the waves on the pilings of the boat landing below. Dave claimed to be splitting his time between here and doing research in Olin Library, but his deepening color and the beach towels drying on the patio railing said otherwise. It made me sad that he thought he ought to fib. He had earned this siesta.

"You could go down one weekend—"

"Nope, I'm in rehearsal."

Dave walloped the dough. "Everyone is *always* in rehearsal."

Behind that sour reaction was his frustration that Gavin wasn't spending enough time with him. If it wasn't rehearsal, it was a design meeting about the next play, or a fundraising dinner at a trustee's house that his barely legal "housemate" couldn't show up at. He complained that I saw more of Gavin than he did. I don't know about that, but I did see how Gavin grooved on the madness of the theatre. Every day he ran a two-room kindergarten, one for the scenes, the other for the musical numbers. I was having a great time, and the Senators were bonding like a real team. Because of my long arms and big beak, it was decided that Lud had to be second baseman. I didn't get the nose connection. I was just flattered they'd put me in the infield.

"Flour that rolling pin, or there'll be heartache ahead," I said.

"The directions don't specifically say to."

I gave him a look. He reached for the canister.

"Larry's apartment is minuscule," I said. "Two rooms just off the lobby of his building. He said it was probably the trunk room back when people traveled by steamer. It's maybe one-third the size of mine here."

"People there make life work in tinier spaces."

Dave could say that; Gavin had five rooms, a tub, and a queen-size on Morton Street. Larry had a single bed and a shower only. He called his Hangar apartment an environmental luxury.

"The only time Larry has lived with a boyfriend was fifteen years ago, in grad school," I said. "For four months."

"So?"

"So, don't you think more practice on his part would be a good idea? Before I pull up stakes and move to a place I've never been?"

Gavin had had two long-term lovers; both clocked in at nine years. I assumed that Larry had been feeding me these specifics about Gavin's life as a way to keep me from coming up with Dave's idea on my own.

"If it feels right, Cary, it is right."

He sounded like Dr. Joyce Brothers with a call-in. Things with Larry felt nice, which is not the same thing as right. We were busy. I'd slept with him a total of four times. One time was just sleeping, which I'd decided was mature of us.

"I don't think I'm smart enough for Larry," I said.

"*What?*" Dave hated whenever I hinted that there was that difference between us, so I don't suggest it often. "You're plenty smart, smarter than a lot of the bozos I just graduated with."

Unlike Judy, Dave didn't tell me what to do with my smarts. I liked his way better. Judy made me feel they would shrink, or get stale, over time. Dave made me feel like I was stockpiling them for the right occasion.

"What do you and Larry talk about?"

"I don't know. I tell him stories about what's going on at Harold's or at rehearsal, and he tells me who's gay in Hollywood."

"Does he make you feel stupid, Cary?"

"Not at all." That was the truth. Larry's questions made my days sound almost interesting. For example, Kristy's life seemed tougher, and her way of handling it, braver, when I pieced it together for him. What I told him about Robin just made him laugh—he said she was a purely literary figure.

"He's eighteen years older than I am."

"That's just experience. Experience is not a concomitant to intelligence."

Concomi-*what?* Dave statements like that crack me up. "If you say so."

"I mean it, Cary. Don't write Larry off just because it's easier to let his age be an issue."

"Fine. I won't."

I was about to ask him how smart he thought Gavin was, all things considered, but I noticed that there were no other ingredients out on the counter, just the cookbook, the dough, and the rolling pin.

"Hey, Dave, pie or quiche?"

"I haven't decided yet," he sniffed.

That was also hilariously Dave. Too much history of science, I thought. Too much data control. Next would be cocktail sauce without the shrimp. Baked Alaska without the ice cream. Oyster stuffing without the turkey. A Bailey banquet of perfect half-measures.

"What's so funny?"

"If you're making pie, it helps to seal the crust with beaten egg yolk. The filling won't bleed, and the crust doesn't get soggy."

"And with quiche?" said Dave, daring me to continue being the expert.

I smiled, wet a finger, and repaired a break in the dough. "With all the eggs in quiche, it really doesn't matter."

I looked up. He was wagging the pin in my face, Brother Knows Best.

"You know, Cary, you could always cook in New York," he said, absolutely reading my mind. "There are thousands of restaurants there."

"Pie or quiche," I repeated blandly. He'd gotten me, and he knew it.

"I don't know. Check the fridge."

Eventually, I sharpened my location management skills. I bought a duffel at Harold's for my script, my harmony cassette tape, a change of underwear and socks, work shirt and badge, a toothbrush, deodorant, and a mini umbrella. I could now go from Larry to rehearsal to home to the Army-Navy in any order and not have to backtrack or compromise my hygiene.

I went to Larry's only by invitation. On the next company day off, I woke up early, did a load of laundry, then brought breakfast down from Collegetown Bagels. I wanted Larry's opinion of the local product. Although my poppy seed with ham and cheese stood in clear violation of the Torah, he approved of his sesame seed with cream cheese, a slice of tomato, and black pepper. And my standing there in skimpy cut-offs was going to make an ideal second course. Finishing a new *Pudd'nhead* scene had put him in the mood. I myself am a fan of daytime sex. Dave had alerted me that testosterone levels peak in the morning, not a problem, he said, for our age bracket, but useful to know for older guys.

I showered a second time, put on jeans, then headed to the Commons. Lola and the Senators had a demo/photo shoot for *The Ithaca Journal.* Summer weekends in this town are full of free entertainment—acrobats, fire-eaters, jug bands, magicians, cloggers, unicyclists—so we expected a crowd. A couple of the New Yorkers had been griping that this was a potential union infraction, but I knew we were all psyched to be performing for anyone besides ourselves. We had had our first Act One stumble-through the night before. I was amazed at how it was pulling together. Six Senators, but not me, thank you very much, had dropped their bats during the soft-shoe. That may not sound like much, except at a certain point, we had to balance them vertically on our palms for a count of twelve while we grapevined left and right. Look at your feet, even for a second, and—CLUNK!

I didn't drop my bat on the Commons either. The people in front of Home Dairy stamped and whistled. Robin was there, looking wan in lime pedal pushers and her red cat-eye glasses, her giant cup of Wa-Wa coffee tracked with lipstick—I wanted Jon Camilleri to meet her and vice versa—and Kristy had taken a break from lunch prep at Simeon's to come cheer me on. Judy begged off, afraid maybe that I'd introduce her to the music director and try to get her on board.

Our uniforms were still under construction in the costume shop, so at Gavin's insistence, we wore our tightest, whitest T-shirts and our tightest blue jeans. The *Ithaca Journal* photographer kept re-arranging us around Suzy Skurnik, who sat on top of a stepladder in a bustier and black fishnets. The idea was to gaze up at Lola with wonder at her unbelievable hotness while she filed her long, blood-red nails. The photographer, an old perv I knew from the Common Ground, re-positioned us fifteen times, clearly wanting to cop feels.

Suzy finally kicked off her pumps and said, "That's enough of that." She motioned to the assistant stage manager to fetch her dance bag.

Suzy Skurnik was a piece of work I'd steered clear of after an early attempt during a break to ask, for Judy, whether she had been on Broadway in *They're Playing Our Song*. Suzy narrowed her eyes, removed a nozzle from her mouth—the New Yorkers all toted water bottles for some reason—looked me up and down, and said, "Are you onstage or backstage?" Triple ouch. I mean, why be such a c-word when you don't have to? Since then, if forced to acknowledge my existence, she'd widen her eyes a tad and exhale in my direction. Forget about her ever learning the names Cary or Lud.

Of course, Robin, who regarded Suzy as competition, just had to go up to her after the photo shoot and introduce herself as the actress who was playing Gloria Upson in *Mame* over at the Strand Theatre. She so hoped that their performance schedules would allow them to see each other's work. (I cringed whenever Robin called acting "the work." *Hamlet*, maybe, was work. If you're Hamlet.)

Suzy, still buffing her nails while everyone packed up around her, looked at Robin as if a horse had just released a load of road apples at her feet.

"Is that a professional company?" she said.

"How do you mean?"

"Does the Strand Theatre pay?"

Robin was too stunned for a comeback.

The upside to Suzy's c-ness here was that it allowed Jon Camilleri, standing right there, to ride in for a rescue. The three of us went for lunch at the Dewitt Mall, but not to Moosewood. On the way in, I dropped a dollar into the flute player's instrument case in front of The Bookery.

For Kate, the owner-chef of Café Dewitt, to give me a hug in front of Jon was the upside to being a townie. Jon had begun calling Ithaca "Sprouts With Everything," as opposed to where he'd grown up, grimy, crumbling Paterson, New Jersey, which he called "Diesel On That."

Waiting for our meal, I let Robin and Jon get acquainted and watched Kate manage the seven orders on the rack, with just one assistant. Why hadn't I ever thought about a restaurant job? At the better joints in town, waiters made a ton in tips, but I knew I'd rather prepare food than hype or serve it. I'm no salesman. Even at Harold's, I preferred stocking shelves to pushing one brand of jeans over another. Every choice has its good points is how I see things.

The conversation had circled back to our leading lady. "She's miscast," Jon was saying.

This was interesting. I had thought Suzy had been great in the stumble-through. "How so?" I asked.

"She's funny, but she's not sexy enough to be Lola."

"She can sing," I said.

Robin fluffed her bangs. "Anyone can sing Lola's material," she said. "Even I could."

"Of course you could," said Jon. "You would make a great Lola."

"I missed the auditions," said Robin, a lie. Then she did her Liza Minnelli bubble-giggle from *Cabaret*. Like I said, Jon was her type, and he had basically just told her she was sexy.

"Gavin miscast her," said Jon. "She's just a Jappy cow from Bethpage, Long Island."

I felt I should defend Gavin, who was my sort-of brother-in-law. "He must have had his reasons. He cast me too. Even after I sang a sex song in German." This was a dig at Robin's audition suggestion.

"What?"

"You know…'in dem bordel, wo unser Haushalt war,'" said Robin, picking up her cue to be exotic and bilingual, town and gown, Sally and Liza.

"What?"

We explained my *Threepenny Opera* gambit, which Jon found so wrong he wouldn't let us leave the table until I sang a few lines as proof.

Next up for me was the Bookery, but Jon peeled off. He was going to work out at the Y, then sunbathe at Buttermilk Falls with some of the cast. I couldn't shoehorn Robin into that plan, because I had a Harold's shift and couldn't go myself. So, I asked Jon whether anyone was going dancing that night at the Common Ground. By now, most of the company went there to burn off energy, but between the store and rehearsals, I was working eighty-hour weeks. It felt like forever since I'd been out and about.

We looked at one another. There were shrugs, maybes, but no commitments and no exchange of phone numbers.

I had made my second-to-last Darwin payment and was giving Jack Goldman a recap of Dave's reaction to his graduation present when Robin butted in.

"Here's your next big gesture, Cary," she said.

She handed me a leather-bound copy of *Pudd'nhead Wilson*. There was a bust of Twain stamped on the cover in gold leaf; the page edges were gilt; the endpapers were marbled in a five-ink paisley; best of all, behind a tissue paper veil was a full-color plate of Roxy getting the news that she's been sold down the river by her genuine son, Tom Driscoll. It's a big moment in the book, so crucial it was the act break in Larry Brownstein's adaptation.

"Yours for only twenty-four hundred dollars."

My jaw dropped.

"It's part of the Stanfield Edition of Twain's *Complete Works*," said Jack. "Thirty-seven volumes."

No need to ask about breaking up a set. I said goodbye to *Pudd'nhead*, gently placed him in front of Jack and looked at Robin. I couldn't believe she'd be this mean to me.

"Why—" I stopped.

"Why what?" she said.

"Why show me this, when you know I could never afford it?"

"Because, Cluck, you're a cluck. A big dumb cluck."

She swanned out of the store. I followed.

"What are you talking about?"

"He's hot for you, stupid," she hissed. I could hardly hear her with the flutist tootling next to my ear.

"Jack Goldman?"

Here she might have done her best Liza/Sally sells the fur to pay for the abortion, but she was too upset. "No, Cluck. Jon."

"Jon Camilleri?"

She poked me in the chest with a red fingernail, the one feature she shared with Suzy Skurnik. "Yeah, and you can tell him from me that he should change his last name. It sounds like Camel-Hairy."

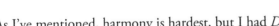

As I've mentioned, harmony is hardest, but I had *Damn Yankees* down cold. Lyrics had never been a problem for me until the next day, in the middle of our Act Two stumble-through. The Senators sing a number, "The Game," in which they pledge abstinence before a crucial match-up with the Yankees. The running gag is that the men trade spicy stories, get hot and bothered, and then throw cold water on each other in the refrain and "Think about the game, the game, the game."

Lud had a solo story he starts telling Petey. I knew my lyrics until I locked eyes with Jon Camilleri. Robin's complicating verdict at the Dewitt Mall had led me to avoid Jon, not so easy when changing down to jockstraps in a tiny group dressing room. I hadn't even said hello. I wasn't trying to be junior high about the situation. Robin, despite her sophistication, was fallible, but suddenly there he was, two feet away onstage, cap backwards, in Petey's catcher's pads, a fellow actor focused on what I was communicating to him in the moment.

LUD: "There was that Pullman car that I got lost in/ On a sleeper out of Boston…"

MEN: "Yeah…yeah…."

I looked at Jon's lips, his thick neck, the hair at his throat, and—he was so hot, I froze. I dried. I corpsed. I forgot my lyrics while the piano played on.

LUD: "……………" Two measures? Ten measures? "…………"

An actor can bullshit his way through a dialogue flub, but a singer? Forget it. Songs keep time. Lyrics rhyme. I stared into Jon's face and babbled nonsense syllables—abba dabba yabba dabba doo—until my brain clawed its way back on the chorus.

The show went on; I was backstage and onstage, on and off, in a burning haze of shame, ready for Gavin to strip me of my uniform. The Big Apple had just lost a promising line cook. Judy would be crestfallen. Dave would be incredulous. I would hide out in my hogshead until the year 2000.

Waiting to make another entrance, I felt a pair of arms cross around my shoulders from the back. "It's okay," Jon whispered. "It happens to all of us."

I didn't believe him. "No, it doesn't. Not really," I said, wriggling in his hold.

"It does, Cary." He locked his hands on my sternum—Heimlich Maneuver time. "I promise." I relaxed for a split-second and leaned into him. Our ears brushed; I felt his breath on my cheek as he repeated his promise.

During notes, Gavin laughed at my flub and said don't worry about it, Lud, but *don't* do it again. After everyone had dressed and headed back into town for dinner, Jon and I went over to a lonesome picnic table hidden behind a stand of poplars between the theater and the lake, tore off our clothes, and fucked, as the saying goes, like bunnies.

◢━━━━━━━━ ● ━━━━━━━◣

Something else I had not done: played the field. (Ha.) As the days went by, make that fields plural, because Jon Camilleri's trip was outdoor sex. He must have thought he wasn't queer as long as he didn't screw a man on a bed in a room. He never said that, but he did say once that doing it in the woods, or on our picnic table, or on a ledge overlooking Cascadilla Gorge, or on a granite sculpture by the Cornell Observatory was like being his pre-teen self again. The twelve-year-old Jonny had figured out what he had down there and wanted to use it, but indoors was crammed tight with eleven other Camilleris, a crucifix over every bed, and only one bathroom. No one he knew could locate him outdoors.

He was twenty-five now and shared an apartment in Astoria with three other struggling actors, and pretended to be straight for showbiz reasons, and kept an old comforter in the trunk of his Dodge Dart. Standing naked outdoors, across from me in the water, with the sun or the stars above, seemed to him like the most private, special place in the world.

I think what turned my head, in addition to Jon's Italian combo of totally butch and totally tender, was the unspoken knowledge that I had to be there for it to happen. I heard it behind his words—Jon was a talker—and behind the press and push of our bodies against rock, wood, earth, and brick. I guess before Jon, I'd felt part-onlooker, part-assistant during sex, but these exchanges were mutual. What happened, happened between us, not just to him, or to me. "I am here with you," I once said into his neck, not as a reminder, but as a discovery. He pulled back. The moon gleamed behind his head, but I was able to watch his teeth in the dark as he replied, "Of course you are, carissimo. Where else would you be?"

"Why me?" I'd wonder. Was it because, as a townie, I knew the best outdoor spots? I asked him just that on the picnic table, after a sudden cloudburst. Sex during a warm summer rain, with fireflies after as the cherry on top—whichever Greek god or goddess was in charge of the weather was on our side that night.

Jon found that funny. Water pearled from his forelock onto my chest, puny and hairless next to his. I really couldn't fathom why he had picked me.

"You're my dowsing rod, Cary."

With Jon, I got my definitions upfront. "What's that?"

"It's a forked stick that prospectors use to find a source of water," he said. "It means you lead me to water." He pointed to our clothes in the wet grass.

"I lead you to chigger bites and scraped-up arms and legs."

He halted further discussion with another dive for my fork and stick.

The question I couldn't ask was how did Jon make do during the winter months. Did the great outdoors shrink to the dimensions of a stopped elevator, or an empty law office on Wall Street where he temped, or the famous alley on Broadway that connected the Plymouth, the Golden, and the Royale Theatres, or behind the all-night diner in Astoria, Queens, with the cook who made him a bacon-and-onion omelet?

⊢———·——⊣

Though I might have preferred to, since deception wasn't really part of my nature, I didn't stop seeing Larry Brownstein. If outdoors was Jon's way of not being queer, then outdoors was my solution for two-timing them. With no exchange of promises or hopes among any of us, I wasn't technically cheating. (Or was I? "We have a caller on line one, Dr. Brothers.") I had also started typing *Pudd'nhead Wilson,* and that meant occasional nights at

Larry's. I couldn't quit the gig for no reason or duck his advances. He was a great guy, and things were still fun. I vowed that if I started feeling guilty, I wouldn't charge him for the typing.

What I didn't like was not being able to have a catch-up. Robin would have been best for that, but I wasn't going to pull Jon out of the closet and confirm her suspicions. No one besides Dave and Gavin knew I was with Larry. Judy didn't know I was queer. Having endured years of it with Wayne, Kristy would come down on me like a sledgehammer. She thought cheaters should be castrated like steers.

After watching the final dress of *Damn Yankees*, Larry was enthusiastic about "my work" (interior eye roll here). He had noticed and commented on little moments I had created for Lud, fine fine, but what I wanted to know was what he thought of everybody else. He privately agreed that Suzy Skurnik wasn't the sexiest of Lolas, but she had a good set of pipes. We went down the Senators roster. He said that Petey, the musclebound catcher, had a case of "proscenium pelvis," an expression I knew wouldn't be in the Tascher's encyclopedia. Larry said that it usually referred to actresses, but it meant that wherever Jon happened to be onstage—up, down, facing left or right, his pelvis unconsciously swiveled as near to center stage as possible. It needed to be putting itself out there front and center all the time.

"Is it a good thing to have?"

"Some of the greatest stars have it," said Larry. "It's not part of an actor's training, like voice and speech."

"Is it upstaging?"

"No, it's involuntary."

"Would it bother Jon to hear that he had it?"

Larry considered this. "He's probably never heard the term. It's very old-school."

Around us, the cast was packing it in, pulling their bags and windbreakers off the empty seats down front. Tomorrow night our first audience would be sitting in those rows, so everyone was advising everyone else to get some rest, drink tea with lemon, no milk, it coats the vocal cords, nap in the afternoon, go over your lines, sing half-voice, good show good show good show. I wanted a strap for my duffel so I could sling it over my shoulder the way they did. I squeezed Larry's hand goodnight and let him go give his notes to Gavin.

Jon passed by with some of the guys, slapped my butt, Petey to Lud, but flashed a Jon to Cary "picnic table" look. No getting that kind of rest for him—he was rabid after a run-through. We all went outside and stood in the gravel approach to the theater, beat but too keyed up to disperse. Five crates of soft drinks and four boxes of snacks were stacked in two towers at the concessions stand just inside the giant sliding metal doors. The lawnmower had done its first pass of the season that afternoon, so the air smelled of freshly cut grass. Moths whirled under the floodlights shining on the twenty-foot sign painted with all the shows of the season. When we returned the next day, our headshots would be stapled alphabetically on the cork bulletin board next to the doors to the theatre. My face would be in that crowd, equal size to everybody else.

Before Jon and I could work out a plan for where to park our sordid selves, Dave came crunching up the gravel, mad as hell that Gavin was staying on for a production meeting.

I hadn't known that Dave would be at final dress. I introduced him to my teammates. His tie to Gavin was common knowledge, so they were eager as puppies to get his feedback. As far as Dave was concerned, *Damn Yankees* had become the mistress beneath mention, so he gave them nothing, which was shitty of him. He was deaf to their fishing and to their praise of Gavin—on purpose or not, I couldn't tell. Dave was so deaf and so shitty, Jon packed his car with as many as could fit and took off, leaving the two of us to walk all the way to Purity Ice Cream.

I ate mocha chip and listened to Dave rant about the fights he'd been having with *his* two-timing man. It was clearly not the moment to do Gavin the favor I had promised him, which was to explain, brother to brother, how the demands of being a director meant that there would be stretches of time when he wouldn't be able to meet all of Dave's emotional needs. Things would get even hairier on *Pudd'nhead Wilson,* because it was a new play, and he hoped that Dave could get used to the process. Otherwise…. More than anything Gavin had said or done so far, his worried look let me know how sunk he was on Dave. His visible distress was worth a thousand outrageous compliments.

So that topic was off the table, as well as what Dave had thought of my performance. Odd how I'd just blown off Larry's praise but found myself suppressing a need for Dave's approval. In the past, it hadn't mattered whether he'd even come to my Strand shows. Jon told me that Lud, the way I played him, was an "unspoiled rookie from the sticks blind to his strengths." That made me laugh, since it sounded like a baseball variation of every report card I'd ever brought home to the Gabelsons. I told Jon that Petey was the glue—the *hot* glue—of the team. The joke around this truth was that summer stock sets were built with hot glue, balsa wood, and chicken wire. All the pros told horror stories of rippling backdrops, flats falling over mid-scene, and doorknobs coming off in their hands.

Judy had called the Hangar a step up; for me, it felt like a graduation into something. I was putting myself out there, hitting my marks, balancing the bat. It was like what was happening with Jon, who wouldn't need to tell me why he'd just spun out of the parking lot with no goodbye. I had seen what he had seen, and we agreed as a couple on what that was without putting it into words. Dave Bailey could be a selfish asshole.

I sucked at my little paddle spoon, wishing I were riding stick in the Dart while Dave revealed his latest honeymoon surprise. Gavin was expecting him to get a job in Manhattan, and bigger surprise, they would be splitting the rent and expenses on Morton Street. Although we both knew that Dave would wind up doing *something* in the city, I had assumed he would simply seek and find the best next display case for his genius. Whether a decent salary was attached to that location was beside the point. Love was his latest free ride.

"You've never had a job in your life," I said.

"I've held several fellowships."

"But what can you do?" That just flew out of my mouth.

"Don't be stupid, Cary. I can do lots of things."

He never called me stupid, or he hadn't since I had gotten busted for pot possession and also hot-wired Hugh's car in my one wild, tenth-grade year. I could have punched him or pushed him off the stool and into the gravel. I snapped the spoon between my fingers instead. He needed to know that I could be with Jon Camilleri, younger and hotter than his boyfriend, right now. I stared at him until he apologized.

Then all you could hear was crickets and cars, the kids wild with excitement on the way in, their faces sticky and their bellies full on the way out.

————◆————

In thinking about what came next, I understand why people keep journals. Events piled up during the three weeks of the show, but their exact order escapes me.

Damn Yankees was a big fat hit. Every bat stayed aloft opening night, every patron stood, and every review made room for the "lovable" "adorable" "endearing" Senators. Judy sent me roses, the first I'd ever gotten, and said she'd never seen me so at ease onstage. The Gabelsons came back twice. On one of our rare daytime outings, Larry had seen me inspect a Rookwood trivet. He'd gone back to the antique store for it and wrote me a note about how he expected he would never meet another twenty-year-old with a taste for art pottery.

When something good happens in Ithaca, people hear about it. For twenty-one days we were mini-celebrities. The radio stations played "Heart" and "Whatever Lola Wants" and plugged the show non-stop. Men spotted us at the Common Ground, where we'd arrive in a pack after performances, send us drinks, and ask for phone numbers. People I'd seen around all my life would come up in the Army-Navy and say they loved the show. Jack Goldman at The Bookery said we equaled the original Broadway production.

I'd wake up in the morning stoked to perform that night. If I was walking up 89 to get to the Hangar, cast members with cars, even the leads, would stop and make room for one more. My favorite moment to play was the solo I had flubbed in "The Game." The Pullman car that I got lost in stood in for my secret with Jon. I was told I got laughs, but I didn't hear them, so intent I was on driving home to Petey who Lud had really wanted to bunk with on that sleeper out of Boston.

Being non-pro, the Strand could rehearse whenever; on a day off, Jon and I went over to catch Robin in a *Mame* run-through. All that needs to be said about that production is that Barbs Burgess, longtime artistic director, saved the best parts for herself. Annie Oakley was one thing, but Mame Dennis was an impossible stretch. Barbs was all bark and no swank. I knew maybe two-thirds of the cast. A lot of them were just walking through it, or stoned, or up to their hambone tricks, trying to get each other to break character, things I used to do. A couple of them even waved to me from the stage during the run-through.

We made sure to tell Robin again and again how terrific she was, because she knew she was in a turkey. Although I wanted to hang out there and preen with Jon, she dragged us to Simeon's lickety-split. It was as if she feared all hell would break loose if a pair of adorable endearing Washington Senators from the rival show was spotted in the Strand lobby.

Unable to relax until her second screwdriver, she kept us howling with the backstage shenanigans at *Mame* and vowed that this would be her farewell appearance at "Barbs' Big Top." Jon reached over, placed a hand on hers, squeezed, and said, "Well, you know the first rule of the theater."

Robin, for once, didn't pretend she already knew something. "No, what is the first rule of the theater?"

"When everything is fucking up around you, save yourself."

We fell out on that. Our laughter fed on itself; it escalated in waves. Other diners started staring, which made it more hilarious. We were becoming one of those tables I hate in restaurants, but I didn't want to settle down. The insider feeling was too good to stifle. Across the room, Kristy, a tray of dead dishes balanced on her shoulder, made the "slit your throat" gesture with her free hand. She'd get canned if the two underage drinkers she served got too rowdy, so we ordered food.

In public, Jon played it straight. He'd slept with enough women to know the moves. Throughout the meal, he touched Robin's arm, bumped shoulders, took a fry, leaned in to listen, got her jokes, showed teeth. Jon was also running an act with our leading lady. At some point after opening, he had decided that Suzy Skurnik was such a horror, he had no other choice but to make her want him before closing. He wolf-whistled her outfits, held doors, carried her bag, told her what roles she *must* one day play, spoke racy-sounding strings of Italian that he wouldn't translate, rubbed his fingers over her cheeks to even out her stage makeup, did anything he could to race her motor. Even though her Lola never changed a hair, he fed Suzy a constant line about all the new discoveries he saw her make with the part.

The attention paid off. Suzy started seeking him out. She learned *both* my names. One night at the Common Ground the three of us danced together to a Supremes medley. The secrecy of what Jon and I were really up to—the *stakes*, another theater term I learned from either Larry or Gavin—sent us into the john for a hot minute, Jon for once not seeming to care who saw us swap spit between the chipped porcelain sinks. Day by day, Suzy's pelvis swiveled closer round to his, but as long as Jon's thigh was wedged against mine under any given restaurant table, I felt that his double life made us an even hotter couple.

He didn't think the same of mine. Robin, stimulated and confused by Jon's attention, blew my cover that night at Simeon's. On our third round of drinks, and that was all Kristy would permit, Robin asked me how *Pudd'nhead Wilson* was going.

"It hasn't started rehearsals," I replied.

"No Cary, how is the play?"

"How would I know? I'm just typing it."

College-bound Robin hadn't taken typing, so she wouldn't know that reading the text reduced your speed.

Her smile was dazzling. "If Larry asks what you think, tell him it's brilliant. Even if it isn't. You have to get him talking about it."

"I think he's happier to not have to think about it every single moment."

"Think again, boychick," she said, sounding pissed. Maybe she had figured Jon and me out. I had never told him that Robin had pegged him for queer from the get-go.

Jon caught up. "You're typing the script for *Pudd'nhead*?"

"At two-fifty a page," said Robin. "Plus the occasional waffle and sausage breakfast at State Diner." She squeezed her cast-off hamburger bun to emphasize this point. "When you think about it, Cary is living his own personal 'Ballad of Immoral Earnings.'" She turned to me. "You could kill with that song *now*."

We let that one lay there until its smell faded away. Jon was looking at me funny.

"Larry Brownstein?"

I could issue no denial. Jon could, and pardon me for Dave's verb, *evince* no jealousy in front of Robin, but his opinion was easy to read: old, bald, short, nellie, *say what*?

I rotated my plate. I swirled my glass, capped the ketchup, reunited the salt and the pepper, reached for his thigh with mine, found it missing, scraped dried mustard off my napkin with a fingernail. Then Robin bested Suzy Skurnik in the c-word stakes by asking whether Larry had mentioned anything yet about my moving to New York.

"No," I half-lied. Larry hadn't used the word "move." He'd gotten as far as "see." He would like to see me in the city, which I interpreted as my showing up for a weekend with a return bus ticket.

Robin drained her glass and waved Kristy over. "You better get to work then. "Cary and Larry," she giggled. "They even rhyme."

I vowed to myself then and there that if I did move to New York, I would never ever call that jealous bitch. But you know, after Jon and I kicked Robin Tascher to the curb on Buffalo Street, we had the best sex ever. Other than to give him directions to Libe Slope, the only reply I could make in the car, stomach quaking like I'd just killed a man, was "Larry isn't you."

Jon pressed my hand to his mouth, then rubbed it against his stubble. My opinion: stacked, butch, mine: *say yes.* For two hours we ground it out like demons on the north side of the Cornell Art Museum, not needing to talk until finally Jon slipped up between innings and moaned, "What am I going to do without you, Cary?"

Now that I took as a direct invitation to *Go Greyhound.*

⊢——•——⊣

Larry helped my decision the night I finished typing *Pudd'nhead Wilson.* We were celebrating in bed after a steak dinner, and I paid some extra attention to his ears. Maybe his ears had never been worked over that way, or it had been years since the last time, or maybe the sight of that 117-page first draft on the nightstand primed his ears for the experience, but he really really dug it. I claim no special skills. Eventually, I moved on, and he said, "Keep that in the repertory."

I froze, but not so long for him to notice. I had been having sex for two years, and no one had ever said something like that to me. It made it sound like a routine, and that was wrong. I had done Larry's ears *freely* because I thought he'd like it. I had enjoyed doing it, liked that he liked it that much, but then he'd liked it so much, he'd gone and put a higher value on it. It wouldn't be *free* on my part ever again; it would be expected, it would have to be worked in. And hey, guess what? It didn't need to be said. I had ears of my own, and with them I had heard how much Larry had grooved on the tongue-to-ear move, so I would have added it to the permanent repertory anyway. But telling me to do it took away my choice and screwed things up. With five words Larry reduced what we had been doing—sesame bagels, the blue jays bickering outside his window in the morning, a hip bump at the door—to a menu. It wasn't fair, I suppose, but I decided during my little freeze in the sheets that he was an older man, and I was a younger man, and his shift was over. Not only that, I had earned that typing money and would be keeping it.

⊢——•——⊣

Dave was leaving on August 20th. Three weeks before that, on the last day of July, I was going to beat him there. I called the bus station several times to re-check fares and schedules, then began planning my move to the tune of "I

Guess the Lord Must Be in New York City."

Kristy was supportive. Judy less so. I hit both of them up for storage space in their basements but can't recall who came first that day.

Judy, pulling dandelions in her back yard, sensed my pants-pissing excitement and so didn't let on how she felt about the decision. Instead, she started with the practicals. I told her I would only lose a month's rent, which had been paid out already as my security deposit. I would certainly give my two weeks at Harold's so as not to jeopardize a positive recommendation. She advised me to write down the addresses and phone numbers of my landlord, my boss, and Ithaca High School, because they asked for those things on job applications. I could switch banks after I compared rates. Change-of-address forms could be found at every post office. Was I able to pull together a jacket, tie, white shirt, and dark slacks combination for interviews? I was. Did I need a loan? Nope, I said, giddy because she hadn't felt the need to ask me what I thought I was going to do. She believed in me. Harry Nilsson started singing, "By tomorrow, I'll be on my way...."

Judy then sat back on her heels and asked me where I was going to live, since the cost of living down there was astronomical.

"Some friends from the show live in Astoria. They say rents are cheapest in Queens. If I get stuck, I'll rent a room out in some old Italian lady's house."

"I thought you liked living alone, Cary."

I shrugged. "It's New York. It's worth the hassle. You know that."

Judy tucked some hair under her sun hat. "Do you want to be an actor? *Damn Yankees* has given you a lot more confidence, but the theatre is an incredibly tough business; you'd need real training and—"

She stopped, a pained expression on her face.

"What? What is it?"

"Are you going because of Dave?"

"Dave?" That was my shock.

"He doesn't even know I'm going," I said.

That was her shock. When I went on to say that Dave could be a selfish asshole sometimes, she dropped the dandelion weeder into the basket like it was on fire.

"What?" I said. "He'll be in Manhattan. I'll be in Queens. Judy?"

She was staring at me, as if my face were melting off in the same fire. "Don't follow him, Cary."

"I'm not."

"Are you sure?"

Sure what? Of my move? That Astoria was in Queens? That Dave wasn't a selfish asshole sometimes? Dave and I had already been separated fifteen different ways. Dave hadn't taken my suitcase out of the closet and opened it; I had, and I was following Jon Camilleri on my own steam.

I should have come out to her right then as the corroborating factor, but I was too upset. Getting up to go, I pointed out a torn screen on a back window, said I'd fix it when I came back with my stuff for the basement, and left her to burn in the grass.

Kristy, who did know the corroborating factor, sniffed it out instantly. "Please tell me it's not that old guy."

I sighed. "Don't say that, Kristy. Larry's been incredibly nice to me."

"He's not right for you."

"I didn't say it was him, did I?"

"You didn't say anything, Cary."

I sauntered away from the register and headed to the wall of jeans.

"Get back here!"

I hummed Harry Nilsson as I straightened and re-sorted inventory, an easy job in June and July. Thank God I'd be gone before back-to-school season started. There'd be too much merchandise, too many idiotic questions, and as muggy-as-the-Amazon August wore on, never enough pants or shoes in the standard sizes. Every night at closing time, the store looked like a cyclone had hit.

"Who is it then?" she asked, poking my ribs with a plastic hangar. Her eyes were lit with excitement. Wayne and three kids by thirty hadn't killed her looks or her belief in romance. "Who who who who?"

At first, I would only allow that he was a Washington Senator, not helpful when she hadn't seen *Damn Yankees*. I had bought her a pair of tickets for the final weekend, and she was taking her mom with her as a special treat. Things eased up for the Schroyers in the summer; no heating bills, and the Farmer's Market donated all its unsold dairy and produce to the food pantry.

Kristy, her mom, and the girls would eat crazy-quilt dinners on Monday, and they never lacked for clover honey.

"You're leaving me high and dry, Cary. You have to tell me."

So, I said it was the Italian she had served with me at Simeon's, and her disbelief that so studly a guy could be queer filled me with pride. I told her the whole story—it felt great to spill it at last—and when I'd finished, she said, "He treats you right, Cary, that's all I care about." I wrapped my arms around her, and she wondered whether Jon had a brother. An older brother with a good job. Who liked kids.

I figure that some of you have been in plays, and so know how a closing night feels. After every laugh, at the end of every number, during every crossover onstage and costume change backstage, you think, "That's the last time for that. This will never happen again." With some shows, it's a relief. With others, you're fighting tears. Robin's theory is that it depends on how you feel about the makeshift family you've created for those weeks. I'll admit I lost it a tiny bit in the final curtain call. Suzy Skurnik was as red and leaky as a busted fire hydrant.

At an after-party in the lobby, Gavin announced that *Damn Yankees* had broken Hangar box-office records. He said this kind of community support for a classic musical would help underwrite the development of important new work like the upcoming *Pudd'nhead Wilson,* which would be starting rehearsals in two days. We cheered long and loud at the continuity of our artistic achievement, or something like that. We cheered for everything and everyone that night. Off in a corner, Dave clapped politely—Gavin would go missing again on Tuesday. I have to say it felt *excellent* to belong to a world that Dave didn't understand. The shoe was on my foot just this once.

Larry Brownstein found me in the drinks line and asked, very directly, why I had disappeared. I said that after the script was typed, he could have called me. The look on his face made me feel awful, so I promised myself that come September, I would take him to his favorite coffee shop in Manhattan and explain everything, except for his unforced error about keeping his ears in the repertory.

We were a habit, Jon liked to say, so he turned up eventually, slurring his words from drink, high as a kite with great news. First of all, Suzy Skurnik had practically sat on his dick backstage. Even better—and here was the real payoff —Suzy's agent had been in the house, and of all the Senators, he'd picked Jon out as "a big talent." Last and best of all, the agent wanted Jon to come in when he got back to the city.

"Come in?" I said. I'd learned Bernini and Luddite and dowsing rod and proscenium pelvis and stakes, but the New York showbiz lingo had largely escaped me. I didn't know that getting your first agent was like losing your cherry.

"He wants me to audition for him."

"Oh Jon, that's amazing," I said. "You're amazing."

He lifted me in the air, not caring who saw us. As I slid down his body, he growled, "Let's get out of here."

<hr />

He was too drunk to drive, so I took the wheel. He talked the whole way about what he should sing, and say, and wear for his audition.

I'd never need a car in New York, I thought, psyched with the insider knowledge. I'd learn the subways, the buses, all the transfer points. Dave and Gavin would come out to Queens for brunch. I'd grow chives in a window pot and snip them into their omelets. I'd meet Judy in Rockefeller Center; I'd sneak into second acts of musicals; I'd help Jon learn his lines and prepare for auditions; with my home skills, I'd build us a loft bed and make our tiny space seem huge and comfy.

I drove up State Street and idled in front of my house; there was beer in the fridge, but Jon refused to come in, even to empty his bladder. So, for our last hometown hump, instead of baptizing my wrought-iron bedstead, I drove us to a spot I'd been meaning to show him. I took East Avenue through the dark campus. I pointed out the Andrew Dickson White House on the right, and the back of Lincoln Hall, where I'd sung *auf Deutsch* for Gavin back in May. Only seven weeks in the past, and so much history since. Life was amazing. I turned right on Forest Home Drive, went just past Beebe Dam, and parked the Dart in the spot reserved for the Dean of the College of Human Ecology.

I led him by the hand to that courtyard fronting the Family Life Development Center in Martha Van Ren Hall. The location didn't exactly spell romance: the grass was thin and the bushes scraggly from a lack of consistent sun. But still, by the light of a weak quarter-moon, you could see the outlines of a log cabin and a jungle gym bolted into a playground covered with pebbles.

"Where are we?" said Jon.

"This—" I paused with an emphasis I had gained from sharing the stage with Equity actors—"is where I was born."

"Huh?"

I took the comforter from his hands, shook it open and lay it out near the cabin. I set him down and told him the story of my life, according to me. I skipped over my birth mother and her interoffice mail cart, because once I reached that part, I couldn't decide whether my mother had been more like Roxy, protecting her real son from peril, or more like Kristy, seventeen and pregnant and refusing to abort. I focused instead on my bond with Dave, and the Gabelsons watching us through the two-way mirror in the model kindergarten, and Judy's choice in the Buy One, Get One Free Orphan Deal, and Professor Bailey's legal kidnapping. My story was leading to the revelation of my latest, greatest chapter, a dramatic, life-changing move to Queens, but Jon, pulling cotton batting from a rip in the comforter, had drifted away.

I stopped, and he said, "Wow, that's rough." Then he went in again on what to sing for Suzy Skurnik's agent. I said he'd kill, no matter what song he chose. He laughed and pulled me to him. "I guess this is the last time. I'm going to miss you so much, baby."

"Last time in Ithaca," I said. "I'm moving to the city at the end of the month."

There was a very long pause. Jon rolled away, then sat up. "Did Larry Brownstein give you the go-ahead?"

A blank stare was ineffective when the truth couldn't be read by the light of a weak quarter-moon.

"New York is expensive," he said.

I held myself very still. It felt like Judy playing just the chords for me on her piano. My second tenor line was lost in a bundle of notes, and I couldn't find it.

"You know, Cary, just because you have your play done in summer stock doesn't mean you're famous. There are thousands of playwrights in New York."

Just like there were thousands of restaurants.

Jon Camilleri was pretending he didn't know why I was moving.

Options. Weep, scream, smother with comforter? No, no, and no. Explain? Not remotely possible.

Final option. If it's going to be the last time, then you make it last, so it will last in your mind for later, for as long as you need it to.

We were going at it, big and strong and outdoorsy, when I heard some bushes rustling. There wasn't any wind, but I paid this no mind. Then there was the slap of shoes on concrete. Jon stopped, but I kept going. Then there was a flashlight upon us. Jon started to move, but I held on. Then the crackle of a walkie-talkie, then a second flashlight. The order to freeze was, I found, unnecessary.

That one phone call rule is true. Since Jon called Gavin, and I called Dave, we could have saved a quarter. Gavin swept in, twenty miles of charm. I don't think those cops had ever met anyone like him. On no invitation, and with no encouragement, he began to talk. He started with the history of his life, then the history of American drama since Eugene O'Neill, moved on to the history of *Damn Yankees,* the history of the Hangar Theatre, touched on aviation in general and on his boyhood dream of becoming a pilot, and then, putting a bow on it, spoke of his plans to build—with the help, God willing, of Cornell and the State Legislature and the National Endowment—an arts center on the lake to rival anything else in The Empire State. The snow job of a lifetime, it was a fundraising appeal spliced onto his Telluride "Artists and Experts" lecture.

Winding down, he referred only once to the reason why we had gathered together in an airless holding pen deep in Barton Hall. He cast our misconduct as a "boys will be boys" incident, no different from two drunken undergrads experimenting with their confused feelings in the dead of night, college is the place for that, no literal children were in the playground, no harm done to anyone, no harm at all, the boys had learned their lesson, exposure was punishment enough. By the time we staggered out of there, further charges pending, any ranking officer on the Cornell University Police Force had two complimentary tickets for any performance of *Pudd'nhead Wilson.*

The brothers needed a heart-to-heart, so Gavin dropped us off at Huck's hogshead. Dave was going to spend the night at his mother's. While he called her on my phone, I took lemonade out to the porch. As far back as junior high, he referred to Leigh Bailey as "Mom" only when he thought I was out of earshot.

We rocked on the glider and sipped in silence, skins searching for a breeze until it felt safe to talk. There was plenty to say on both sides, and it didn't roll out smooth. As far as I was concerned, both Gavin and Dave had pimped me out to Larry Brownstein. That's a strong verb to use for a person like Larry, an actual gentleman and a genuine listener. It made sense that Gavin hoped his closest friend could experience what he was having with Dave. You want happiness to catch on. The same went for Dave, who also wanted, he said, to help steer a path for me out of Ithaca, because he believed in my potential. He said he wasn't going to just leave me behind, so yes, he had put the bug in Gavin's ear, but that didn't constitute pimping me out.

I had to admit that a part of me had been sleeping with Larry so I wouldn't disappoint Dave. I had taken the bait our first double date—he bakes! he refinishes! he types! No one had forced me to clamber into the back of a two-seater convertible for a drive to the lake between a man's legs. It didn't look comfortable, and it wasn't, but I had gone along with it. Dave slips a Frankenstein mask under my jacket, I don't rat him out. Dave puts a gun to my head, I'll take it out of his hands and use it my own way. Anything to keep him shiny.

It got rougher when Dave expressed his contempt for the other man, meaning meat-headed, sweet-talking, straight-acting, closet case Jon Camilleri. I had been used. What he'd been having with me—and this was Gavin's term—was a classic "showmance," as flimsy and perishable as a summer stock set. I didn't want to be a classic anything. Classic means "over." And, ideally, showmance was going to be the last expression or reference I'd hear from any man for the rest of my natural life. But once again, I had to admit that a showmance was no different from a work shift, the problem here being that Jon Camilleri punched out first. Dave maintained that Jon had never punched in, but I knew different. Some things that happen between two people cannot be faked.

The entire time we were detained in Barton Hall, Jon had apologized a hundred different ways to Gavin, but not once had he looked at me. Saying goodbye, he obeyed the first rule of the theater and told Gavin he felt he had grown tremendously as an actor in *Damn Yankees* and hoped that Gavin would call him in for any auditions he might be holding—for musicals *or* straight plays—for the coming season. He didn't acknowledge my goodbye. Dave and Gavin and I watched him open his car door. His face was ashen under the ceiling light. Jon was about to sit and key the ignition when he spotted something. I watched him lean right, watched his big, tender arms fish around in the back seat. Then, just before closing the door, he pitched my duffel onto the asphalt.

In the summer, you water at night, so your plants don't fry. I got up for my begonias and herbs. I went into the kitchen to fill the watering can, Harry Nillson's lyric "seeing my prayers gone unanswered" ran over and over through my brain, like a dead branch had gotten stuck in that paddlewheel banjo sound I loved and feared. The pain I was feeling about not ever seeing Jon Camilleri again was so intense I had to clutch the edge of the sink to keep from buckling over. Had Jon ever punched in? Would I ever know?

When I made it back to the porch, Dave ordered me to stop messing with the flowers, he had more to say.

You don't get to be a genius by ducking the tough questions, even if it can take years to find the words to ask them with. He asked why had I destroyed his old bunk bed once upon a time?

"Destroyed?" I said with genuine surprise. "Hugh and I took the beds apart."

"No, Cary. You took an ax and tried to chop my bed into kindling."

It didn't sound like me. "What are you talking about?"

Dudley Do-Right was staring at me under a funnel of gnats at the porch light. Charges might be pending up the hill, but he wasn't going to let me off this hook.

"Judy told me years later that right after I'd left with Leigh you ran into the basement and got an ax and went crazy with it. She said Hugh had to roll you in a rug to calm you down."

It still didn't sound like me. I'm not an angry person. "I wanted more room, maybe?"

"Don't try to be funny. I *know* you."

"This was what, ten years ago? I don't remember."

Even by quarter-moonlight, I could see his eyes were glistening. He kept opening and closing his hands, like the truth was in a bucket on a rope he could pull out of my throat if I would just open wider.

"I'm leaving Ithaca in a month, Cary."

"I'm sure you have your own theory, college boy," I replied, jealous as shit at the mention of his move. Jon Camilleri had stabbed me in the heart, back, and head while Dave, who got everything, always, would get to live on love with Gavin Steeg.

"I do."

"Well?"

Dave drained his lemonade like it was a cup of hemlock. "I think you wrecked my bed, so that if I changed my mind, and wanted to come back, I wouldn't be able to."

"That's—"

If we couldn't be separated at five and six, why did anyone think it was a good idea to do that to us when we were ten and eleven? I heard my feet pounding on the basement stairs, saw the ax shining above my head on Hugh's pegboard, felt its handle in my fist, heard it crack again and again against the stepladder to Dave's bunk, heard glass breaking when it missed and hit a lamp. I felt Hugh tackle me to the floor and then all I was were muffled screams inside a wall of wool.

Now my head was screaming again, with its own question years in the making. I managed to control the volume by listening to the crickets, to the humming window fans next door, to the tires thudding over potholes, and the sideward metal creak of the glider as I reached over him for his empty glass. On the return, needing room, I put another foot of distance between us.

"Why did you say yes?"

He knew what I was asking. "I didn't have a choice, Cary."

"Bullshit," I said softly, shaking my head. "You did. You know you did."

He even knew the question beneath the question, that's how smart Dave can be: How could you have left me behind? I stood with our glasses, to give us both more room.

"Leigh wanted to be my mother for real."

I don't cry, but Dave started, as I knew he would. I set the glasses on a table in the hall and fetched him a linen handkerchief monogrammed with a *D*—Dunkler or Dave—from the top drawer of Judy's cherry wood bureau. I was sorry we wouldn't be having that lunch for three before he left town. I tucked it between his fingers and picked up my watering can.

"Do you even love the guy?" I asked. "Gavin?"

"Of course I do."

I should have asked him how he knew; it might have helped this rookie from the sticks, but I was beat. Instead, I offered Dave my opinion that he didn't need Gavin Steeg to get him to New York, or anyplace else. He would be a star wherever he went.

⊢————•————⊣

So, I didn't keep my nose clean. In addition to the dropped charges of trespassing and illegal parking and indecent exposure and disorderly conduct and disturbing the peace and underage intoxication, feel free to add petty theft to my townie accomplishments this summer. Reasoning that, what with my imminent move to Astoria, Queens, I could never afford to pay for, much less house, the thirty-seven volumes of the Stanfield Edition of Twain's *Collected Works*, I went into The Bookery one afternoon during the run of *Damn Yankees*, greeted Jack Goldman like the friend he was, moved back two aisles, found, then whisked the frontispiece from *Pudd'nhead Wilson* into a manila folder waiting on top of the change of underwear in my duffel. Color plates of this vintage are pasted, not sewn, into the binding, so Roxy pulled right out, like she'd been waiting all along for me to set her free. To pay her bail, I slipped a one-hundred-dollar bill behind her yellow tissue curtain.

I had her mounted and framed at a store in Triphammer Mall, rather than down on the Commons. The plan had been to present Roxy as a parting gift on Larry's opening night, but, events being events, I wound up putting the package, wrapped and ribboned, inside the screen door to his apartment on Tioga Street while the premiere was going on next to the lake.

With Dave gone now, I figure I can finally apply to Cornell. I have solid experience in stocking sweatshirts and such. I might even get used to selling them. I would also feel confident cooking on the line at Noyes or Willard-Straight or Clara Dickson or Risley. Leigh Bailey, in a first favor to me, used her pull to get my name expunged from the campus police records. So, when fall semester starts up, I'll call Day Hall for an appointment with personnel, and she'll have made another miraculous save.

Part Two

Kristy Schroyer & Isa Vass
1982

"It's a gruesome thing that man learns only by what he has between the one leg and the other! Oh, that short dangle! We corrupt mortality by its industry."

~ Nightwood

Kristy Schroyer was twelve hours into a Friday double at Simeon's when her mother dropped dead. Her eldest, Janice, phoned her at work, a cardinal no-no. Taking the receiver from the wall extension next to ten gallons of simmering stock, Kristy expected the worst. Maybe Wayne had tried to kidnap the girls again or make off with whatever in his twisted mind he thought was still precious to her. Last time it was a Christmas sweater—the sequins, she figured. He liked shiny things.

"Mom, I'm so sorry—"

"What's wrong?"

"Gram fell down on the rug, and I can't wake her up."

Kristy wasn't expecting this worst.

"TV room or the living room?"

What kind of question was that? Her mother was dead. She watched a new prep cook—Luis?—toss celery tops into the stockpot, then start on a crate of carrots.

"The living room."

Good. They'd still be able to watch television without that visual. A horrible thought, and she knew it.

"How's her color?" Kristy had once wanted to be a nurse.

"All white."

"Is there blood?"

"I didn't see any."

"Okay. I want you to hang up now. Close the door to the living room and send your sisters over to the Montleys. I'll be home in two shakes."

Kristy didn't dither. But neither did she fly. First, she called 911. With a corner of her cocktail apron, she wiped steam and perspiration from the receiver, dropped a handful of carrot dice into the pot to be helpful, and then, rather than involve her supervisor in the drama, found a co-worker to cover her tables for the rest of her shift. She walked the six blocks home in her uniform, and when Janice unlocked and unlatched the door, she remembered to tell her that she had been very, very brave.

Her mother, born Louise Camille Petka in 1911 and now no more, lay on her side in her pajamas. A book and a pen were on the sofa, but there were no dents in the cushions, so Kristy figured her mother must have just set down her crosswords before stroking out. The fall had dragged her wig forward over her face and had caused her left heel to twist out of its old blue sneaker, unlaced because of the diabetes. Oddly, her right arm was stretched straight as a stick under the sofa, as if it were reaching for something important. Holding her breath in case of smells, Kristy crouched by the body and followed the plaid flannel sleeve for corroborating evidence: a dollar bag of sandwich cremes, a roll of waxy chocolate mini doughnuts, a pint of rye. Louise had kept up the bad habits of her era and upbringing, but there was nothing she was pointing to now, except this surprise way out.

Kristy had never touched a dead person. She braced one hand against the arm of the sofa and, with the other, dared herself to cup, then squeeze her mother's shoulder. It was cool, but still pliant. "Jiggly" was how Penny, her youngest, who liked nothing better than to pet the flesh of her grandmother's upper arm while they watched TV, put it. Kristy and Louise had never discussed death, or what came after; life was hard enough, but Kristy was certain that her mother, cheerful, flinty, proud of her chickadees, had loved her time on earth. I should have died first, Kristy thought, with a flare of irritation. The girls would have had a better go of it with their Gram. But wasn't that always the case—hate your parents, love your grandparents? She tried to remember the last thing she and Louise had said to one another. We're low on jelly. Take the chicken out of the freezer—an out the door in the morning exchange.

Kristy tugged the pajama top collar into place and stood. It was going to be some night on the phone: her brother, her snooty sister in Albany, the aunts, uncles, and cousins. Tomorrow would be Louise's poker buddies, St. Stan's, State Farm, Social Security, and a funeral parlor. She'd have to concentrate on getting the order right. If Cary wasn't baking, he could keep an eye on the girls, take them somewhere, give her the room to feel something, to—what was the word?—*process* the event.

Kristy knew not to move the body, but couldn't she sponge that dirty heel before the ambulance arrived, or adjust the wig? Should she try to close the eyes, a job that fell to official types in the movies? Should she start a pot of coffee for the cops? In this way, Kristy Schroyer was completely her mother's child. Always in motion, Louise could stuff eight hundred cabbage rolls for a church festival without a pee break. Once, in a couples counseling session, Kristy recalled her mother's prom night suggestion that if she hadn't anything better to do while waiting for her date, she might as well empty the dishwasher. Kristy complied without hesitation, careful of her press-on nails, and opened the door to Ron Stevens holding a stack of cereal bowls. The therapist didn't find this memory as funny as Kristy had.

The approaching wail of a siren down Seneca Street struck Kristy as a male waste of noise. Her mother was dead and gone. For lack of anything more decisive to do, she clicked the pen on the couch shut and put it in her pocket. How was she going to keep Wayne away from the wake, the funeral, the interment? Fresh occasions for his maudlin dad act. One thing was sure. The rings couldn't go into the ground with her. There was no money for anything, and now, with this catastrophe, there'd be even less.

⊢————◆————⊣

Her girls always knew how things stood. Typically, Janice of the Startling Announcements announced at breakfast two days after the funeral that she was going to quit school and find a job. Washing Penny's hair over the sink, Kristy willed herself to stay calm. Things went better when she didn't torpedo Jan's ideas right away. Jan had a B+ average at Ithaca High, plenty of decent friends, and wasn't boy crazy. So, it couldn't be that she wanted a job as a first step toward getting knocked up by a store manager the way Kristy had back in the day. At some point, she'd sit the girls down and poke the necessary holes into Wayne's version of their everlasting love. Jan should learn she had been conceived next to the Pirro's Pizza time clock mere minutes after Kristy punched out on a bitter December night in 1966.

"Ready for the rinse," she said to Penny. "You're fifteen," she said to Janice. She had been sixteen when she became a mother, and stubborn would be an understatement.

Kristy's neutral tone left Jan unsure of a reply. In the meantime, Kristy checked on her middle daughter, Darcie the Dreamer. Elbows on the table, she was staring at the wall, a length of toast crust dangling from her fingers like a dead stem. Darcie was twelve, and from year to year, depending on her teacher, was either a genius, or, for lack of a kinder term, a dumbbell. Further tests were recommended, but Kristy refused all offers to locate her on someone else's scale. Darcie took after neither parent and, so far, seemed hardest hit by Louise's death. Kristy wasn't sure when she had last heard her voice.

"Nancy Chavette has a job," said Jan.

"Oh, I know. She sweeps up hair in her aunt's beauty parlor."

"Sometimes she washes hair."

"And gets fifty cents for her trouble. *If* the customer remembers and isn't a cheapskate. Are the lunches made?"

Penny twisted under the spray faucet. "Is this trouble for you, Mommy?" she asked.

"No, baby. It's a good job for me because I'm your mother." And I won't always be here, she nearly said, in imitation of Louise, now no longer here.

"I packed them last night," said Jan. "Bologna and cheese and pretzel boxes and an apple."

"I like grapes better," said Penny.

"Grapes are expensive," said Jan, a beat ahead of Kristy.

School lunches were another system they were going to have to figure out. Kristy lifted Penny from the stepstool, set a folded towel in her hands, and felt for her own pulse, even though, truth to tell, she couldn't remember how to count it.

"Do you have an aunt with a beauty parlor?" she asked Jan.

"I could work at McDonald's."

"Provided you lie about your age."

"I'll be sixteen in three months."

Janice couldn't get a job. Her job was going to be minding Darcie and Penny until kingdom came and went, or until Kristy found a knight in shining, salaried armor, not a wage earner. No easy thing for a not-divorced-enough mother of three in Tompkins County without a college degree.

"Who's going to get you there and back? Who's going to pay for gas? Who's going to look after your sisters when I'm at work?"

Janice rapped Darcie's head with a teaspoon. "Darcie will."

Other than a quick shoulder hunch, Darcie made no reply. Kristy was going to have to carve out some time alone with Darcie or fix her favorite meal. Which was what? When going through her mother's things, *effects* being too grand a term for the costume jewelry and Catholic charms Louise kept in an old tin button box, Kristy had been hoping to find a list of instructions and warnings, like a prescription insert, for each of her daughters. One of them had a shellfish allergy. One of them was terrified of pinecones, and so forth.

"Darcie is too young to watch Penny while you're slinging hash on 89."

"McDonald's doesn't make hash," said Janice.

That got a laugh out of Darcie, so at least she was listening. Kristy sighed. "A job is one thing, Jan, but you are not ever quitting high school. You were too young to remember how I almost lost my mind getting that G.E.D."

"I do so remember. You were nursing Penny and crabby the whole entire year."

"McDonald's makes hash *browns*, Jan," said Penny, the unconscious peacekeeper. "Yum."

Janice and Kristy shared a look over the breakfast things. Each could read the other. Janice: We have to do something. Kristy: I *know*. Give me a fricking *minute*.

Eventually, the dishes found their spots in the drying rack, Penny's hair was tangle-free, and the school bus had sent a warning honk to the two younger Schroyer girls.

"Darcie, honey?" asked Kristy.

Always last out the door, Darcie turned. Her lunch bag, heavy with the apple, swung in her hand like a pendulum.

"You eat shrimp, right?"

Darcie smiled and shook her head.

———————

Levelheaded Cary Dunkler, a rock for Kristy despite their ten-year age difference, had talked her out of her nuttiest idea to keep food on the table—stripping at Liberty's in Binghamton like Arlene Sands. Not that she wouldn't be great at it, he was nice enough to say. Cary had been a rock with the funeral arrangements. Kristy had fallen apart in the middle of costing things out. Cary had been able to track down a misfiled copy of Louise's burial policy at the State Farm office—saving her thousands—and then he had sweetly reamed out an assistant at Fontana's Funeral Parlor who had tried to guilt Kristy into a casket loaded with extras. All this when Louise had never warmed to him. Her mother had been too old school to be able to figure out what a "gay" could offer Kristy besides a rinse and a set.

Kristy's other job was Associate Manager of Harold's Army-Navy on the Commons. It was early May, and they were posting discount flyers to capture Class of '82 commencement dollars. Cary hadn't worked at the Harold's in months, but she knew he loved walking around Cornell and so offered him seventy-five bucks for the day. He agreed, but only if she got her rear end out of the store and went with him.

Kristy could handle students when they were ordering lunch at Simeon's or buying a T-shirt downtown, but she felt judged on both Ithaca campuses. Today her dull brown hair felt especially coarse, her face, wind-burned; her clothes were sloppy. She felt an indistinct, unaccomplished thirty-two and was ready to apologize to any co-ed who met her eyes. Cary, on the other hand, breezed around the Arts Quad, pointing out which academic department went with which fancy stone pile. He had no problem wading into the class-changeover crowds to staple-gun flyers over magazine offers, frat party come-ons, and calls for political action on the bulletin boards.

They followed a faded trail of green claw tracks around the statue of Cornell founder, Andrew Dickson White. Cary explained that they were a remnant of Dragon Day, a celebration held every March by the School of Architecture, Art, and Planning. The first-year students designed and built a gigantic dragon out of papier-mache and suchlike, then torched it in a drunken bonfire in front of Sibley Hall. Kristy kept her opinion on that kind of waste to herself. A TV special she'd once watched on Tibetan monks sweeping away their mandalas had made her physically ill.

"We're coming to my favorite place on campus," said Cary.

They walked into Goldwin Smith Hall, then down a short flight of marble steps on the left into a rectangular space about forty yards long. Students thronged a double row of tiny tables. Along one wall, a line of them were waiting to buy coffee, sandwiches, and baked goods. Cary nudged her. "Look up, will you?"

Kristy gasped. Training her eyes on her feet, she hadn't noticed coming in that the room was two stories high, or that circling its perimeter, on an elevated gangway, was a parade of colossal white statues. Greek and Roman, that much she knew. The winged gods and goddesses were sort of obvious, but there were soldiers too, and discus and javelin throwers, a rearing horse, and just to Kristy's right, a man in a toga, at least twenty feet tall, holding a wreath in both hands like a steering wheel.

"Are they real?" she asked.

"No. They're plaster copies made for the art history department back in the twenties. They call this the Temple of Zeus. Cool, huh?"

Kristy, silenced by the centuries, even cast in plaster, nodded. She found it hard to fathom how the students could possibly study and eat and argue here. She wondered whether the streets in Rome were like this. Once upon a time, Louise had been saving up to get the Pope's Easter blessing in Vatican City.

"You want a coffee?"

"God no," she said.

"Wait here then." Cary handed her his flyers and staple gun. "I have to pick up my order."

She watched him weave his way down the stairs and disappear through a bead curtain behind the cash register. Cary had left the Army-Navy to apprentice at Clever Hans, a new European-style bakery that had opened up close to the lake. It made sense to Kristy that Ivy Leaguers would load up on the fancy pistachio tarts and Linzer squares from Clever Hans. Townie kids went for doughnuts, twists, and bear claws. Cary sometimes brought over a bag of day-old product for the girls. Louise hadn't resisted him then. Kristy herself wasn't much for sweets, but in her last years, her mother consumed sugar in all forms, like a fruit bat.

She ducked under an iron handrail and perched on the base of the statue of the man with the wreath. A Caesar maybe, she thought, but she was too self-conscious even to read the ID tag on the front of the base. She rested her head against the hem of his toga, but rather than provide comfort, the contact dredged up an awful memory of Darcie's school pageant two years back. Kristy had been so busy with inventory month at Harold's that she wasn't aware of the preparations going on at home until she showed up at Cayuga Heights Elementary. The theme was "Life on Mount Olympus." After what felt to her like an endless parade of mumbling fifth graders wearing cotton-ball beards and tinfoil crowns, Darcie entered as Hestia, goddess of the hearth. Kristy watched her lips move but having spotted the cut-up bed sheet sacrificed from the linen closet—those were arm*holes*—she was too furious to register anything Darcie said.

She and Louise had scrapped for days over Hestia's toga. Kristy remained unaware of the triumph of her middle daughter's original declamation until her teacher brought it up in a parent conference as ringing evidence of artistic promise, fifth grade being one of Darcie's "genius" years. Kristy had tried to sweet-talk Darcie into a repeat performance, or a copy of the speech, but no dice.

Kristy scanned the airy upper reaches of the Temple of Zeus, hoping that Hestia might herself might descend from Olympus and tell her how to repair her shattered hearth, but instead of the healing wave of an olive branch—or a fireplace poker—she felt a shower of hammers from all the gods rain upon her. She was an ignorant mother, and she had been a selfish daughter. She would never be able to seek Louise's forgiveness for the toga ruckus, for having dropped out of high school, for the umpteen last chances she'd given Wayne after it was clear he was batshit crazy, for draining her nest egg, for the years she and the girls had cost her, taxed her, aged her, bled her dry, the years Louise might have spent visiting other children and grandchildren, relaxing, seeing Vatican City, *enjoying* life. Her mother had been swept away faster than a mandala. She would never hear her voice again, argue with her about how chemicals were in everything now, laugh about men and their idiotic ways. Kristy, unable to afford tears downtown, put her face in her hands and began to cry.

Cary brought her to, with paper napkins and a different flyer. This one read:

Responsible College Student with Car
Seeks Room for the Summer of '82.
Special Skills: Babysitting. Yard Work. Spanakopita.
Heavy Chores. Light Housekeeping. Light Comedy. Pig Latin.
Call Isa at 420-1756

In crafting her appeal, Isa Vass had very nearly added "Please Don't Make Me Go Home To My Parents," but her roommate, for whom "Pig Latin" was already quite enough, had talked her out of a second cherry on top. (Isa had a tendency to overdo.) This summer, though neither would cop to it, Isa's parents were splitting up, and she knew she couldn't spend her days acting as their buffer while also meeting the needs of several thousand laying hens. Let it be her brother's turn.

How Isa Vass, a vibrant girl from Southern Illinois, wound up in the Finger Lakes region of New York majoring in theatre was a tale easier to share with Kristy Schroyer than how her father, engineer George Vassiliotis, had wooed and married her mother, Olga Kaletsos, in Alexandria, *Egypt*, and wound up on an egg farm ninety minutes southeast of St. Louis. The two women were sitting with coffee on a bench in front of Home Dairy, an iced moon cookie between them. It was one of those balmy spring afternoons when the Ithaca Commons feels like paradise, or a Grandma Moses rendering of a tidy, tending-to-Socialist hamlet.

Isadora Vassiliotis had been her own comedy act since before she could walk, so it had been her change-of-pace dramatic performance as Annie Sullivan in a competitive, half-hour version of *The Miracle Worker* her sophomore year that began her path out of the butt end of the Land of Lincoln. The show advanced to the state meet in Springfield, where Jacksonville High received second place, beating many a snotty high school from the Chicago suburbs. Isadora did even better, winning a Best Actress citation and a two-week Rotary Club scholarship that summer to an acting camp at Western Illinois University.

Macomb is only marginally less podunk than Jacksonville, but the acting camp was, again, a statewide affair, so in addition to voice, speech, improv, text analysis, and scene study classes, Isadora met (and in two instances, screwed, though this detail she kept from Kristy) snotty Chicagoland boys. The suburban girls were even more useful. She took note of their quiet voices, their subdued makeup, their subtler ways of getting boys to do things for them, even something as simple as busing their cafeteria trays. Isa had been a full-service girlfriend from the get-go. Most important, they were all making plans—if not college, then stewardess or beauty or secretarial in Chicago. One way or the other, these girls were getting out of their hometowns.

The WIU faculty encouraged Isadora to believe that she possessed that alchemical quality known as a talent for the stage, so the "funny Greek girl" decided at the end of those two weeks in Macomb that she was going to go to college to study theater. With a farm girl's resolve, she made it happen. She spent her junior and senior years waitressing, typing, harvesting soybeans, baling hay, babysitting, wiping butts at the Jacksonville VA. She graduated first in her class, with cash prizes from the Rotary Club, the Jaycees, the Kiwanis, and the Knights of Columbus. She rejected the marriage offer of her mystified boyfriend; rejected Western's partial scholarship, took on a stupendous loan load, and headed to Ithaca...where Isadora Vassiliotis became Isa Vass and where for three years running she had been typecast by the department—when she was cast at all—as the "funny ethnic," the gal pal with haywire hair and a boisterous laugh. With Annie Sullivan still her most challenging role to date, Isa fretted on bad days that she was back at square one, but sixty grand in the hole.

"You're not saying college has been a mistake, are you?" asked Kristy, impressed with Isa's command of her own history, which seemed a straight line next to Kristy's zigzag. Spouses and kids could be mistakes, and job changes, but she had never heard anyone say that college had been a waste of time.

"I can't say for sure, Kristy. I could head down to the city tomorrow and start auditioning, but New York is money I don't have. Plus, it means I'd be throwing all this education—macroeconomics, child psychology, an affair with a professor—down the tubes." Isa got the laugh she was after, but then worried she'd gone too far. She might be caring for this woman's children. "Don't worry, Kristy. I would never bring a boyfriend to the house."

"It hadn't crossed—"

"That's why God invented the car."

Kristy laughed again, despite herself. "Do you have a boyfriend?"

Isa shook her head. "I'm waiting to see whether the Hangar has cast me in a show this summer."

"Why would that make a difference?"

"Because actors are the worst men on the planet, and I go for that."

She could tell Isa wasn't entirely joking. Somebody, probably Cary, had told Kristy that real comedy comes from a place of truth. Truth led to trust, and Kristy, who had hired dozens of young people at Simeon's and the Army-Navy, decided that she could trust Isa with her girls, provided Janice didn't have an instant allergic reaction. She invited her for dinner that night and accepted Isa's offer of bringing dessert. Just before they parted, Isa took hold of Kristy's hand and told her that she was really sorry about the loss of her mother.

⊢———◆———⊣

"What's a 'gimcrack'?" asked Darcie, reading in dim light on the Friday after Isa moved into Louise's old room. At the other end of the TV couch, Penny was curled up with "Sunt-Sunt" (her stuffed elephant), eyes closed, thumb in mouth.

"Hmmm?" said Isa. She was tired after an hour of long-distance with her mother. If you believed Olga, her father was now screwing the teller with the overbite at Jacksonville Federal Savings, and the vodka empties were piling up behind the egg washer higher than an Indian burial mound. Isa would compare notes with her brother, Ken, but not tonight.

Darcie held up the copy of *The Philadelphia Story* Isa had checked out of the Ithaca College library. "Your line says 'knickknacks, gimcracks, and signed photographs.' What's a gimcrack?"

So far, Penny had been an angel with Isa, while Janice flounced around pretending that they were the same age, but in different social cliques. Darcie was the curious Schroyer, asking her questions about farm life and the habits of chickens, and Isa's heritage. She couldn't believe that someone would change her name from Vassiliotis to Vass. She vowed to take up Isa's rejected syllables one day and become the great spy Dora Iliotis.

Isa stood and clicked the standing lamp a notch higher.

"A gimcrack is a gewgaw."

Darcie laughed. "What's a gewgaw?"

"It's a gimcrack."

"C'mon, Isa. Tell me."

"Go get the dictionary."

"We don't have one."

"Well all right," said Isa, concealing her surprise. Kristy had claimed a strong belief in education for her girls. Isa was too tired to drag out her own *Webster's*, still stowed in a tower of milk crates. "In cases like these, an actress needs to be specific. So, you can look up gimcrack at school on Monday, and I'll look up gewgaw at the office."

With Kristy's okay, Isa had taken a side gig subbing for the theater department secretary eight hours a week. Any over-the-table money beyond that would jeopardize her scholarship status. The good news was that in July, she would be playing Liz Imbrie, tabloid photographer, in *The Philadelphia Story* at the Hangar. It was a sizeable role, funny, but with room for wistful, and a man at the final curtain. The bad news was that Ash Rickwood, her acting prof, ex-fuck, and all-around terrible idea, had been cast as Uncle Willie, who carries a torch for Liz in the play. Ash had her left a note of congratulations in her pigeonhole at school, saying he looked forward to being her scene partner.

She shuddered at the thought of those rehearsals. Above his elaborate and strangely girlish wicker headboard, Ash had hung a copy of a portrait of Napoleon on a charging steed. He had painted in his own face for Bonaparte's. Isa was dying to share this creepy detail with her girlfriends— and oh what a mistake it had been to giggle at it in front of him—but that would give them away. Ash would never tell her his real name. Was it Asher or Ashley, or something ordinary, like Bob? After he had ended things *and* given her a B in Acting 312, Isa decided that Ash, which was both the color of his penis shaft and the smell of his breath, was short for Ashhole.

There was a sound of a key. The front door opened, but the chain lock held. Darcie's eyes got huge. Isa muted the television.

"Let me in, Darse." The voice was sweet, lulling.

"I can't, Daddy. It's not your night."

Darcie dropped the book and ran from the room, but not toward the door. Penny could sleep through everything.

"It's not?"

"No. Mommy will kill me if I let you in."

Isa knew who Wayne Schroyer was, but Kristy hadn't given her instructions on how to deal with him if he turned up.

"Is Jan watching you?"

"Jan's at a baseball game."

Darcie turned off the kitchen light, a weird response that made Isa think of that Audrey Hepburn movie where she's blind and doesn't know she has drugs in her apartment until the dealers come hunting for them. With knives.

"It's not that faggot baker boy, is it?" asked Wayne. Even on the slur, his voice was tender, lulling.

"It's not, Daddy." Darcie's voice was fainter now, as if she were crouching under the kitchen table. The missing drugs—heroin, Isa remembered—had been sewn into the stomach of a cloth doll. It was a terrifying movie.

"Now honey, you shouldn't be all alone with Penny…."

That was enough. Isa snapped the hall switch on the way to the front door. It was too bad that the Schroyers were renting the ground floor of the tiny house. Higher up would keep them safer. She stood back from the chain, folded her arms, and searched in the darkness for Wayne's eyes.

"Who are you, lady?"

"I'm Isa Vass."

"Babysitter?"

"You could say that. I'm living here all summer."

"Huh." Wayne paused, seeming to calculate how that might have come about and how he should play it. "So, you and I will have to get used to each other."

"If you like."

"She's Greek, Daddy."

Darcie had crept up alongside. Isa put her hand on her shoulder.

Wayne began drumming his fingers on the doorjamb, below the chain. "How are you, baby? I've missed you so much."

"It's only been a week, Daddy."

Darcie reached over and pressed his fingers down. Wayne flipped his hand over and swiftly laced his fingers through Darcie's. Isa flinched, but Darcie giggled. It looked to be a game they played.

"Isa's real last name is Vassiliotis," said Darcie, holding on a little longer.

"Aha. That's cool. What did the Greek bride say to her mother-in-law?"

"I don't know."

He laughed. "You better not ever know, baby girl. I was asking Isa."

If his daughter weren't standing there, Isa would have supplied the gross punch line to the joke. Instead, she said, "Oh, I've heard them all, Mr. Schroyer."

"Call me Wayne."

"Okay, Wayne, what can we do for you this evening?"

He held up a white paper bag. "I know it's not 'my night,' and Kristy will have my head on a platter for breaking 'the rules,' but can't a lonesome old dad bring his little girls Purity ice cream when he wants to?"

"Ice cream!" shouted Penny, now behind them, dragging Sunt-Sunt by a back leg.

And it was all over at that point. Watching them dig in, Isa leaned against the countertop, arms crossed again in a bid for neutrality. Wayne was a hazel-eyed, cigarette-ad charmer. Lean and long, with appealing butt dents in his jeans, the kind of four-handed man who could split wood, make a lay-up, cop a feel, and smoke a cigarette at the same time. Her father, the egg farmer with a PhD, had been like that until he started drinking. When she herself was Darcie's age, Isa had been on George's side against Olga until the afternoon she found him in *her* bed with an "Up with People" singer who was lodging at their house for the weekend. That was the beginning of several ends.

Rinsing bowls while Wayne put the girls to bed, Isa promised herself that she wouldn't get in between this mom and dad. This time the kitchen was all she was going to clean up.

<hr />

Although it was heresy to think so, considering whom she had replaced, by Flag Day, Kristy felt Isa Vass was Hestia come down to earth in actress form. She checked homework, packed the lunches, donated a dictionary and taped "Words of the Day" on the fridge for the girls to put into sentences. She painted rooms, sanded two perpetually stuck doors, dismantled and cleaned the S-pipes under the sinks, and whipped up dishes with eggs, kidney beans, and ground chuck—the house proteins of necessity—with no effort Kristy could discern, dishes the girls ate without complaint. Darcie and Penny were vying for the daily crown of "Neater Bedroom Half." Isa's gift of a couple of calico sundresses and her old Doc Martens completed Janice's thaw. With the addition of a headscarf, Jan went off to school looking like a migrant grape picker, a classic Ithaca look. She might not say so, but Kristy knew Jan had decided Isa was cool. There was no more griping about not getting Gram's old room or talk of working at McDonald's. Isa had been deftly putting the college bug into her ear.

With less to worry her and none of the maternal friction Louise couldn't help but generate now and then, Kristy had some leisure to think about herself. If she had even one-third of Isa's determination, she might look into taking some nursing pre-recs at the community college. At Simeon's, the new prep cook, Luis, had been flirty, if adding extra garnishes to her orders and tossing garbage bags into the dumpster for her could be considered flirting. He was persistently cheerful—he had great teeth—and sexy in a hangdog way. Or so she thought. Kristy had gone so long without she worried she might be making that part up. She had no clue how old he was.

Isa loved intrigue and came over to the restaurant to inspect Luis. Kristy, pretending to interview her for a hostess position, gave Isa a kitchen tour. Isa so charmed Luis with her high school *español* that they wound up arm-wrestling on the butcher's block. Kristy felt a flicker of jealousy, another new old feeling, but sharing an umbrella on the way home, Isa assured her that Luis really did want to tongue-wrestle with Kristy.

"Do you think maybe I should?"

"He's got boogie, but you should definitely hold out," she said.

"For what? More? Hold out even longer?"

"No, Kristy, hold out for better." (Isa Vass often dispensed this advice to girlfriends, but never herself followed it.)

"Why?"

Instead of Louise reasons, which would have included bills, daughters, the age gap, the language barrier, and possibly a green card, Isa said, "Because you're hotter than he is."

"Really?"

Isa stopped walking. Kristy felt the rain spatter her hand. "Absolutely. Two jobs, three kids, and those looks? You're like if Meryl Streep had starred in *Norma Rae*."

The compliment floored her; Kristy teared up. To rescue them from feeling, Isa took a typically (for her) lower road. "My advice is to mash with Luis, break the tension, then see where it goes."

Kristy's wild tilt of the umbrella splashed them both with rain runoff. "*Mash?*" she said. "What's that?"

"Mashing is making out against a car. You mash against each other hot and heavy until you both…um…come."

"Right," said Kristy. Before he was able to lure her into the back seat of his Impala, Wayne would center her between the door handles on the driver's side and mash away. They should have stopped there. Janice had been an accident she went through with over everyone's objections. Darcie they had let happen, because Wayne, a lineman then, was pulling down a lot of overtime, and they were still crazy about each other. Penny was the surprise disaster, a condom failure during a ten-month separation in which Kristy had gone off the Pill with the superstitious hope that no protection would mean no more sex. But, she reasoned, shivering a bit in the rain, if she had kept out of Wayne's Impala once upon a time, she wouldn't have these three amazing million-piece puzzles to solve. She teared up again.

"Are you okay?"

Kristy nodded. Isa righted the umbrella and began moving, worried that she'd said too much too fast. A farm community like Jacksonville, Illinois, with spying eyes and one drugstore, didn't believe in birth control, so Isa had learned to be sexually creative from the start. When she got to IC, Isa discovered she had far more experience than anybody she met, including the boys. She had lost a Catholic suitemate freshman year to her frankness, but she didn't expect to upset a mother of three. In fact, she had been hoping that Kristy might help her achieve some balance in the area of sex and romance.

"It's just been a long time, you know."

Isa didn't know. "How long?"

"The last time—it was Wayne—was five months ago."

Five months was twenty weeks was 140 days, inconceivable to Isa. "They say sex with an ex can be really hot."

"It's always a mistake. He just knows how to get me. Then I get his hopes up, and then he starts scaring me all over again." She sighed. "I wish we could afford to move."

Isa was still processing 140 days. "Did he cheat on you ever? Or does he now?"

"He used to, all the time, but he's stopped for some reason," said Kristy. "I've told him to find somebody else and move to Wyoming, but he says that the girls and I are, quote-unquote, his only possessions."

"Are you going to get a divorce?"

"Lawyers charge by the hour. Getting rid of Wayne will take millions, believe me."

Isa wondered who her mother would be if she didn't have George to martyr herself to. Her father would have no trouble post-divorce; Isa could visualize a line of casserole-bearing women from all over Morgan County snaking down the driveway. Who was going to take over the farm? Olga was the competent one who got things done.

Pausing across the street from the Moosewood, Kristy tried to change the subject. "Well, if I'm Norma Rae, you're Mary Poppins."

"Julie Andrews? Thanks a lot."

"No, Mary Poppins is amazing. She cooked, she cleaned, she cared about those kids."

"Little Jane and Michael Banks."

"That soup you made with Darcie tonight was so so good. What did you call it?"

"*Avgolemono.* You've slept with other men, haven't you?"

"Not so many. A few. They're just...."

"They're just what?" asked Isa.

They're not Wayne, thought Kristy, ashamed to still feel this way after all the years of crap. She stamped her foot. "They're not marriage material."

Isa stifled a laugh. Her girlfriends who had gotten married out of high school had pages of complaints. Todd Willetts drunk-dialed her once a month, whining that his bride wouldn't do any of the things Isa used to do.

"If it's been five whole months, lady, you better get mashing the next time a line cook makes you a radish rose."

They both laughed. Like a pair of Doc Martens, Isa's advice made Kristy feel with-it, and Luis's attention made her feel in the game. It was time to get back in the game.

⊢————•————⊣

Ice cream Wayne gave way to batshit Wayne on the last day of school. Darcie and Penny had come home at noon, and Isa put Penny's third-grade graduation certificate on the fridge. It was wet outside, so after lunch, she took them into her room and tried teaching them to knit. It would be a useful, realistic activity for all the hours they spent playing "Little House on the Prairie."

The needles were too long for Penny to manipulate, so Isa tried to interest her in re-rolling a package of yarn into a ball for Darcie. When that got too boring, Isa set Penny up on the floor with a crochet hook and some aqua angora yarn. Making a "fuzzy blue caterpillar" proved just as frustrating, so Isa went and dug into her closet for the watercolor set she had used for a costume design course.

Jealous of her big sister's skill, Penny scooted over to the bed, reached up, and began knocking Darcie's arm to make her drop her stitches. Darcie, expert at blocking out distractions, soldiered on. Finally, Penny pulled on the yarn tail at the corner of Darcie's little knit square in a bid to undo all her work; Darcie took up an extra needle in self-defense just as the pressure of Penny's foot in the act of standing had caused the rag rug to slip out from under her.

Penny fell forward and speared an eye on the knitting needle.

There was a stunned silence, then Darcie screamed. Isa leaped from the closet, pulled out the needle without thinking, and covered the injured eye with her hand. Tearing through the kitchen with Penny, who was rigid with shock, she whisked her keys from the table, pulled a tray of ice cubes from the freezer, and yelled to Darcie to get a pillow.

Blood was spilling through her fingers as she set Penny's head on the pillow in the back seat. Isa tore off her T-shirt and wrapped it around the ice tray. She placed the cold compress on Penny's head, made Darcie hold it there, and drove to the hospital in her bra. By the time they reached the emergency room, her roaming hand had tracked blood all over her chest, neck, and face. At first, the attendings didn't know whom to treat.

During the emergency surgery, she rocked the trembling Darcie with a susurrus of *It's not your fault it's not anybody's fault you didn't mean it it was an accident she'll be okay she'll be okay she'll be okay* and waited for the rest of the family.

Wayne showed up first. The nature of the accident made "eye for an eye" threats irresistible. He paced the length of the room, marking the tongue-colored chairs with his hips like a coyote, and cast blame, going so far as to accuse Darcie of causing her grandmother, the old Polish bitch, to stroke out like that. Darcie wet herself with fear. Isa wished they were closer to the reception desk so she could signal an orderly for a stun gun or a hypodermic. Barring that, why couldn't a next emergency emerge and distract Wayne long enough for her to be able to hustle Darcie back to the car?

When she got there, Janice perceived the hostage situation instantly. She strode over to her father, stood on tiptoe to kiss his cheek, then suggested that they go outside for a smoke.

"You're not smoking now, are you?"

She shrugged.

"What have I always told you about smoking?"

"Nothing."

Jan couldn't quite mask her contempt, so with a great curse, Wayne grabbed her by the hair and twisted it, as if he were tightening the reins on a horse. She smacked him back. With his free hand, he taunted her for more. "C'mon, hit me. Hit your old man. You know you want to." Isa worried she might have to get in there to keep Wayne from shoving Jan against the candy machine, but Kristy, arriving with a nurse, set him flying with a vicious kick up the ass. Magazines whooshed in the air as he crashed into an end table. His sprawl was worthy of a Popeye cartoon, but unfunny in the current setting.

"Where the fuck have you been, Kristy?" he screamed. He stood, snatched at the table, but the legs were bolted into the floor, which further stoked his anger.

Kristy ignored him to tend to Janice.

"Why are there knitting needles in the house?"

"I'm sorry, Mr. Schroyer—" began Isa.

"You ought to be, you stupid stupid cunt! My precious baby girl has gone blind because of you!"

Isa sensed Wayne was jumping straight to blindness to justify his mayhem. She had dated enough boy-men and had been in enough acting scenes with them to know that a part of Wayne was getting off on his fury. Not exactly counterfeit, it was enhanced, like projecting the voice to the back row of the theater. Despite their Mediterranean heritage, Isa's parents fought with the icicle swipes of people trained in disappointment. She found she preferred Wayne's chair-kicking, pre-school fire. Now he was tearing out magazine pages and threatening to take the girls away from their incompetent mother. Jan was screaming that she would shoot her father through the eyes and go to jail for it before she'd ever go live with him in his rat hole apartment when the sight of a white coat silenced them instantly—again, funny on a sitcom, but not here.

Things could have been much worse. The doctor said Penny had a surface tear of the sclera, the white part of the eyeball. The cornea was mildly lacerated, which would be a major discomfort. The doctor told them to think of it like a speck of dust in the eye magnified exponentially. The post-op dangers were infection, perforation of the globe, and, worst case, sympathetic opthalmia, a condition in which the fellow eye reacts to the trauma in the same way as the damaged eye. If not aggressively treated with steroids and immuno-suppressants, complete blindness could result in both eyes. At this reveal, Wayne crumpled onto a couch cushion with a sob and reached over for Kristy's hand. She smacked it away.

Penny could return home after three days of observation.

In a dramatic about-face, familiar to his loved ones but astonishing to Isa, Wayne offered to take them all to dinner at the Triphammer Mall Friendly's. Rejection was swift. Kristy would wait, *by herself,* for Penny to wake up in recovery. Isa drove Janice and Darcie home, leaving a deflated, dungareed King Lear to rage, rage in the parking lot.

—————————————•————————•—————————————

Isa's reward—*The Philadelphia Story*—began rehearsals on July 7th. Gavin Steeg held the first reading at the Hangar, on the set of *Man of La Mancha,* which had opened on the 3rd. To prepare for the part of Liz Imbrie, Isa had researched the history of American tabloids and, because she had decided that Liz's covert super-objective was to become a serious photographer, she looked at books of photos by Margaret Bourke White, Dorothea Lange, and Berenice Abbott. She also read as many reviews as she could find of Gavin Steeg's directing gigs in New York to work flattering references in as needed.

Isa arrived a half-hour early on the big day and helped the stage manager, Dale, set up the coffee works and space the pencils and scripts around the table. You always want the stage manager on your side. Isa learned from Dale that she was the only college student in the fifteen-person cast; definite bragging rights come fall. Even better, the experience would give her points toward her Actor's Equity card, and theatre connections to use (judiciously) when she inevitably moved to New York after graduation.

Fanning the sugar packets into a semi-circle on a chipped china plate, Isa thought about Hazel, the stout, pestering TV maid from afternoon reruns. Hazel had been played by Shirley Booth, who was the original stage Liz Imbrie in 1939, the same Shirley Booth who, a decade after *The Philadelphia Story* and a decade before *Hazel,* had won a Tony Award *and* an Oscar for the same dramatic lead in William Inge's *Come Back, Little Sheba.* Miss Booth could play comedy and drama, leading and featured, had fame and the respect of her peers. And like Isa, she wasn't pretty. For a few trembling moments, alone on stage while Dale answered the phone in his office, Isa allowed herself to feel that it was all going to start happening for her now. She wouldn't be an actress if she didn't, or couldn't, hope that these five weeks as Liz Imbrie constituted the first step in a long and brilliant stage career.

One of her IC buddies had written a fan letter to Stephen Sondheim about how earthshattering he had found *Sweeney Todd* and had gotten back a handwritten note from the composer-lyricist. Isa wondered how she might track down Shirley Booth. If she were still alive, she could write and ask her to recall any insights about playing Liz, especially her tricky first scene with Macauley Connors, her on-again, off-again journalist boyfriend. It wasn't that wild an idea. Movie and rock stars might be unapproachable, but theatre people left New York apartments six days a week to get to their jobs a half-hour before the curtain went up. Plus, they were said to want to pass on their stage wisdom, mentor youngsters coming up in the business. And what a business—$125 dollars a week to play make-believe in costume. George and Olga Vassiliotis would never understand her hunger for the stage.

Alas, by the end of that first day of *Philadelphia Story,* Isa felt the need of Miss Booth's advice to the tenth power. With such a short rehearsal period, it was practical to be "off book" as quickly as possible; eager to begin, Isa had run her lines so often with Darcie she had them memorized. She knew enough not to say so; the other actors might think she was showboating, but her readings gave it away. She was louder than the rest; she anticipated her cues; she wasn't listening to her scene partners. Seeking results, she wasn't in the moment, and so she bombed. The ten-year-old girl playing little Dinah Lord had gotten more laughs than Isa did.

Gavin Steeg took her aside at break and told her not to push; it was just a reading. "Make them come to you," he said. His tone was friendly, but his eyes weren't. He didn't touch her arm or shoulder the way she'd seen him do with other cast members. He walked away before Isa had a chance to thank him for bringing new life to the Hangar Theatre. Just as well, she thought. That speech would sound as canned as her Liz Imbrie. Usually a cast sparkplug, Isa felt alone, and as green as a lime Lifesaver.

Isa took her seat and feigned a protracted interest in the sharpness of her pencil for the rest of the break. Comedians of all ages push. They can't help it. Her fourth-grade teacher had told Olga in a parent-teacher conference that little Isadora tried too hard. Her intensity frightened some of the other children. Olga thought this a compliment when recalling it to her daughter, but Isa, younger then than Darcie was now, knew it for what it was. She was too needy. Need was a condition as impossible to conceal as Robby Little's harelip. But if you could make them laugh, they wouldn't discard you so fast, or want to make fun of your voice when you talked.

Isa's reading went in the other direction for Act Two: quiet, tentative, and again, crickets from Gavin and the rest of the room. The actors on either side of her edged their chairs away, as if she were emitting a talent-sapping gas. When they were finished, and the cast was pushing back from the table with stretches and easy goodbyes, Isa leaned down for an extended scratch of her ankle.

She stalled further by re-buckling her sandal strap. She straightened up to make her escape and saw that only Ash Rickwood was left.

He knew what she was feeling. "Dial it back, don't you think?" Uncle Willy had gotten his laughs. Gavin had even snorted at a couple of Ash's deadpan takes.

"I don't know what you mean," she lied.

"This is a Phillip Barry comedy of manners, not *Saturday Night Live*."

"Thanks for the heads-up." To keep tears from gushing forth, Isa remembered that Ash's toenails were as yellow and ridged as potato chips. "But from now on, Professor Rickwood, I am going to take my notes from the director. Just the way you teach us in class."

It was an aggressive move. Ash loudly set his knuckles on the table, causing a pencil to roll in his direction. He picked it up and, as he talked, prodded the air with the pointed end.

"Miss Vass, you should know that I, or rather the theater department, has more riding on your abilities than even you do."

"How do you mean?"

"This season, Gavin was obliged to cast a certain number of majors from IC and Cornell."

"Obliged?"

"Ties to concrete production opportunities are beneficial to the Hangar and to both college programs. A picture of you and I, as Liz and Uncle Willie, would, for example, look great on a recruitment brochure."

Isa, seeing where this was headed, felt sick to her stomach.

"Last summer, the Hangar ran a deficit. You never want those piling up. Gavin reached out to us last November, and we came to an agreement."

"I gave a good audition, Professor Rickwood."

He smiled. "Of course you did."

"Gavin could have put me in the chorus of *Man of La Mancha*."

"As far as I or anyone knows, you don't sing, Miss Vass."

"Then he could have cast somebody who doesn't sing. I could be a maid in *Philadelphia Story*. But I'm not, I'm Liz Imbrie."

"Yes."

With that, he left her.

Taking deep breaths, Isa gathered her bag and script and pressed them to her chest. She said goodnight to Dale, who was showing his assistant the proper way to sweep a stage, then staggered into the evening air via the landing dock. Passing her car, she threw her things through the open driver's window and kept on towards the lake. She heard bats cracking as they met the ball and shrill cries at the pony league fields at the other end of the park. Ending their picnic, a family man emptied a bag of ice on a grill and set off a hissing shower of steam. His wife clapped her hands for attention, and their children began folding up the lawn chairs. They drooped into each other happily as they made their way back to their car.

Isa sat in the grass at the edge of the lake. Expanses of water soothed her: the quiet slap-suck of the waves, the pointed tops of the pines on the opposite shore, the breeze, the white sails like torn envelope flaps gliding north. Sometimes she wondered whether the tragicomedy of her parents stemmed from their having removed themselves from the Aegean. Growing up, she had been told tales of great-aunts who salted fish and pounded squid for hours until it grew soft enough to eat or sell, of great-uncles who would catch a tuna and grill it on a beach for the whole village to feast upon. George and Olga had packed up, then packed themselves into the level earth of Illinois, with bottom-feeding catfish the only reminder of what they had given up. And all of it for eggs.

She tried not to think about being a token.

By the time Isa got up to leave, baseball practice was over; the stadium lights had flicked on for the actual games. She'd have to get the car out of the Hangar lot before the *Man of La Mancha* crowd hemmed her in. She thought she might ask Cary Dunkler, who would be coming in with his Clever Hans delivery, for tips about working with Gavin Steeg. Kristy and Darcie still raved about *Damn Yankees* from two seasons back.

A man sitting on a picnic table called out her name.

She had the crazy notion that it might be Gavin, but it was Wayne, come to apologize for using the c-word on her at the hospital. Janice had let on that Isa had gone to her first rehearsal. He said he'd spotted her sitting at the edge of the lake but thought he'd wait, because she looked like she needed to be alone. Maybe she still did; he could go.

"Free country," said Isa. She sat on the bench attached to the table.

Wayne's right leg swayed toward her. His jeans were rolled up, like a teenage hood. "Hey."

She looked up. He fished in his shirt pocket and pulled out a couple of pills.

"You want?"

"What are those?" asked Isa, looking in his palm.

"Painkillers. Takes the edge off."

She shook her head no.

"Clean teen?" he said.

"Something like that," said Isa.

Wayne laughed, popped one, and swallowed. After a silent moment, he gripped the edge of the picnic table with his hands. The light was nearly gone, but Isa could still see the play of the muscles in his arms as he leaned forward to murmur in her ear.

"I don't think so. Not you, Greek girl."

There was that voice again, the profane and the tender folded together in a thick, rich batter. You should go to radio school, she almost said. She counted seven lightning bug flashes before Wayne spoke again.

"I've got something else that maybe you'd like."

She knew what it was, and this she did want. Hadn't Kristy told him to find somebody else? She counted another three lightning bugs as his fingers traced a slow path up her spine. Let's go to Wyoming, she thought, drawing up his T-shirt to palm his stomach.

For ten days, Penny wore a half-sphere bandage that made her resemble, in left profile, a housefly with Shirley Temple curls. The nurse had cut the tape away, and then, after Penny said she could see perfectly and the doctor tested both eyes, the girls celebrated with cake and ice cream.

Then came the bill. Twenty-three hundred dollars that Kristy couldn't hope to raise, so ridiculously high an amount, like Monopoly rent on Park Place, that at first she could only laugh and zip the envelope into an inside pocket of her purse. But after a few days, the sum began to prey on her thoughts. She had always paid her bills. She had never been on public assistance.

She had no health insurance. Her emergency fund stood at two hundred and sixty dollars. When Louise was alive and they got into a crunch, the balance would sometimes miraculously appear on the kitchen table, but there was no way Kristy would ever ask her brother or sister for help, or appeal to the priests at St. Stan's. All Wayne was worth was his standard eight-dollar apology, a bouquet of pink carnations from the Pic-n-Save, one currently drying out on Penny's nightstand.

Forget about the banks, or a loan from Harold's Army-Navy. Despite her years put into his store, the time to sleep with Harold Scharf was over. He had a new young wife, a second batch of kids to support, and now ran the business from Jersey City. Cary would lend whatever he had, but it wouldn't be much, and borrowing from a kid would be humiliating. There remained Liberty's strip joint in Binghamton, but her weekend tips at Simeon's were huge. The thought made her smile. Customers still left phone numbers on their credit card slips. Kristy finally calmed down by reasoning that the situation wasn't like having to bury Louise. The hospital wasn't going to re-puncture Penny's sclera for non-payment or send them all to debtor's prison.

Ithaca is a merciful town. Kristy went to the hospital to plead her case to Mark Shinner, a billing counselor, gave him her two hundred and sixty, and got asked out to dinner. Neither the debt forgiveness nor the invitation seemed above board, but she wasn't in a position to refuse this surprising act of charity.

"Look at me, Ms. Schroyer," he had said, extending his hand. "Need is not a crime."

She shook his hand. "Okay."

Not wanting him to see where she lived, nor let the girls or Isa know she was going on an actual date, Kristy met him in front of the Chanticleer Lounge, then Mark drove behind her to the Rongovian Embassy in

Trumansburg. Except for cash reconciliations with her boss, she couldn't remember the last time she'd sat at a restaurant table with a man. What would they talk about? Turning into the parking lot, Kristy recalled Isa's "Male Gas Test." In the miscellany of advice she had brought to Seneca Street, Isa had told Kristy that, when on a first date, to check her watch when the guy asked a first *real* question about her. The average was an appalling forty-five minutes. The older the guy, the longer the gas.

The Rongo, as it is more commonly known, was the spot in Tompkins County to hear musical acts from all over the world, but this was early on a Wednesday, so both the bar and lounge were quiet. Kristy would have preferred a blues singer or a jug band as distractions when the conversation faltered or dried up.

Mark Shinner was new to Ithaca. He was thickset, and the chin area of his beard was gray, so Kristy put his age at forty to fifty-five. An AV Club type in high school, she decided. If there was a sport in his past, it was wrestling. Or he'd been a baseball catcher. Other than something of a throat-clearing tic, he was mellow, with nice manners and a deep dimple in his left cheek.

Mark aced The Male Gas Test. Kristy thought he already knew too much about her from the billing interview, but when he asked at a mere six minutes what was the toughest thing about raising girls, she relaxed some and talked about how, more than anything, she wanted them to be the owners of their bodies, wanted them to be in charge when the man on the street, or the playground, or in the alley, or behind the desk, not to mention all the boys in homeroom, came calling. In other words, what she wished for her girls was the warning her mother had failed to ding into her when she was their ages.

Kristy began making an accordion of the paper napkin in her lap. Busy hands might stem the tears. Sometimes, when she heard Isa open her bedroom door, her heart swelled to think that Louise had just come back from a restful trip to the Adirondacks.

"Your mother hasn't been gone all that long," he said.

"Not even three months," Kristy replied, confused by his intuition. She watched him adjust his glasses by spreading his hand across the entire frame and pushing it up with his thumb and middle finger.

"You mentioned her death in my office, Kristy."

That brought up the humiliation of her bill, which Mark had insisted was not up for further discussion. They looked at each other for a long moment. Mark cleared his throat.

"Do you have kids?" she asked.

"No."

"Ever been married?"

"No. Right now I'm looking after my brother and trying to finish my doctoral dissertation."

She hid her disappointment. A man with degrees would never want her. She'd have better luck with the grizzled elbow-benders under the elk's head at the bar. Getting men to talk about themselves was never a problem, so she asked him the subject of his work-in-progress.

"Colonial land jurisprudence," he replied.

"What does that mean?"

"Zoning regulations in the Massachusetts Bay Colony." He made a snoring sound. "I fall asleep myself trying to explain it."

"You mean like the Pilgrims?" Kristy could sort of picture Mark standing over a turkey in one of those big-buckled hats.

They got off that subject and ordered more wine. That she didn't feel any spark made Mark easy to talk to. Edgar, his kid brother, had fallen into an empty swimming pool when they were teenagers, suffered a partial spinal injury, and had become paraplegic. He had taken over Edgar's care when their sister needed Mark's space for a third child, moving west from Hartford and locating a house for them to share in Lansing. After he'd gimped it out— Edgar's term—with rails and ramps, Mark had found his admin job at the hospital.

Wheeling someone around all day long sounded beyond depressing. Kristy, always attuned to the cost of things, wondered how the brothers made do. Was there public assistance for the handicapped?

"My brother is the Associate Dean of Students at IC," said Mark.

"Oh."

"His *completed* dissertation was on the Bonus March of 1932. It's a book now."

Here was another against the odds success story that made Kristy feel that any potential she ever had had been ground up in the sink disposal years ago.

75

Jan was going on to college even if Kristy had to sell her eyeballs to pay for her books.

"Edgar keeps *me*. I'm just there to bring in the groceries and make sure he doesn't stop breathing."

Maybe she should marry Edgar. If things got dicey, she could outrun a wheelchair. She tried not to giggle. That was the wine, she figured.

Before the check was paid, Mark asked her for a second date.

"Why me?" blurted Kristy, covering her face with a hand. She stood, took an unsteady step, and did her best to keep from bumping the diners next door. Where had all these people come from? A Mr. Green Jeans-type was on the stage, picking his banjo at mic height to test sound levels. She was glad they'd be gone before the hootenanny started. Mark would insist they had to dance, and then be terrible at it.

"You've waited on me at Simeon's. If there's a lamb special, I tend to order it."

Kristy blushed. "I'm sorry—I should remember customers—that's so rude of me."

"It's not rude, Kristy; it's efficient."

He made efficiency sound appealing. She gave him a longer look. Without a beard, and better eyeglass frames, or contacts, he'd still look like a math teacher. She remembered Isa's verdict. You could do better.

"When you came into my office this morning, I thought I'd risk it. I'm glad I did."

She was supposed to say, "Me too," but it wouldn't be true. Mark adjusted his glasses to cover her silence, and they made for the door. Out by their cars, he kicked gravel against her tire and said, "I know I'm not going to finish it."

"Finish what?"

"The dissertation." He sounded so lost she instinctively put her hand to his shoulder for a quick second. There were worse things than a math teacher.

<hr />

Once inside the Temple of Zeus at Goldwin Smith Hall, Darcie acted as if she'd been set loose in Candyland. Weaving among the nearly empty tables, she ran from statue to statue, identifying them by sight. Hermes, known as Mercury to the Romans, with winged sandals; Artemis, Diana to the Romans, with a deer; Poseidon, King of the Seas, with his crown and trident; Cerberus, the three-headed Hound of Hell; Hades, who wasn't permitted to leave the underworld and visit his relatives up on Mt. Olympus.

Isa followed, checking Darcie's work against the ancient labels. Darcie's excitement reminded Isa of the time she had taken a backstage tour of the St. Louis Rep after a school matinee of *Our Town*. Emptied of actors, the dressing rooms had been a kind of temple. Their spans of mirrors framed in bulbs and patched with opening night cards and photos, their counters a repeating frieze of make-up kits, folded towels, jars of cold cream, and bouquets of brushes, eyebrow pencils, and floral tributes.

Darcie couldn't identify Hippolyta and Ganymede, but shrugged off these lapses, explaining to Isa that the Amazon Queen and Zeus's cupbearer weren't ranking members of the Greek Pantheon. Ganymede, Darcie declared, was just a kid, and besides, cupbearers were basically water boys, like the townie teens who relied on the waitresses at Simeon's for a cut from their tips.

When they had finished with the plaster parade and had come around to the treats counter, Isa bought an iced coffee, and a root beer for Darcie, and two chocolate mint brownies. "Who do you want to sit by?" she asked.

Darcie knew what Isa meant. "Hephaestus," she said instantly, pointing to the corner furthest from the stairs.

"Sure thing," said Isa. "Why—uh—her?"

Darcie sucked her teeth. "*Him.*"

"Him," said Isa. "I'm not as smart as you about these things."

"You're not?" asked Darcie, surprised.

They sat down. A shadow cast by the god of fire's arm and hammer ran down half their table.

"My favorite is Hestia, but she isn't here. Neither is Demeter."

"That's interesting," said Isa, who didn't know Demeter from Doris Day but understood Darcie's impulse to catalogue. She herself kept a goal starting in eighth grade to learn every Best Actress Oscar recipient from Janet Gaynor to Faye Dunaway. This year had been Sally Field's second win, for *Places in the Heart.* Her "*You really like me*" acceptance speech, so needy, so easy-to-spoof, had made Isa burn in shameful recognition.

Darcie took a pull of root beer. "Hephaestus is blacksmith and armor-maker to the gods. He reminds me of Daddy."

Isa's stomach lurched at the mention of Wayne. "Is that so?" she said. Darcie was on this field trip to the Temple of Zeus to compensate for Isa's guilt at what had happened on that picnic bench. She had permitted Jan to have a male friend in to watch television, and for Penny, Isa had made red, white, and blue cupcakes.

"Hephaestus is strong and smart, but he's crippled, and that makes him angry."

"Your father isn't crippled, Darcie." Quite the opposite, thought Isa. Even at forty-two, Wayne was as fit as any farm boy she'd ever fucked.

"I know," she shrugged. "Hephaestus has a club-foot; Zeus made Aphrodite, the Goddess of Love, marry Hephaestus against her will, so she cheats on him with Ares, the God of War. And others."

"That's pretty racy stuff, Dar. They taught you that in school?"

"I read up," said Darcie, smoothing a finger of mint frosting across her lower lip like a starlet. "They didn't have divorce on Mount Olympus."

Darcie made Aphrodite's dilemma sound modern. Isa didn't ask her how she would feel if Wayne and Kristy actually finally got divorced. Darcie avoided direct questions or took so long answering them that her mother and sisters tended to move on. She wasn't so much dreamy, Isa had tried explaining once to Kristy, as she was an old soul. Darcie had recently told Isa that she'd decided that life wasn't a line or an arrow going in one direction; life was like drops of colored ink that bled and flowered into each other on a piece of paper every which way. No matter how attractive she might turn out to be post-puberty, Isa knew that pronouncements like these might help scare off the boys with back seat ambitions. Being the weird girl has its advantages.

Wayne had pretty much said so himself as he and Isa, hustling back into their clothes by the lake, small-talked about his daughters. Serious talk, had Isa been capable of it, would have begun with this is the biggest mistake of my life. This is fucking the maid. This is fucking the *au pair*. This is George Vassiliotis fucking the Up with People girl. This is—and here the chips fell for Isa in the shadow of a god's mighty arm—fucking my father. After three days of missing this oh-so-obvious connection, the thought made her physically ill. Her father was only five years older than Wayne. She scootched back her chair and rested her forehead on the table. That the sex was incredible to boot made the situation worse than tawdry. It was chicken-fried-hayloft tawdry, and she wouldn't be able to escape the fallout until she had fled back up the hill to IC in September.

"Are you alright?" asked Darcie.

"I feel a little light-headed."

"Is it your period?"

"No," said Isa.

Darcie broke the strange silence by asking Isa how play practice was going. Isa shot up and laughed, wildly, as if she were playing a scene from *The Bald Soprano*.

"What's so funny?"

"I haven't heard that for a long time." Isa reached for her glass and drained the water from the ice. "That's what my mom always called it. Play practice."

When is play practice over tonight? Do you have play practice tomorrow? Do you need a ride home from play practice? It wasn't a sport, Isa had tried to explain, so it wasn't practice. And it wasn't a *skit* for God's sake, she'd snap at her father, it was a *play*. It was a work of *dramatic art*. Her parents had never seen her on a college stage; forget their crossing the Ohio River Valley together to see *The Philadelphia Story* during the endgame of their marriage.

"Then how are your rehearsals?"

Darcie's la-de-dah tone made Isa laugh harder.

"Fine. Better. Pretty good."

Summer stock is perpetual panic. Putting a play up in twelve days allows no time for character exploration or textual interpretation. Isa hit her marks, kept track of her props, and maintained a low profile. She got along with the MFA actor who played Macauley Connors, and her reactions to Uncle Willie's butt pinches got laughs—you could hardly call it acting—but the magic she had been hoping to have with her professional debut hadn't happened. Ash Rickwood's unspoken word "token" had drained her of the confidence to generate it. She pitched in with the production assistants or did the crosswords while she waited for her entrances.

Darcie went to trash their cups and napkins, but instead of coming back to the table, she used another chair as a step stool to climb onto the runway, stage right of Hephaestus.

"Dar? What are you doing?"

"*I am Hestia, Goddess of the Hearth*," she announced, eye-level to Hephaestus's waist.

"Come down from—" Isa glanced swiftly around. The nearest students, noses in books, were yards away. She looked back at Darcie, nodded, and put a finger to her lower lip to signal her to keep the volume down.

Darcie clenched both hands to her sternum and went on:

> *"My mother was Rhea, my father was Cronus. I am sister to royal*
> *Zeus, Poseidon, Demeter, Hera, and Hades. It is my duty to*
> *maintain the fires of the Olympian hearth with fatted cows and*
> *goats.*
> *I would not marry Poseidon. I would not marry Apollo.*
> *I vowed to remain a maiden, opposite in aim to my unchaste*
> *cousin,*
> *Aphrodite the Beguiler.*
> *To keep the peace, I gave my seat at table to my nephew Dionysus,*
> *God of Wine and merriment.*
> *I am not so merry, but I am kind."*

Here Darcie opened her hands in supplication, swung out her arms, but kept her elbows against her ribs. It looked to Isa like a Martha Graham move.

> *"Great Homer sings to me in invocation,*
> *So that I may protect your hearth too:*
> *'Hestia, you who tend the holy house of the lord Apollo*
> *come now into this house, come, draw near,*
> *and bestow grace upon my hymn.'"*

In a pause, Darcie dropped her hands. She pivoted her right foot inward, as if she might begin to dig a hole she could disappear into.

Isa was amazed. "You didn't just make that up, did you? You *wrote* it."

Darcie shrugged. "Except for the Homer part."

Struggling to keep her balance getting back down into the chair, she was once more an awkward seventh-grader. Isa pulled her from the platform and gave her a big hug. "That was incredible, Dar."

"You could understand me?"

"Absolutely." Some of the speech, she was sure, was in blank verse. "Do you have it written down?"

"It's somewhere."

"It's on my refrigerator," said a familiar voice.

They turned. It was Wayne. Hip against a chair, surly, and selfish in every way but one. Despite all of the lectures she'd given herself since the picnic table, seeing him made her crave an immediate second helping. Isa set Darcie down.

"It is *not*, Daddy. What are you doing here?"

"Visiting my old pal Vulcan."

"Hephaestus," snapped Isa. How long had he been tracking them?

"Vulcan to the Romans," corrected Darcie.

Wayne turned to Isa. "Ha," he said. "You think I don't know my gods and goddesses?"

"What are you doing here, Mr. Schroyer?" It was a terrible line reading.

"Studying for my finals."

"Come on, Daddy, don't be silly."

"I saw you pass by on the Commons, and I decided to track you like Harriet the Spy." (This didn't pass the smell test, but Isa was flattered nonetheless.)

"Pretty amazing, huh?" he said to Isa. "Her speech."

"There's definite talent there," said Isa.

"Gets it from me," said Wayne. "Shall we?"

She didn't want him following them, but couldn't say so, so down they went, all the way down Buffalo Street to the Commons.

⊢———————•———————⊣

Until she could decide what upset her more—father, daughter, and *au pair* eating ice cream in Wayne's apartment over the Danskin store, or Isa getting to hear Darcie's world-famous oration—Kristy kept her feelings under wraps. First off, she wanted to ground Darcie for giving her father the Hestia speech. It deserved better placement than his refrigerator, empty, she knew, of anything resembling nutrition. She was mad at Isa for knowing how to make Darcie happy, and worse, how to make her *talk*. When Kristy had proposed a return trip to the Temple of Zeus, just the two of them, Darcie looked at her as if she'd suggested she set her hair on fire.

"She calls her 'Dar' now. And Darcie calls her 'Izza.' Or 'Izard.' It makes me nuts." Kristy tightened her leg around the stool as she slid her glass forward. She'd cut a thumb in the kitchen on her shift, and it was still smarting from the lemon juice she'd scrubbed her hands with. Kristy and Mark Shinner were sitting at the bar in Simeon's. She was too tired to care whether co-workers spotted her drinking with a customer. She lived in this town too.

"Can you think why?" asked Mark.

She ought to tell him sometime that his therapist-y manner was the opposite of sexy. He was like Mr. Deaver, the fruity guidance counselor at Ithaca High who'd asked her to write her dreams down onto different color note cards and pin them above her desk. That way she could look up at her dreams while she did her homework.

"Because it leaves me out," she replied. "I know that. I hated all that secretive crap girls did in school. Diaries. Passing notes, special languages, secret clubs. My sister Sheila was so gung-ho about her college sorority, my mother and I thought she'd become a dyke."

"Are you sorry you didn't get to have those kinds of experiences? Wayne cut you from the herd at a very young age."

Kristy signaled Francis for another 7&7. "So now I'm a heifer."

"Not just *any* heifer," he said. "You're the prettiest cow in the pasture."

He covered her hand with his, a move so sudden it made her laugh. She swiveled on the chair for a better look.

"What?" he asked.

"You really do need a new pair of glasses. Those aviators make you look like Kojak."

Mark drew his hand away to adjust the offending lenses. "I'd say that's about right, time-wise. My prescription hasn't changed for years."

"Styles change, Mark."

"Right." He frowned, as if that were a lesson he'd tried to follow his entire life. "So, would you help me pick out a pair?"

God, what was going on in his head? He wasn't playing her. This was why *Cosmo* was always urging its readership to go for older men. She ran through their reasons: established, done with kids, less to prove, giving in bed. "How old are you?"

It was Mark's turn to laugh. "Thirty-six."

"Only thirty-six? Really?"

"Honest and true."

"What about contact lenses?"

"I have astigmatism."

Whatever that meant, everyone said it. It was like fatties claiming they had glandular conditions, or waiters in Mexican restaurants who warned you to watch out, that plate was *hot*. She reached over and clinked her glass against his. "It's a deal then, four-eyes."

When Cary showed up with a bag of unsold Clever Hans, he listened to her gripes and declared that Wayne was her "millstone," so of course he'd try to pit Isa against her. What's more, she wouldn't know who she was if Wayne weren't somewhere in the picture. He was all she knew. He was her photo negative, a bed of nails, black wallpaper in the bathroom.

Nor did Cary see what the problem was with Isa and Darcie's bond. It was hero worship, a crush, it was anything but a conspiracy to steal her from Kristy. Darcie had become more outgoing; her head wasn't forever in a book, and that was all to the good. If Cary played prosecuting attorney, then Mark was the judge, whose alert head nods, and the sober way he pressed his chin whiskers with his thumb and index finger, meant he was taking everything in.

Upset at being cornered, Kristy turned on Cary when Mark went to the gents. "Why did you say all that shit about Wayne?" He was supposed to be weighing in on Mark instead. "*Black* wallpaper?"

Cary shrugged. "It's a Charles Manson thing."

"Wayne is *not* Charles Manson."

"He is to me, Kristy."

"For how long?"

"For like always." Cary bit the head off a gingerbread man. Kristy grabbed and pulled off a leg.

"Why are you telling me now?"

They stared at one another, chewing. She spotted three dead bulbs over the bar and resisted the urge to run and scare up replacements from the storage room.

"I'm telling you now because this Mark guy likes you, and it frightens you."

Kristy choked on her gingerbread. "Bullshit, Cary."

"Bullshit that he likes you, or bullshit that it frightens you? You have to take Wayne out of the picture."

Why did everyone sound like a self-help book tonight? The two Kristy had managed to start, *How to Be Your Own Best Friend* and *Your Erroneous Zones*, loaded gifts from snooty sister Sheila, hadn't helped. Maybe if she had the luxuries of childcare and a catered month on an island beach, she could pause and reflect and—ugh—"work on herself."

"Why am I eating this? It's too sweet for me."

"Then have a rhubarb muffin." Cary pushed the bag toward her. "I think he's cool."

"Seriously?"

"I do. I really do. He's mellow."

"I think he bats for your team," said Kristy, double-checking Mark's sexual preference with an expert.

"With those eyeglasses? Please."

"I know, I know."

"And that belt?"

"Stop."

"It's vintage Korvettes."

The tension was broken. They were bent over laughing and spitting crumbs, their heads knocking between the stools, when Mark returned.

"What did I miss?" he asked.

They looked up. A fresh fit of laughter took Cary right off his stool. "We're going eyeglass shopping," he whooped from below.

"Tomorrow," said Kristy. "And then you're getting a haircut."

"And then we chop off your beard," said Cary.

"And then we give you a perm," said Kristy, dizzy with laughter. She nearly toppled onto Cary, who was trying to pull himself up by her calf. She gripped the edge of the bar for dear life as she scanned Mark's torso. His belt was brown, braided, utterly male, and fucking hilarious.

As their affair continued, Isa began to tally the ways in which Wayne Schroyer was *not* like George Vassiliotis: He lacked chest hair. He didn't wear cologne. He didn't have a doctorate, and he didn't speak Greek. That was pretty much it.

The sex, generally late morning quickies at his apartment with a Tab chaser, was intense, but not violent, and good and loud. Wayne's signal was a honk on his horn as he slowly drove past the house. If Penny were inside, she'd spring to the window and wave him forward like a border official. From the couch, Darcie might manage to raise and waggle a sympathetic arm, but her eyes stayed glued to her book. Isa would invent a theater-related reason to leave the house for forty minutes. That's all the time they took. She'd set a plate of contraband cookies next to the toaster for the girls, re-check the stove burners one last time, and hustle down Seneca.

The situation was so ill-advised, Isa sometimes saw the humor in it. Climbing the creaking stairs to his third-floor apartment, she cast herself as Hazel performing a morning chore for Mr. Baxter. She'd pause at the dusty coffin niche embellished with a plaster Virgin Mary and cross herself superstitiously, unable to recall whether there had been a *Mrs.* B. on Shirley Booth's famous sitcom. Wayne would open the door wearing a ratty pink hair towel tucked around his waist. She'd whisk it off, resisting the urge to stow it in her backpack and reunite it with its matching bath towel and washcloth in Kristy's linen closet.

His stripped-down quarters—three mismatched chairs, a metal and Formica table, a mattress/box spring combo on the floor, a TV, and his father's acoustic guitar on a stand—was like a boxcar in the wilderness. It made Isa feel as if Wayne lived on sex alone and that their daily dose was his basic nutrition.

The guilt she felt at abandoning the girls was the one shaming thing. She tried resisting him one morning, but within twenty minutes, he was ranting on the phone, threatening to march across the Commons to Harold's and spill the beans to Kristy. He was such a baby. His good looks had gone to Jan. Darcie inherited the brooding self-absorption that turned to actor's ham under pressure.

One night, after a draining tech rehearsal, Isa went to Wayne's before home. While she showered, he sat on the toilet and picked out "Half as Much" on the guitar. She thanked him for the serenade, and he told her that his father used to sing Hank Williams songs for his kids when they were taking baths.

"Did you do that for the girls?"

He shook his head. "I wanted to. Tried once or twice, but—I'm no singer."

Isa felt the ghost in the room. Guys don't turn out like Wayne because they had decent fathers. She remembered him taunting Jan in the emergency room—"Hit your old man. You know you want to."

They went up on the roof and screwed under the swoop of bats on the hunt. Afterward, with time on their hands, they sat up together as if they were tucked in a bobsled. Isa let her head fall back and rest on his collarbone. The moon was a sliver, little more than a darning needle. His breath tickled her forehead, but instead of talking, he slowly drew pictures, or spelled words, on her stomach with his index finger.

She drifted home to find Kristy smoking in her nightgown on the front porch. With their crazy schedules, they had been seeing less of each other. Isa hoped this wasn't an ambush.

"Looks like your date went better than mine," said Kristy.

Isa whisked her backpack to her stomach to quell the panic. "How so?"

"I didn't get lucky."

"Did you want to?" asked Isa.

Kristy shrugged. It would certainly relieve Isa if Kristy had bedded Mark, and not just because of the Wayne situation. No mistaking that Kristy had cooled towards her. She no longer checked in with her when she came home from her shifts or marveled over how clean the house was. Worst was the night she'd taken the girls to the Ground Round for a splurge and didn't ask Isa to come along. Isa hated to think ahead to August. *The Philadelphia Story* would have closed; Wayne would continue to wait for her every morning, and Kristy would figure things out by wifely osmosis. If she hadn't already.

"I sure wish I had your energy," said Kristy in a gloomy tone.

Isa began over-explaining the long tech process and a midnight snack at the State Diner with some of the cast and her plan to replace the contact paper in the kitchen shelves in the morning, but Kristy, not really listening, flicked her butt over the railing. Isa stood in a tense silence for a moment more, then said sweet dreams. As she turned, Kristy grabbed her hand and squeezed. "Get your rest."

Isa squeezed back with relief.

┠───────•───────┨

Wayne was also not like her father insofar as he saw her play Liz Imbrie in *The Philadelphia Story*. Moreover, he showed up to the women's dressing room after the second performance bearing pink carnations, earning him a modest kiss on the cheek in front of the other actresses. Apart from prom corsages, no man had ever brought Isa flowers. Pat Staples, who played Mrs. Lord, pulled a dime-store vase from a box under the common sink. "There are always some of these on hand."

Isa set the carnations on the counter and arranged her mother's card and Penny's glittery, hand-crafted congratulations on either side of the vase. Kristy and the girls had come the night before; Isa had let Jan drive her car for the special occasion.

Wayne earned a genuine kiss when he told her how pretty she'd looked onstage in her hat and heels. And then, for a final magic trick, he solved a mystery. They were heading from the dressing room to the parking lot. The plan was a quickie, then a drop-off for Isa at the Common Ground for a cast after-hours party. Amidst a crowd of well-wishers in the lobby, Isa slowly swiveled this way and that, long enough to allow the gathering to recognize her out of costume and praise her Liz. No one did, so she took Wayne's arm.

They passed behind Ash Rickwood, who was signing programs in front of the photo board. A local favorite, he did several shows every summer at the Hangar. In August, he would be playing Bluntschli in Shaw's *Arms and the Man*. Wayne stopped, cocked his head like a spaniel to listen to Ash's falsely humble thanks to the playgoers, then tapped him on the shoulder.

"Hey Otts," he said. "Good job tonight."

Otts? Who was Otts?

Isa watched Ash draw up his spine. He turned, but he did not shake Wayne's extended hand. Seeing his acting student and former fuck on Wayne's arm added to his obvious displeasure.

"Come on, Otts. You know me. It's Wayne Schroyer, Class of '58. Go Skunks."

"Hello there."

"I almost didn't recognize you, Otts, what with that accent. Your skin cleared up too."

87

What kind of name was Otts?

"You did all the plays back then too. Even with your pizza face, we all knew you were going places."

"Yes I did."

"Why did you change your name, Otts?" asked Wayne, playing dumb for Isa's benefit. It was absolutely delicious.

Ash had turned back around to face his fans. "Oh, professional reasons," he said airily.

Wayne, who had five inches on him, leaned way over Ash to peer at the program in his hand.

"What are you doing?"

"Just checking."

"Checking what?"

"Ash Rickwood," he said, sounding out the syllables like a beginning reader. Then he paused to milk his moment. "I guess 'Ash Rickwood' does sound more professional than 'Otto Novak.'"

Otto Novak? Strike three. Ash was down for the count.

"We called him Otts back when he was an Ithaca High Skunk," he said to the crowd. He clapped a hand on Ash's back so that his pen tip jiggled and tore the program page. "What I'd like to know is, how do you sign your checks?"

Later, they laughed so hard at Isa's debrief of Otto Novak's intimate quirks that Wayne rolled off the box spring and toppled the guitar from its stand. He tried to play her a Hank Williams tune, but would stop every few measures to croak the word "Otts" and fall out laughing. Maybe it wouldn't be impossible to be with Wayne in the fall. Isa vowed to provoke this goofball side in him for as long as they lasted.

┣━━━━━•━━━━━┫

The Philadelphia Story wasn't as big a success as *Man of La Mancha*; the musicals always outsold the plays at the Hangar, but Isa's Liz was deemed "crisp and effective" by the *Ithaca Journal*. Gavin gave the cast a warning speech the day after they opened. They must perform the show as if they didn't know it was a comedy. Audiences would drag them down to their level lickety-split. If you start expecting the laughs, you won't get them, and when you don't, you'll start to push for them and wind up covered in egg. "Covered in Egg," jotted Isa on her script, which she kept tucked under her makeup kit in the dressing room. If she ever got famous, "Covered in Egg" could be the title of her autobiography. If she never got famous, they could carve it on her tombstone.

The show ran Thursdays through Sundays, with a Saturday matinee. A crisis struck the company the Monday before the last week of the run. April Maddox, the little girl playing Dinah Lord, was unaware of her bee allergy until a sting on a hike in Buttermilk Falls had sent her to the emergency room. Gavin had visited the hospital on Tuesday to see whether she would recover enough to be able to play the final four shows, but, as he put it in phone calls to the company (uncharitably, Isa thought), April's head was now the size and color of a boiled ham.

Darcie, the easy solution, needed no coaxing. She had seen the show twice and knew a fair amount of Dinah's lines from having helped Isa prep for rehearsals. Wednesday morning, Isa took Darcie to the Hangar and read with her in front of Gavin and the stage manager. Darcie wasn't nervous; there were no hesitations or flubs; Dinah's lines in French flowed like a real foreign language, and she belted out her verse of "Lydia, the Tattooed Lady" like a pro. Dale vouched from the back row that he could understand her every word. When they were through, a beaming Gavin asked Darcie whether she knew April Maddox at school.

"No, sir. I'm two years older than April. Why?"

"Because you're so right for the part, doll baby, one might think you'd sent her a box of bees in the U.S. Mail."

He winked, but Darcie didn't catch his meaning.

Kristy, who heard the blow-by-blow at dinner, knew what Gavin meant. She found the remark offensive, and also disparaged his use of the word "doll baby," which she found creepy.

Mother and daughter argued all through dinner about the offer from the Hangar. Other than to apologize for not seeking her permission to let Darcie audition, Isa, who couldn't fathom why Kristy was trying to keep her off the stage, didn't need to advocate; Darcie countered every objection, half-baked or not, with Hestia-like steel. The quieter she was, the louder Kristy got. A wide-eyed Penny and Jan ducked their heads and sped through their food.

At one point, Darcie crossed her silverware on her plate, blotted her lips, and then folded her square of paper towel with a disdain that only turned up the flame in her mother. She stood, pushed in her chair, and said perhaps it was time to call her father and request his permission to be in *The Philadelphia Story*. Kristy beat her to the wall phone, blocked it with her body, and raised an open palm to ward her off. Wayne had referred a couple of times to a batshit side of Kristy. Here she was, thought Isa, red-faced and ready to pop.

"He has no authority in this house, young lady," she said.

"He remains my father nonetheless," said Darcie with excruciating serenity.

Kristy's eyes were slits. She bent at the waist to get closer, to drive her points faster through the air to her middle child. "If the man had ever earned the right to be your father, if he paid for anything besides cartons of ice cream and the occasional pack of barrettes these last ten years, he might get a say. But he doesn't, so he won't!"

"I told you I'll be earning a hundred dollars; that should please you for once. I'll give you all of it."

Kristy looked stricken. "I would never take your money, baby. How could you think I'd ever do that?"

"As you wish, mother."

As you wish, mother? What kind of hoity-toity talk was that?

"Jan and Penny can split my wages then. I will perform the role gratis."

"What the hell is gratis?"

"Latin, meaning 'for free.'"

"Speak English in my house!" Kristy's raised her hand again. "Haven't I told you never do anything for free? Didn't Gram tell you that too? Why would you do this for free?"

"Because the show must go on."

Kristy sneered at the cliché. "Is that what Izza says?" she said, drawing out Darcie's pet name for Isa until it sounded like a skin condition.

What could Isa say or do in the face of a battle ran that ran deeper than four weekend performances at the Hangar, when she didn't know all of what theater people call "the given circumstances" of the situation. Onstage, she would know what to do with her hands. Here, in real life, without lines or blocking or even prop silverware, Isa felt soldered to the kitchen chair, her hands sweating in her lap.

It was Darcie's scene to play. While her mother remained half-crouched by the phone, she moved back to her seat, picked up her plate, shrugged, and, en route to the sink, where her spooked sisters were staring at the water coursing over the dishes, said, "Grandmother warned me that this would happen."

A classic dramatic reversal, power play, a bolt from the blue, a left to the jaw—however one defined it, the force of Darcie's remark floored Kristy. A cancer diagnosis would have hurt her less than this sudden, posthumous message from Louise. When she had managed to recover her senses, Kristy begged Darcie, over and over, to tell her what her grandmother had predicted would happen, what *this* meant, until the grief and rage inside her could be relieved only by hurling the gravy boat at the wall. She fled to the porch, leaving Darcie, in her triumph, to righteously sponge the wall and floor and Isa to sweep the greasy china chips into a dustpan.

That high-stakes conflict was eclipsed twenty-six hours later. Before she left the house the next morning for the Army-Navy, Kristy could hear Isa and Darcie running Dinah's lines in Gram's bedroom. She reserved a ticket over the phone, bought flowers at the Dewitt Mall at lunch, wrote a card, and made it to her seat at the Hangar just as Gavin Steeg was announcing from the stage that a brand-new local actress was making her debut that night as little Dinah Lord. She heard Wayne whoop from somewhere else in the darkness and muttered "Sonovabitch." Of course she'd called her father. He would always be in their lives, always.

This time Kristy paid attention to her daughter on stage. In the opening scene, Darcie's dress, made for April, was a tad short, and tight through the shoulders, but she moved freely around the set, tossing out her lines while she examined wedding presents and made faces at the ones she didn't like. It was a second dose of the unruffled, high-class girl who had challenged Kristy at the dinner table. Darcie's physical reaction to the surprise entrance of her ex-brother-in-law, C.K. Dexter Haven—a run and full-on leap into the actor's arms—had the grace of Nadia Comaneci sticking a floor vault.

For her second entrance, Darcie flounced across the stage in a tutu blithering French at breakneck speed and finished with a deep curtsey to Isa (as Liz) and the actor playing Macauley. The pair drew back from her as if she were radioactive, and there was a huge laugh from the audience. In that moment, Kristy realized that Darcie, the mousy, klutzy, silent Schroyer, had been playing Dinah Lord the night before. She had been in character, with borrowed courage and a highfaluting tone. Good for her, Kristy decided, filling up with pride. Except for the gravy boat, no harm done.

Kristy focused on Isa for a bit. Her ability to repeat her performance, with the same gestures, moves, and vocal inflections Kristy had seen opening night but without seeming mechanical, amazed her. This was what Isa had called technique. Neither Isa nor Darcie gave any indication that they knew each other in real life. This wasn't Harvey Korman and Tim Conway cracking each other up on *Carol Burnett*. It was balls-out, focused, professional make-believe, a situation she found exciting, but because it left her out of the pact, made her feel jealous again. As the performance went on, Kristy cheered herself by imagining that Louise was surely watching down from heaven. By intermission, she had decided that Darcie had invented the horrible warning from her grandmother. That wasn't Louise, and that wasn't Darcie. Things at home would settle down once the play had closed and Isa had gone back to college.

At curtain call, Gavin presented Darcie with roses and made her take an additional bow. In the instant before the cast disappeared into the wings, Kristy watched Darcie wipe her eyes and Isa take her hand. She vowed to be generous to Isa backstage.

Kristy knew from Cary's turn in *Damn Yankees* how to reach the dressing rooms. She charged Darcie, held her tight, and, drawing in the sweet, damp scent of her hair, asked for her forgiveness, she was so so so sorry. When Darcie said, "Of course Mommy," Kristy pressed her hands to her daughter's shoulder blades and began weeping. This, this was not make-believe.

It couldn't last forever. Both went rigid when they heard, "Where's my little star?"

"Your father is right for once," whispered Kristy. "You are a star."

Darcie broke their hold. "Really?"

Kristy began tucking Darcie's hair behind her ears. "You're my little star too. Really and truly." She pulled some Kleenex from a box and moved off, nodding at Wayne, who was crowding in with a plastic-wrapped bouquet of Pic-n-Save carnations. "That's our girl," he said, clearly expecting some family time with Kristy, perhaps a group hug and a photo shoot.

Kristy made a beeline to the corner where she had spotted Isa removing her makeup. She began an apology about not understanding how important this experience was to Darcie, etcetera, but stopped mid-sentence when she noticed another bouquet of carnations, also pink, in a vase next to Isa's wig on its stand. Clipped to the stick was a card. Kristy didn't need to decipher the handwriting. Isa looked up in the silence, stopped rubbing cold cream into her forehead. Their eyes caught in the mirror, held on.

Although confirmation wasn't necessary, Kristy thought there was something that nevertheless needed to be said. "You've stolen my daughter and my husband."

She was wrong on both counts, Isa thought, but this wasn't the place for a showdown. "Can we go someplace to talk?"

"Pack your things," said Kristy.

"Absolutely," said Isa.

"Gone by tomorrow."

"Got it."

Kristy ran her hands through her hair as if she were already rid of her.

⊢———•———⊣

Ithaca is picture-pretty in autumn too. It was the first Saturday of October, windy and just this side of chilly. The sky was a bright, enameled blue, Greek blue to Isa Vass, and only the maple trees had yet to release their leaves to the season. Descending Danby Road, Isa listened to dried hydrangea blooms itch the sides of clapboard houses and watched funnels of leaves swirl and settle against latticed porch steps, only to be taken up again with the next gust. Some pumpkins sat out on stoops, waiting quietly for the end of the month to be carved into beings.

Isa wanted to get to the Commons early, so the store managers would be fresh and receptive. Her backpack held posters and two rolls of masking tape. The departmental powers that be, Ash Rickwood (né Otto Novak) presumably included, had finally given her a good part, no, make that a great part: Beatrice in *Much Ado About Nothing*. Isa was having a ball with it. A director from Boston had been jobbed in, and he made his approval of her acting choices clear to one and all. She made such clean sense of the verse that the director was having her coach some of the less experienced cast members in scansion. She amazed her pupils when she demonstrated how English speakers naturally fell into iambic pentameter. "Go to the store and get some milk and bread"—was her go-to example. Meter was not the enemy; they must think of it as a tide pulling them forward; the iambs made the lines easier to memorize, to get into the body and stay there.

From her summer gig, she made conscious use of Gavin Steeg's very first piece of direction: "Make them come to you." Beatrice was a sophisticate, Tracy Lord this time, not Liz Imbrie. Her character image for herself was an unopened bottle of champagne draped in a fine linen towel. Benedick unwrapped her slowly, foil first, then the wire untwisted, the cork pushed and prodded, finally popped at the end of the play. For rehearsals, she lassoed her unruly hair into a severe bun, had her corset cinched as tight as it could go, and insisted on high-button shoes.

Isa being Isa, she also helped hang lighting instruments and chaired the publicity committee. It was in this capacity that she was down on the Commons that October morning. At Rothschild's Department Store, she left a poster with a salesgirl. The owners of Isle of You and House of Shalimar let her hang them in their windows straightaway. A counterman she often flirted with at Home Dairy gave her a cruller on the house. On she went, the Ground Round, Top of the Ladder, the Smoke Shop, Corner Books, First National. She crossed back and forth, affixing posters to telephone poles and community message boards. Shakespeare was an easy ask, even at Lewton's, the fancy "Haberdashers to Men & Women" she'd never set foot in before.

Harold's was getting closer. Isa knew she couldn't skip it. So many different kinds of potential audience members shopped at the Army-Navy. She hadn't seen Kristy Schroyer since fleeing Seneca Street at the end of July. If she still opened Saturdays, Isa expected to find her there.

From the door, she saw Kristy bent over the cash drawer. She hesitated, hoping she might straighten up, see Isa, then, like an acting partner, give her a physical cue—beckoning or banishment. But it had been Isa's mess, so it was her scene to start. She nerved up and went in. Isa drew in a breath of the familiar scent—roach powder and packing peanuts, according to Cary Dunkler—and marched to the counter.

Kristy looked up on Isa's approach. She didn't mean to slam the cash drawer shut, but that's the sound it made when she saw her first customer of the day. It rang in their ears while each tried to gauge the other's reaction.

"Hey, Kristy."

"Hello, Isa."

Kristy's tone was neutral, so Isa went on, so jittery as she wrestled her backpack that she asked five questions in a row without waiting for the answers. Yes, she could put some *Much Ado* posters in the windows, the girls were fine, Kristy was fine, it *was* gorgeous outside, and the Columbus Day Sale was underway.

Kristy, unused to seeing Isa fumble anything, reached across to pluck a roll of tape that was threatening to dive off the counter.

"I've got that," said Isa, but Kristy already had it. She motioned with her head to the front of the store and began moving there. "Bring yours too," she said.

"You want to help me?" asked Isa.

The question itself, compounded with Isa's burst of volume and tone of wonder in its utterance, threw their summer months into high, terrible relief. Each was relieved not to be facing the other as they snaked their way through circular racks of athletic shorts and waffle-weave undershirts.

Isa had humbled herself in coming into her store. The next move was Kristy's, and she found it simple to make. "You helped us out, Isa."

"Umm."

"You don't even know."

Conversation stalled at the store window. Outside, an old hippie, who went by the name of Kunat, was playing Frisbee with his chocolate Labrador, his bedroll and guitar case posed on a stone bench. He'd get out his guitar when the foot traffic picked up. If so inspired, he'd make up a quatrain about you on the spot. From her years put into Harold's, Kristy knew every conceivable rhyme for 'blonde,' for 'hair,' for 'lovely,' and for 'jewel.' When the cold really came, she piled Kunat high with lined gloves and long johns from the remainder bin.

Each woman hung a poster—there were two versions, one designed from Beatrice's point of view, the other one from Benedick's. Isa rolled careful tape loops and affixed them on the corners of her poster. She winced to watch Kristy tear off strips with her teeth and run them in uneven diagonals on the window. She remembered that "Done is best" was one of Kristy's life mantras. She also reminded herself that Kristy wasn't the actress lucky enough to be playing Beatrice.

Her poster up, Kristy frowned at something on the floor. She slipped off a white nurse shoe and began dusting the metal floor ledge with her sock.

"I filed against Wayne," she said.

"You did?" asked Isa.

"On August 12th." Kristy couldn't yet look at Isa, so she kept dusting. "What he did to you kicked something off in me."

"Did to *me?*" Isa was astounded. The encounter she knew she'd have some day with Kristy had involved one-way groveling. She braced a hand against the window. "How about what I did to *you?* Not to mention the girls."

"Only Jan knows what happened." Kristy changed feet. "It was easy for me to forget that you're as young as you are, Isa." She frowned. "Mark says it's a pattern I have, trying to make friends with young people, because I never got to be young myself."

Maybe, maybe not, but Isa did like hearing the word "friend."

Kristy was moving west, foot-dusting and picking old scotch-tape fragments off the window with her fingernails. "Wayne told me that he did what he did with you for—"

"Leverage!" burst out Isa, almost giddy with the opportunity to abase herself with Wayne's actual term. "Leverage. Did he say he was screwing me to get leverage with you?" It was the rock-bottom thing Wayne had said to her in the one drunken phone call she'd made to him since school had begun.

"He did." Kristy stopped her work. "The sick fuck." Here Kristy looked back and their eyes finally met. "So, I thought if he could do that to you, forget about me, how would he treat my girls when they actually needed a father, a decent man to trust?"

"Okay then."

"I'm going for full custody."

Isa clapped her hands. "Use me for evidence!"

"Don't be silly."

"I'm serious, Kristy." Isa had sworn off sleeping with daddies of all varieties, and she'd be glad to say it in court, under oath, if it strengthened this vow of her former employer.

The women looked at each other with more ease. They had been friends, after all. They couldn't let him win. Both felt it.

"These windows are filthy," sighed Kristy.

"Got any vinegar?"

Kristy cocked her head and asked with the surprised air of a television housewife, "Is that what you use?"

"It's cheaper than Windex and cleans most anything."

"I'll be sure to tell Jan." She sighed again. "The house is a wreck. The girls miss you."

Isa nodded, afraid to speak. She hoped that this last admission might lead to an invitation. If given the chance, she would love to clean and cook her sins away, give the girls two months' worth of Words of the Day. With no funny way to frame her betrayal, she had kept the details of her summer to herself. She had also begun practicing patience during her calls home to Illinois. She needed to do better by her mother. In happier days, Olga would say to her, "A son is a son 'til he gets him a wife, but a daughter's a daughter all of your life."

Kristy plucked tape bits from her hand and fingers and gave them to Isa to deal with. "I don't want my girls to end up marrying dicks like their dad, because that's the only example they had around. They'll still get to see him," she added, almost to herself.

"That's good," said Isa, crafting a tape ball in her palm. She wondered whether Mark Shinner was in the picture. He was decent and trustworthy, so probably not. Isa wondered if she herself would ever be mature enough for a math teacher-type.

"I think we're done here."

Isa took this as a dismissal. "Okay," she said. She pushed up her sweatshirt sleeves and held her hand out for a goodbye.

"But I'm dying for a cigarette." Kristy raised her arms and called to the back of the store: "I'm taking a break, Doug. Come out and watch things."

Doug appeared from the stock room, looking all of fifteen years old, dragging a cardboard box by its flap just the way Penny used to drag her Sunt-Sunt around the apartment on Seneca Street. Isa thought of the tiny scar just inside Penny's eye socket that she would bear forever. Someday a boy would get close enough to ask her what had happened. Penny had already inflated the knitting needle event from a scary accident into a deliberate attack from Darcie. In ten more years, she might get around to—and, depending on the kind of woman she turned out to be, get laughs from it—by blaming Isa Vass, the slutty Mary Poppins who fucked her dad one crazy Ithaca summer.

"Tuck in your shirt for the customers."

"Yes ma'am." Doug set down the box and started tucking.

"And when she gets here, I want you and Pam to fill a bucket and wash the windows. Put vinegar in the water, if you can find some."

"Vinegar?"

"You heard me."

"Yes ma'am."

It had warmed up some, but Kristy smoked with her arms pressed to her sides. She watched the peach butter lady set up her card table in the middle of the Commons; her kids, a boy and a girl, were climbing the monkey bars nearby.

The hippie's dog ran up to them. Isa crouched and let him lick her face. He could use a vinegar rinse too. The collar tag beneath his yellow bandanna bore the name Brigham. Maybe Kunat was Mormon.

"Have you ever taken the bus to New York City, Isa?" asked Kristy.

"A couple of times to see shows," said Isa.

"Are there bathrooms on the buses?"

Isa stood and hooked her second arm in her backpack. "There are. It's a five-hour ride. I think it's the law."

"That's what I said to Darcie, but she didn't believe me," said Kristy. "Of course if you had told her, it would have been holy gospel."

Kristy regretted the sour note in her voice. Managing Darcie post-Isa had been a trial. Cary put the blame on puberty. Kristy felt Darcie was too young to get the full report on Isa's disappearance, so Darcie had started eighth grade under a cloud, had even refused Kristy's offer to take her grandmother's room ahead of Jan, saying it would remind her too much, not of Gram, but of Isa.

"Are you two going into the city?"

Kristy checked her watch. "Cary is going with her in about an hour."

Here Kristy hesitated; saying it could spoil it. "She has an audition."

"An *audition*?" cried Isa. "For what? How did that happen?"

"An agent came to the last weekend of *Philadelphia Story* and took her on, uh, signed her up."

"Really? Really?" A huge smile broke over Isa's face. "What for?"

"Commercials and soap operas, and what have you. Tours of *Annie*. I drove her down twice for meetings, and that was enough of New York for me, thank you very much. Cary was happy to take over for me. He gets to see his brother Dave when he's down there."

Isa threw her arms around Kristy with such force that Brigham began barking. "That's incredible! I love it. I just love it. What's she going in for today?"

"A shampoo commercial."

"National?"

Kristy disengaged and drew her cardigan closer. "I don't know. Breck?"

"*Breck* shampoo? Do you know what this means, Kristy?"

"Kind of." Good fortune scared the crap out of her.

"If Darcie gets a national commercial, you'll have enough money to move; you can quit your jobs—Jan can apply out of state—"

"Oh, I can't not work, Isa."

"No, but you can go back to school!"

"I never went to school."

Isa laughed. The quibble was very Beatrice and Benedick. "Then you can *start* school. For a nursing degree."

Kristy tightened her lips. Mark had said the same thing. "I'm not counting any chickens."

Isa was ready to run laps around the Commons to burn off her excitement. She pulled Brigham, still barking, up to her waist by his paws. "Good boy, good boy. That's a good dog. My god, Kristy, this is the best thing ever."

Ithaca being so tiny, Kristy had figured on running into Isa one day and breaking Darcie's professional news, but she hadn't planned how or when, nor expected it would go so well, or happen in a public space with dogs and shoppers. There was one question left, one that Isa could read in her expression.

"What?"

Kristy went for it. "You're not—"

An actress goes with her first impulse, and Isa got it instantly. "Jealous? Oh God no, are you nuts? Dar is twelve years old."

Kristy flinched at the use of Isa's special diminutive. If she only knew the hours she and the agent had spent talking Darcie out of assuming the professional name Dora Iliotis. If Darcie booked this commercial, and another, and got a soap, and she took her earnings and rescued the family, it would be because of Isa Vass. No wonder she seemed so relieved. Kristy ground out her cigarette. She would have Isa over for dinner soon, share the goodwill, make Darcie happy even if it made her jealous. In bad moments Kristy felt she had lost both her mother and her daughter in the space of four months. Afraid she might rattle apart, Kristy focused on one of the *Much Ado* posters.

"Is it a good play?"

Isa was still giddy. "It's Shakespeare!"

"That doesn't mean it's good."

"It's a comedy, Kristy."

"That doesn't mean it's funny."

Kristy kicked her butt into the nest of leaves that had blown and settled against the bricks. Some goodbyes you were ready for. She looked forward to saying goodbye to the Army-Navy. Simeon's too. And Wayne, even though, as father of her children, he would never get far enough away to suit her. Isa and Mark were right about the money—Darcie's agent, a tough talker hardly out of her twenties, had quoted stupefying, eye-popping, jaw-dropping figures—but Kristy couldn't think about it. "What I mean is, Isa, will *I* get it?"

Isa remembered a woman so careworn she couldn't tell whether a line cook was flirting with her. "If you don't get it, lady, that means we didn't do our jobs right."

Isa skittered away with a bear hug and a promise of comp tickets and a "love to the girls" before Kristy could even think to hang onto her a little bit longer. Before she went back into the store, she listened to Saturday morning on the Commons. Kunat was tuning up. He'd start strumming any moment. Someone with a harmonica would join in before long, then most likely a fiddler, sometimes two. By noon, a band of wayward musicians would be ushering in the autumn. She bought two jars of peach butter, for luck, and quietly slipped one behind old Kunat's bedroll.

Part Three

Judy Gabelson
1987

"Where a woman rules, streams run uphill"

~***Ethiopian Proverb***

Judy Gabelson had never flown further than Chicago. An untroubled sleeper, she had the fantasy that she would be able to snooze through most of the twenty-two hours she'd be in the air. So, after having been presented with nine time zone changes, fluctuating ear pressure, foreign accents, bad food, worse coffee, cigarette smoke, canisters of bug spray released into the air by impassive stewardesses, and rampant insomnia, she could be forgiven for repeating "Am I what?" several times over to her seatmate on the final leg of the journey, from Addis Ababa, Ethiopia to Entebbe, Uganda. Paul Obilil was a young African, dressed like Malcolm X or a Blues Brother in a dark suit, white shirt, and skinny tie. His question was preposterous, but she was too exhausted to say so.

"Are you a spy?" he asked once more.

This time she got it. "Absolutely not." It was possible Judy was too woozy to sound convincing. "How could you possibly think that?"

"According to your story, Miss Judy Gabelson, you have come to Africa to create a theater play with a man you do not know well. Moreover, you have the support of the Swedish government to do so. Moreover, you are not a missionary."

"How can you tell I'm not a missionary?" Now her voice bore the tone of an aggrieved society matron. Why were her responses so magnified? She'd had no alcohol on the flights.

"Your ears are pierced."

"Oh." She thought this over. Dozens of passengers on the Belgium-Ethiopia leg had worn matching acid green "Get Right with God" T-shirts. Ramped-up and chatty, they kept switching seats to praise Jesus and witness to one another. In one surreal moment, Judy, awakening from a doze, had imagined that a tide of chirping Christian goop was pouring through the cabin, consuming all in its path, like in *The Blob*. She hadn't noticed the women's jewelry, or their earlobes.

"If I were a spy, I wouldn't be able to tell you, now would I?"

Paul Obilil laughed.

Judy felt giddy to have reasoned her way out of this, although she was coming to realize that the closer she got to her final destination, the shakier her story sounded. What had seemed glamorous stateside seemed ludicrous 30,000 feet above the actual Equator. She might not even clear passport control. Rank and file Americans did not take a semester's leave to go to Uganda. Equatorial Africa, the cradle of AIDS? *Uganda*, eight years after the end of Idi Amin Dada's reign of terror? To create a musical with a mixed-race man she'd met just once? The notion was lunatic, despite having originated in the brain of a woman generally considered among the most sensible citizens of Ithaca, New York.

Reason for travel, Miss Gabelson?

Education. Business. Creativity.

Permission denied, Miss Gabelson.

Emil Thompson.

Please explain, Miss Gabelson.

The previous July, the Hangar Theatre, where Judy served as Musical Director, had had its first onsite visit from the New York State Council for the Arts. Artistic Director Gavin Steeg had begun looking to expand programming beyond August, so he and Judy had filed a grant application asking the state for money to fund a boiled-down *Romeo & Juliet* to tour Tompkins County middle and high schools. NYSCA sent Redmond Kain, a freelance set designer, to watch their production of *Anything Goes*, interview Gavin and Judy, and file an assessment.

Along with Redmond Kain that weekend was his old Oxford classmate, Emil Thompson. Emil's skin had the color and glow of polished tiger maple. He had jet freckles on his cheekbones, a cleft chin, shamelessly pouty lips, and most startling in a South African (or any Black person she'd met), green eyes. Emil's coif was a dignified arrangement. More wave than curl, it was cropped against the skull, so that one could travel cleanly down his powerful neck to a strong, stocky torso. If Richard Burton had had an African mother, or Harry Belafonte, a Dutch father... "Coloured" Emil Thompson, on summer holiday from the secondary school he taught at in Kampala, was perhaps the handsomest man Judy Gabelson had ever met.

Redmond Kain's bad, British stutter meant Emil ran the NYSCA interview. Judy knew straightaway that Gavin didn't like Emil (a rival charmer), but with funding at stake, Judy watched him pretend that he was fascinating and his advice, useful. Touring the facilities, Emil stopped them short by bringing up his dream project: a Broadway-style musical about the defiled women of Lake Bunyonyi to play at the National Theatre of Uganda.

Defiled women? Defiled how? Set to music? What kind of music?

The idea was so many literal and figurative worlds away from *Anything Goes* that Gavin Steeg merely widened his eyes and left Judy to bite. (An unwritten part of her job was to maintain conversational flow.) This was how Judy learned that Emil, as an advocate of theater for social justice, had as his personal cause writing workshops at the Good Lights School. One of his students had written a play about her grandmother, who had been sent in the nineteen-forties to die on an island after shaming her family with an out-of-wedlock pregnancy. The script, titled *Mango Roses,* needed a composer. Emil had noticed in the *Anything Goes* program that Judy wrote incidental music for Hangar shows—did she happen to write songs as well?

"Lord no," said Gavin, his sole contribution to the conversation.

"Not since college," she countered. Only her mother knew that Judy had taken a music composition class. She had set a trio of Emily Dickinson poems and written a couple of silly folk tunes.

"Are you allowed sabbaticals?" asked Emil.

"I've never taken one," said Judy. "But they do happen."

It did happen. Before Red and Emil had backed out of the graveled parking lot to drive to a *Dracula* in Rochester, Judy wrote out her address on a two-for-one ticket flyer.

Gavin said Emil was gay—mere reflex, she thought—and Judy said it didn't matter. It didn't. Emil's enthusiasm was seduction enough. His first letter, which arrived early in August, reported that the Swedish Embassy had given him five million shillings to help produce *Mango Roses*. (She hadn't a clue about the exchange rate, but it sounded like a lot of money.) In September, she arranged her leave at Slaterville High, where she taught music and directed the various choirs, and, helpful to the core, found her spring term replacement. In October, she got her passport; in November, the tickets. In December, vaccinations from the Cornell travel clinic and a grad student to rent her house on Titus Street. She chased the first dose of her anti-malarial, Doxycycline, with a shot of her foster brother Cary Dunkler's homemade eggnog the day after Christmas.

The one person in town who encouraged Judy's plan was Cary, who bought her a map of East Africa and a wide-brimmed canvas hat on an adjustable choker so it wouldn't sail off her head while on safari. Safari, he had learned, was the Swahili word for "adventure," and he had always been in favor of those for everyone. (But himself, thought Judy.)

The one person in town who might have changed Judy's plan was Mark Shinner. For Christmas, he had given her a diamond tennis bracelet, but he wouldn't, or couldn't, or at any rate, he *didn't* tell her that he wanted her to stay in America, despite her having given him an entire autumn's worth of opportunities. There was a world of difference between a bracelet and an avowal, she thought, twisting her left leg out from under the blankets to cool on her bedspread. Mark generated heat like a furnace but did not, like many big men, snore.

Only Cary was permitted to see Mark's gift, slipped into her carry-on at the very last minute, when he had dropped her off before the crack of dawn— Cary kept baker's hours at Clever Hans—at the Syracuse Amtrak station. Before her flight to East Africa from JFK the following morning, she'd be staying over in Greenwich Village with Gavin Steeg and his boyfriend, who happened to be her other foster brother, Dave Bailey. Dave had gotten them tickets for *The Mystery of Edwin Drood*.

"It's not a ring," said Cary, fingering the bracelet in its case and stating the obvious.

"Exactly," said Judy. A ring would force a decision, not her and Mark's M.O. at all. They had been dating for sixteen months, with cyclic levels of enthusiasm. He was sweet, steady, trustworthy, empathetic, intelligent, attentive...in cynical moments, she thought that just added up to *boring*. But, according to Dave, taxonomist of living things and potential couples, Judy was at best a Betty, not a Veronica, a Mary Ann (if you squinted), but never a Ginger. His larger point eluded her. Gilligan and Archie Andrews weren't the best examples of evolved manhood. Should she settle on Mark, or not?

"He'll realize what he's missing and have a ring ready when you get back," said Cary.

Judy chose not to disabuse Cary of his romantic notion; at thirty-five, she was in no rush to marry, nor eager for children. She was hoping, however, that life on the other side of the world, even a short five months of it, would help her escape running arguments, predictable responses, canned impressions, reliable outcomes, recycled thoughts, and convenient relationships.

As they said goodbye, Cary let her hold him tight, even allowed her a kiss.

"You be careful," she said, always the big sister.

"I always am." Their subtext was the virus. Cary was a loner, but not celibate, and there were still no drugs to take for HIV, unless you got into a study. All she could do was hope he practiced safe sex.

"Passport?" he asked her in a military tone.

Judy smiled. Cary was imitating how every school morning of their childhoods, she had asked of her little brothers, "Lunchbag?" before they left the house for the bus stop. Cary was ready first, but he always let Dave, the shining star, be first through the door. Judy undid her jacket and tapped a buttoned inner pocket. It was the first U.S. passport issued to a Gabelson.

The gesture had made her feel like an astronaut, but now, a half-hour from splashdown, with the plane making its final descent into Entebbe Airport (site of the notorious 1976 Israeli raid on Entebbe), it occurred to her that she and Emil Thompson had never once talked on the phone. Shouldn't she have at least heard his voice a second time? Maybe *he* was a spy and would force her to become one. Maybe he was a smuggler looking for a mail-order bride to help him ferry diamonds and ivory out of the country. A sudden glimpse of a boundless stretch of water looming below made her heart accelerate. Uganda was a landlocked country, so that had to be the Red Sea. They had been hijacked! Bearded men in blue-and-white kerchiefs would soon burst through the cabin curtains with machine guns.

"What is that?" she asked Paul Obilil.

"That is Lake Victoria."

Her relieved laughter, she knew, was that of a madwoman.

A steward began his seat back and tray table position spiel. Judy checked her seat belt and had just popped her ears when through the window, she spotted a burned-out plane in the middle of an empty runway. Its nose was tilted into the ground like an ostrich. Small trees pushed up around it at crazy angles through cracks in the cement.

"What is that?"

Paul smiled, as if aware that the answer would freak her out. "That is Air France Flight 139."

Judy's hand flew to her mouth to keep the words "Raid on Entebbe" from spilling out. She took two breaths, then, in a shaky voice, asked him why the plane was still on the runway.

Paul Obilil looked puzzled. While he considered this, she noticed that the skin under his fingernails had gone purple from gripping the front of his armrest.

"Where would they put it?" he answered just as the wheels met earth.

Where indeed? Through the rattling screech of their touchdown, Judy Gabelson absorbed her first genuine lesson about Africans. They left things where they landed.

┣━━━━━━•━━━━━━┫

For some American travelers, it's the random flash of a turreted castle along the Autobahn that proves that Europe actually exists; for others, it's the slow, twisting climb to the Acropolis that proves that history is more substantial than a paper-and-glue diorama you'd made of it in grade school. Judy Gabelson's twenty-six-kilometer drive into Kampala from Entebbe Airport, crammed into a *matatu* with Emil Thompson, a dozen plus Africans—and yes, a pair of roosters bound by their feet—was a *National Geographic* layout sprung to three-dimensional proof.

Add the fourth dimension of time, Judy thought, because here were sights that had been happening for hundreds, if not thousands, of years. Her colleague, Sally Lamont, in social studies, liked to say that recorded civilization may have started in the Fertile Crescent between the Tigris and the Euphrates Rivers, but humanity began in Africa. For long stretches of the drive, the jungle came to the edge of the road. In its tangled depths, she spotted mud huts, elders sitting cross-legged under banana leaf lean-tos, men hauling stacks of sticks the size of hay bales, women chopping enormous tubers into uniform lengths with machetes, children teasing tethered goats, women with baskets on their head and babies strapped in bright cloths around their backs, women bent and hacking at the bright, orange-red soil with hoes, women tending fires and hauling yellow jerry cans, and children darting in constant motion among the trees. Everyone was engaged with the maternal yet adversarial earth, and much too busy to face the camera.

It was late afternoon, and the air inside the bus was thick with smells of sandalwood and body odor, hers included. Emil's left knee was fixed in the crook of her right knee. By the tenth pothole jounce or slam on the brakes, she'd given up worrying whether she would ever see her luggage, roped to the top of the rickety vehicle, again. There was a constant shift of bodies as passengers got on and off at apparently random stops, but Emil conveyed to the curious group that the white lady—the *muzungu*—must stay next to the window. Several women leaned over him to touch Judy's hair. Others drew thumbs across her forearm as if testing whether the chalk would come off. The men flirted with their eyes and smiles. Never had she seen such strong, gorgeous teeth.

"Muzungu" is the all-purpose Swahili word for "white person"—like "gringo" or "paleface" without the negative connotation. Judy would grow accustomed to hearing the word everywhere she went, but for now, when groups of children spotted her from the road, then gathered to wave fiercely and cry "Muzungu! Muzungu!" she felt like Anna Leonowens being greeted by the royal children in *The King and I*.

The traffic was hazard-filled. Ever since she'd made her plans to go, friends and family and neighbors had outdone one another with worst outcomes. Her father, Hugh, thought she'd make an ideal international hostage. Her mother, Mary, was stuck on her contracting river blindness. Her students went, predictably, for big cat attacks. Her colleagues: malaria, tribal enslavement, rhinoceros goring, packs of ravenous hyenas, sleeping sickness, hemorrhagic fevers, enforced prostitution…on they went. Judy chose not to reveal to these Comforters of Job that Emil had written that the greatest risk to her health in Kampala would be the traffic. There might, for example, be a sudden animal stampede. Or she might be struck by any one of the thousands of *boda boda* motorbikes taking shortcuts through the crowds. There were no such things as sidewalks. Or stoplights. Just roundabouts and perpetual, teeming chaos.

They halted at a crossing and waited for a boy to merge a herd of cattle into the traffic flow with nothing more imposing than a stick. The cattle had enormous, snow-white horns that shot out at tremendous angles from their skulls. The horn span on the largest looked ten feet across.

"Those are Ankole cattle," said Emil, following the point of her finger. "They're from Western Uganda, out by Mbarara."

"They're like the Daughters of Charity." He didn't understand. "The nuns with *cornettes*." Another pause. "Like on *The Flying Nun?*" One last time. "Sally Field?"

Emil shook his head.

"There was a time when I thought I wanted to be a nun," she said, just to say something.

"Ah," he said. Nothing more.

Oh God, she thought with a flash of panic, what were they going to talk about for five months? This man didn't know *The Flying Nun,* luckily so perhaps, since she had just reduced the timeless majesty of Africa with thoughts of *The King and I* and Sister Bertrille. To her left coughed a motorbike with a bunch of green bananas the size of two Christmas trees tied crosswise over its back wheel. She couldn't see how it didn't tip over, especially with all the weaving and sudden stops to its course. Judy vowed then and there not to compare these fruits to the bananas at the Pic-n-Save, and the vehicle to the mini-bike that Dave and Cary had saved up for as kids, and the risk of an accident to something out of a *Bugs Bunny* cartoon. She must refrain from articulating these connections. That was the colonizer's position. A guest of the continent, she must watch, observe, witness, marvel, but strive against facile, Anglo comparisons.

And then, in the briefest of instants, it was pitch black.

"Where did the light go," she asked, clutching at the outline of her passport in her jacket pocket. There was a full-page visa pasted just inside, with her name—Judy Ellen Gabelson—triple stamped and underlined, with an embossed, deckle-edged golden seal tickling her neck in the mug shot.

This Emil could answer. "In Kampala, the sun rises at 7:02 a.m. and sets at 7:02 p.m. If you watch carefully for it, there are about six minutes of twilight at the Equator."

They had reached the outskirts of the capital; the darkness had created an instant, riotous carnival. Strings of electric bulbs lit up swarms of brightly dressed people pulsing into shops that were no more than curtained metal truck cases set on end. Women sat behind carefully built stacks of yams and plum tomatoes and eggplants and artichokes and cabbages and vegetables

Judy couldn't identify. Then, suddenly, for sale was an audience of empty, overstuffed love seats covered in acid primary colors or animal prints. Birds squawked from cages stacked six high. Everywhere, open grills sent up sweet-sour meat smells. The air was filled with the sound of drums, and the population seemed to be keeping time to it. Afraid that this sonic cliché was her own fabrication, Judy vainly tried to find the source of the beat. "These are the hot, wet lands," she murmured to herself, suddenly recalling the term from a unit in her fourth grade geography class.

Women and children were walking so close to the road that, had she the energy, she could have created a quick, flapping bouquet of head wraps with a mere reach of her hand. But she didn't have the energy.

"Why is everybody outside, Emil?"

"Homes are dark, so there is nothing to do inside at night but sleep. Or wait for the rain to stop. This is what your country calls 'Happy Hour.'"

"These are the hot, wet lands," she repeated, drifting off.

Judy woke up under a mosquito net on a single futon—raised from the floor, she hoped—with no memory of having disembarked from the *matatu* the night before. Before she drew the curtains and looked, she listened, as composers do, and she was in Africa to be a composer, to the morning. The air was alive with yips, crows, bleats, squawks, thrums, buzzings, and an amplified, staccato bellow in a strange language. Underneath it all was a crisp, incessant swish she couldn't identify.

Upon parting the netting, she spotted a stool next to the bed on which was placed a glass of juice topped by a curiously webbed skirt. Upon inspection, she concluded its edge was weighted down with metal beads as an insect deterrent. Judy stood, stretched, and sure enough, from the corners of her eyes, she sensed some creatures scuttling for the ceiling.

She was alone in a man's apartment, in Africa. What was the protocol? There was nothing to do but drink the juice—a tart, tongue-curling flavor—and signal her host with an over-exuberant yawn. She waited and took in the bright egg yolk hue of the stucco walls. She'd noticed from the *matatu* ride that colors were far more intense in Africa.

At the lack of response, Judy dragged her bags across the red-tiled floor a couple of times. Then she opened and shut the clumsily hewn top drawer in a hardwood dresser, the third and final piece of furniture in the room. Finally, worried that Emil might have abandoned her, she clocked her passport in her jacket hanging from a nail in the wall, coughed loudly, and pushed open the door. There was no knob.

Just two feet from her, so close that the door grazed his foot, Emil, in a red dressing gown and rope sandals, looked up from a newspaper. The sun angled a slab of light across his neck and chest. Now she was in a man's quarters, a man with thick lashes and dark brown knees and slender ankles. How had she gotten into her nightgown? Who had provided the juice? Where had he slept? Had she been drugged?

"Mango? Guava? Papaya?" she said, with a wild sweep of her empty glass.

"Good morning, Judy."

"Good morning. Delicious."

She meant the juice, not him. Well, not entirely him. He dominated the small space from one of those weirdly overstuffed love seats covered in cranberry velvet, or velveteen. There was a table, two mismatched chairs, another stool, a standing lamp, and a low, hi-fi console like her parents had, with slots for records, and woven acoustic cloth covering the speakers. Emil's copy of Johnny Mathis's *Greatest Hits* confused her. He didn't belong here. She remembered the time Dave told her Johnny Mathis was gay, and she told Dave he was Black, revelations that had left them both speechless.

"It is passion fruit."

Oh Jesus, she thought, of course, and embarrassed herself again by saying, without euphemism, that she needed to go to the toilet.

Emil said something, and a bent woman with a headscarf and matching apron appeared from nowhere.

"This is Alice. The house girl."

Alice shyly curtsied, then gripped Judy's forearm and pulled her into the backyard. The rush of hot air felt like a blast from a wall of laundry dryers, and the swishing sound had grown more distinct. A lizard darted into the shade at their approach to a hot pink outbuilding. It was a three-holed pit latrine. Inside the door, there was a bucket on the floor, a long-handled brush propped against it, but nothing resembling a sink. Over the side of a cinderblock half-wall, she spotted two showerheads. Above them were tree fronds that had grown indoors through the open rectangle of air below the roof and were languidly rotting for lack of sunlight.

Alice drew three pale green paper squares from her pocket and gave them to Judy. Wax paper. Judy couldn't help but smile to touch them. In that other country she knew, they would be wrapped around Christmas pears. Left alone to do her business, she discovered, then decided, that the elemental rawness of it all cheered her. This she had prepared for. She reminded herself to keep her mouth closed when she took a shower and never to rinse her toothbrush with tap water.

Other first lessons: Ugandans shook forearms, not hands. Ugandans spoke a lilting British English and seldom used contractions. Ugandans had extended formal greetings that included asking whether every family member had slept well; Emil said this was because out in the bush, there was no guarantee that one and all would make it through the night. Pre-pubescent schoolchildren of both sexes had shaved heads, because of lice. Even longstanding city-dwellers identified with their home villages. Ugandans were proud of the progress they had made in the near-decade since the fall of Idi Amin. The Ugandan meal, every meal, was a colored plastic plate heaped with seven starches—rice, *posho* (white corn mush), millet, white "Irish" potatoes, sweet potatoes, cassava root, and a gelatinous mass of unsweetened cooked green bananas called *mtoke*, all blanketed with a ladle of ground nut sauce, a lavender protein made from peanuts still in their skins. Ugandans didn't spice their food—that was *West* Africa. The birth rate was 7.5 children per mother, making Uganda one of the most fertile countries on the planet. There were approximately fifty separate tribes in Uganda, the four most prominent being the ruling *Bu*gandans, who spoke *Lu*ganda, the Luo, the Busigu, and the Ankole. If a relative died, you could ask anyone from your tribe—and hundreds might be living in one urban district—for help with funeral expenses. An unattended banana on a desk or music keyboard was fair game for the monkey on the other side of an open window or breezeway. A monkey, alert for poison, would never touch a peeled banana. Nearly all Ugandans had malaria, the non-fatal kind that lay them flat for several days every few months. Ugandans didn't smoke, because they lacked discretionary income. Cigarettes were issued to soldiers as wages. Ugandan men could take on as many wives as they wished, provided they could afford them. Public displays of affection shocked Ugandans, who also didn't smile for the camera. The endless swishing was the sound of women sweeping the dirt.

The best first lesson Judy Gabelson learned was that, because nearly everyone was poor, poverty was neither a source of shame nor a stigma. Even affluent Kampalans were, at most, only one generation away from the daub and wattle huts of their home villages. They sent money home for the school fees of their relatives three times a year. Ugandans were proud to have made it to adulthood, and because poverty wasn't a crime, they respected themselves and each other and always wanted to know what Judy thought of their forward-facing country.

City-dwellers weren't used to and didn't seem to expect or demand a comfortable living situation. The rolling electric blackouts—three to four hours, every other night, it seemed—would complicate Judy's ability to write and orchestrate music for *Mango Roses*. After a couple of surprise disruptions, her suggestion of an organized civic blackout schedule made Emil laugh and iterate his umpteenth "You are on African time now, Judy." This all-purpose justification, explanation, and blandishment for off-kilter occasions, embarrassed her, not only for its similarity to the racist American term, "CPT," but also because AT turned out to be true. Unless a feral dog was charging you, there would never be a reason or an occasion to hurry. On a continent where restaurants don't kill the chicken until it's been ordered, explained Emil, waiting was the default human activity. Judy kept her copy of *Anna Karenina*, the fattest paperback she'd been able to find at The Ithaca Bookery, on hand at all times, but ever absorbed in her new environment, she never got past the first five pages.

———————

Nandie Lubangakene was the high school second former whose grandmother's escape from Lake Bunyonyi had inspired Emil to dream up the idea of *Mango Roses*. As recently as the late 1960s, unwed mothers-to-be were routinely sent to Lake Bunyonyi to die on "Punishment Island." The sole means of escape was for a man, seeking a "free" bride, to rescue her by boat. The themes uncovered in Nandie's classroom assignment—shame, hope, tolerance, family, love, forgiveness—fired Emil up and, Judy would come to suspect, touched him personally. A Johannesburg "coloured" like Emil, although not considered as low caste as the East Indians that Idi Amin had expelled in 1972, was as much an outsider in Uganda as Judy. But for his humorous anecdotes from his Oxford years, Emil never referenced his past. Her life spent growing up in the left-tilting "People's Republic of Ithaca" had educated Judy all about the brutality of South African apartheid. For Emil to migrate to landlocked, dirt-poor Kampala could only mean things had been worse for him in Johannesburg.

To begin work, Judy needed a script. The first shock: there was no *Mango Roses* script. Emil had inflated Nandie's student exercise into a complete play. Well then, what was the plot, and who were the characters? Emil laughed again. After rushed introductions on her second morning in Africa, Emil left Nandie Lubangakene and her friend, Patience Ochom, to her supervision. They would all work it out most marvelously, he predicted, dragging in another chair before rushing off to teach third form English.

For a long moment, no one spoke in the cinderblock vault. Emil's notebooks and papers were stored on an open rack of hanging file folders underneath an ancient fan whose impaired rotation mechanism was blasting cold air onto Judy's neck. Nandie Lubangakene's stocky figure, coloring, and the gap between her front teeth—a mark of beauty—meant she belonged to the Bugandan tribe. She was clearly nervous. Her fingers and purplish palms, splayed upward on the aqua skirt of her school uniform, opened and closed like a sea anemone in the tide.

Judy remembered with a start that she was a teacher. "Tell me about your writing, young ladies," she said, moving to adjust the fan.

"Never turn it off, Teacher Gabelson," warned Patience Ochom. She was bolder than Nandie, and taller, and sat with her knees apart. Her eyes, which did meet Judy's, were Asian. Another mix. Accustomed to adolescent fads at Slaterville High, Judy wondered whether the beauty mark at the outer corner of Patience's lower lip was false or true.

"Why not?" asked Judy.

"Teacher's papers will rot."

"Oh?"

"They will grow wet and smear and clump all together. You will not wish, please, for that outcome."

"Thank you, Miss Ochom."

At that first meeting, Judy pulled teeth to get the barest information out of the pair. Speaking for her friend, Patience said that the play title was a conflation of Rose, the name of Nandie's disgraced grandmother, and the mango tree in whose dense shelter Nandie's father, Dilman Nisumwesiga, was conceived during a rainstorm. Judy also learned that Patience intended to be a movie star and that Nandie—again, via Patience—had never in her life spoken to a *muzungu*. Nandie put her face in her hands, moaned, then giggled to hear this, and, although Patience boasted of having had speaking parts in the Christmas pantos at the National Theater, neither girl had ever seen a Broadway musical, not even at the movies. *Oklahoma, Music Man, Guys and Dolls, West Side Story?* Crickets. (Or rather, the whirr of an office fan and growling stomachs.) Nor had they ever written dialogue. *Mango Roses* was Teacher Thompson's idea. Nandie hadn't even brought in her writing exercise.

All Judy knew about dramatic form was that conflicts were essential, so she asked the girls whom they fought with most at home.

"My brother Emy," said Patience. "He is a spoiled baby brat."

"My Auntie," said Nandie, looking at Judy for the first time, and blowing out her cheeks in annoyance.

Now we're getting somewhere, thought Judy, and instructed them to write a scene of direct conflict—no descriptions, only speech—between themselves and their chief adversary. The girls went right to it, without, Judy noted, the ritual hair and clothing adjustments native to their American peers. While they free-wrote, Judy scanned Emil's desk blotter and calendar for clues to his character and tried to assess the level of her anger at this dramatic pig-in-a-poke he had sold her on. It crossed her mind again that she might have been imported for espionage or smuggling or human trafficking, but the air outside was soft, her breakfast pineapple, white, not yellow, was the most intensely delicious example of the fruit she'd ever tasted, and with her very own eyes, she had spotted a pair of monkeys kibitzing in a tree on the walk to Good Lights School.

From a legal standpoint, Emil could not breach a contract that didn't exist. How bad could things turn out, really? The tough part, getting here, was past her. She was on a sabbatical that she had earned and had only to answer to herself. Judy Gabelson, a born pedagogue with a very long fuse, made the best of situations.

She could still do something about that fan. Standing on Emil's chair, she jimmied the rotator mechanism until she noticed through the window and across a swept dirt quadrangle a squadron of buzzards the size of third-graders, with hideous ivory heads and gray-green feet, methodically rooting through a garbage dump that, judging by the woman tossing scraps onto the pile from a basin, appeared to back up against the school cafeteria. Remembering one of her brother Dave's favorite zoological discoveries, she turned to Nandie and Patience. (As a boy genius, Dave had been allowed to chalk the basement walls with every known constellation in the sky. Now he was second-in-command of the Gorton Fish Sticks account at Ogilvy & Mather.)

"Do you know why buzzards and vultures have bald heads?"

The girls looked up with instant, ingrained obedience.

"No, Teacher," said Patience.

Judy explained the meaning of the unfamiliar term *carrion,* then went on to describe how the evolutionary lack of feathers on a buzzard's head prevented the bird from potential bacterial and microbial infections when it reached in to feed on bloody, rotting animal carcasses.

Gross-out factoids were bonding moments in an American classroom, but Nandie and Patience, obviously waiting for a larger point, remained silent. Judy was set to offer them a ludicrous bromide about the glories of the natural world when the tea girl rescued her with a soft knock on the doorjamb.

Both girls put six spoonfuls of sugar in their mugs of tea. At breakfast, Judy had counted four for Emil, but she had yet to spot an African with less than flawless dentition and so held her tongue. While they drank their tea and gnawed at the dry wedges of carbohydrate that passed for cake, Patience and Nandie read their arguments aloud. Patience's scene ended with her killing her brother Emy with a *ponga,* subsequent to his defacing the cover of her maths notebook with a crayon. *Ponga* was the first Lugandan word Judy would really absorb. It means machete; no home is without several. Used to chop, slice, cut, sever, and hack, the *ponga* is the chief agricultural tool and murder weapon in East Africa. Nandie's scene ended with her poisoning her Auntie Nayamanja because she had made her dig an extra two hours when Nandie wanted to finish her homework instead.

The Darwinian adaptation of the buzzard's head was tame by comparison. "Dig what?" was all Judy could muster in response to these schoolgirl examples of domestic slaughter.

"Dig," repeated Nandie.

"Vegetables?" Maybe minerals, Judy thought.

She would get used to the look from Nandie and Patience, the one that said for all their wealth and power, *muzungus* didn't know very much. The root starches that sustained the population grew year-round. Digging was the first thing a girl or woman did every morning until the work was complete. There were patches of arable land over every inch of Kampala. Any unconsumed cassava or potatoes were sold along the road. It was a help to have many sisters in a family. Men never dug. A mother got two days of respite after delivering a baby, before she returned to her hoe.

Judy tabled her feminist objections in favor of focusing on the idea that dramatic conflicts weren't always settled by homicide. The girls seemed skeptical, Nandie especially, since one of her village cousins had only recently avenged himself by poisoning her uncle's forty pigs over the theft of a chapatti roller, but they agreed to rewrite their scenes as strictly verbal arguments for their following meeting. After Nandie left with the last piece of gritty cake, Patience hung back for a moment to let Judy know that *her* family didn't dig. "My mother is Cambodian, and my father is a missionary from Sudan." Her eyes were proud.

It took a month of thrice-weekly tutorials to hammer out a plot for *Mango Roses*. Judy encouraged the girls to draw from their own experience, gently pushing them to critique a system that would consign Nandie's grandmother to death for a pregnancy caused by rape during a bush uprising. The girls created a pair of twenty-something heroines. There was Rosie, who founded the Open Arms Shelter, a clinic for Kampalan women in trouble, and there was Jamie-Rose, an aspiring mixed-race singer from America who, seeking to discover her African roots, goes to Uganda and volunteers at Open Arms. The news of Grandmother Rose's death kicks off the plot. After seeking advice from a *juju* about whether to attend the funeral, the young women rush to the home village of Nyamirima in an overcrowded *matatu*. On arrival, Rosie must confront her alcoholic father, Rosso, who killed her mother with a *ponga*, while Jamie-Rose shares her dreams of stardom with Rosie's charismatic brother, Petero. No sooner has old Rose been laid to rest than Jamie-Rose's *white* grandmother, Meaghan Braithwaite, comes roaring up in a *boda boda* and, in a recognition scene worthy of *The Adventures of Scooby-Doo*, has a romantic reunion with James Rutamirika, Rosie's grieving grandfather. Meaghan had been the daughter of a missionary who had shamed her family by getting pregnant with the *shamba*, or garden boy. Being *muzungu*, Meaghan had been sent, not to Punishment Island, where Rose had Rosso before being rescued by James, but to a convent in Cleveland, Ohio. At the final curtain, all were reconciled under a mango tree. Rosie would even permit Rosso, who had thrown his ever-present gourd of home brew into the ground with his mother's body, to visit her someday—at her invitation, not his pleasure—in the big city.

The family tree would give Aristotle an aneurysm. For her own dramaturgical peace of mind, Judy concluded that Rosie and Jamie-Rose were first cousins once removed. Their exact tie didn't matter to the girls or to

Emil. All three were indifferent as well to the confusion of having two Roses, a Jamie-Rose, and a Rosso in the same cast list.

After a second day of bunking with Emil, Judy had been moved down the hall to two rooms of her own. The Swedish Embassy picked up the tab, roughly five dollars a week. Judy and Emil shared Alice, the noiseless house girl. Every day, Alice swept, scrubbed their floors, and laundered and hand-ironed every item of her clothing. Judy didn't think her bras and panties warranted such detailed attention until Emil explained that an iron heated in a fire killed any vermin eggs ready to hatch in the cloth.

One morning Alice had set Judy's coffee next to the keyboard (another gift from the Swedes) and revealed, when asked, that she was thirty-six and had four children living in her village, Bukedea, with their grandmother to whom she sent her wages as support. The fathers were in Kampala, but neither one of them lived with Alice. Judy, one year her junior, had guessed Alice's age at fifty-five. That same night, on Emil's porch, celebrating the completion of Judy's first composition, "The Matatu Song," a contrapuntal bus-ride fugue of driver instructions, bargaining passengers, stop announcements, and vendor cries, she asked him whether there was abortion in Uganda.

"This is a very Christian country," replied Emil. "Abortion is a capital offense. Millions were lost under Idi Amin. Children are Uganda's most precious resource."

Judy, who'd read the sentiment on several billboards, gave him a look.

Emil paused and started over. "Abortion is never spoken of. A visibly pregnant woman can go to a *juju* and say she is 'very tired' and ask for something to help her with that. The *juju* will prescribe herbs, and she will lose the child."

Judy frowned. She didn't like the word *juju,* or its English equivalent, "witch doctor." She preferred the Peace Corps term: "traditional healer." It had amused her initially to read in the obituaries in the daily *New Vision* that "witchcraft may have been involved" as a cause of death. Nandie and Patience wore crucifixes, but their chatter was filled with casual references to hexes and spells that their classmates were putting on one another.

"The girls say contraception is illegal too." It had taken Judy two full minutes to explain the concept of preventing a pregnancy to Nandie.

"For both sexes," said Emil, drumming his fingers against his close-cropped skull. "Christianity drills it into their heads that birth control imperils their immortal souls. I am afraid sex is not much fun for Ugandan women." He smiled. "Many European practices have made no inroads in East African culture." The emphasis he placed on the word "East" made it clear that Emil regarded himself as a more enlightened sex partner. Was this something of a come-on? Pushing aside a quick visual of Katherine Hepburn in *The African Queen* (yet another Rose in the bush), she listened to him talk about how "slim disease" was decimating the urban population. He meant it literally—one in ten were infected or dying.

"Slim disease?'"

Emil reached for a toothpick. "AIDS. It is called 'slim disease' because of...."

"Because of the body wasting."

He nodded. "When a sick child's stomach sticks out in this country, it is malnutrition. When it does not, it is slim disease. In the villages, mothers and aunties are taking in thousands of city relatives. So, you see," he concluded, "from the tribal perspective, and with multiple marriages, cousins are cousins are cousins. Villages are as full of orphans as the humanitarian agencies in the cities."

"My brothers were orphans," said Judy, thinking of home for the first time in days. Judy's parents had taken in Dave and Cary as foster children, then released Dave to Leigh Bailey, who legally adopted him when he was eleven. Cary, she felt, sort of stopped trying after that. His life in Ithaca was quiet, and useful, but she'd always wanted bigger things for him. Dave, who would always feel guilty about having left his brother behind, had never stopped urging Cary to move to New York. Judy had an inkling why he wouldn't, but it wasn't something she could share with either of them.

Her first month in Uganda she had been too swept up to pen more than a round of "Having a Blast on a Dollar a Day" postcards, which may or may not have reached Ithaca—this sudden reminder of Cary and Dave facing the slim disease back home made her panicky. What if one of them fell ill while she was away? Dave had Gavin to protect him, but Cary stuck to himself. With neither a street address nor a phone number, Judy's parents and brothers wouldn't know how to reach her in an emergency. Like Cary's birth mother, she was officially nowhere, and although she secretly loved the feeling that the continent had swallowed her up, Judy knew it would be prudent to go register at the American Embassy and disclose her whereabouts to the world at large.

Emil, who knew nothing of Judy's home life, began to sing "The Matatu Song," which cheered her up. The song had made Nandie and Patience, who had helped Judy with place names and curses, laugh. To dilute her pride, Judy claimed to be unhappy with the bridge. Songs weren't supposed to be this easy to write.

Emil poured them each a double tot of gin. They finished "The Matatu Song" in mock-solemnity as the sun took its ritual six minutes to drop in a tangerine and purple blaze behind Naguru Hill, thereby releasing the sharper sounds of the night.

"African men are the laziest on the planet."

You said it, I didn't, thought Judy. In a reception room filled with well-dressed African men, Clara Svoboda hadn't even bothered to lower her voice.

"I mean, why do anything when women will do everything for you?" Clara lifted an exquisitely shaped, piss-elegant eyebrow. Might she be testing Judy's politics?

Judy hadn't meant to engage the wife of the Swedish Ambassador in quite this fashion. She and Emil had gone to a string quartet recital at the embassy, both for the cultural diversion and for a belated introduction to their producing angels. Post-concert, the Ambassador, who was at least twenty years older than his wife, disappeared after wheezy pleasantries, leaving Judy to fill Clara in on how challenging it was to make production decisions for *Mango Roses*. Getting a set of performance dates at the National Theatre was her top priority. Without dates, they couldn't audition and hire performers and musicians, much less publicize the show. Judy felt she had talked to every possible official at the National Theatre, from box office staff to the technical director. Lacking typewriters, each one had listened attentively and taken down her name and request in a slow, elaborate script, as if that were tantamount to closing the deal.

"Did you bring Emil along?"

"No, I *boda*ed over by myself," said Judy.

To get to the National, she had taken her first solo *boda* ride with Isaak, Emil's driver, preferred because he was a devout Muslim who wouldn't be drunk on the road like so much of his competition. Emil had given Isaak her destination and waved them off. Judy kept her arms tightly around Isaak's waist and bucked with him down an off-road hill. They descended through a gully-carved ravine choked with *mtoke* trees, past drab huts and windowless guesthouses in jewel tones and innumerable half-built brick structures and kilns and loose poultry and yellow-eyed old men and women and girls digging. As always, the toddlers waved to her and cried, "*Muzungu!* *Muzungu!*" Older children used their English, shouting out "Hello. How are you?" She shouted back, "I am fine. And you?" and felt Isaak's stomach shake with laughter. They reached another paved road and whizzed alongside an open-air market. After six weeks in the capital, Judy had a clearer idea of what was for sale—everything—from freshly slaughtered goat to strips of flyblown tripe to dried fish to bedsteads to hair extensions. The congested traffic, plus the gigantic potholes, made their zig-zagging pinball passage feel like a chase in a spy thriller.

Judy now knew why men and boys loved motorcycles and the open road, but Clara Svoboda was horrified. "You must never ever *boda*, Judy Gabelson."

"Why not?"

"They are dangerous. You are a woman."

Judy pursed her lips. She had seen plenty of other solo females on that first ride. Many of them sat sidesaddle, and a couple of them applied makeup with a dexterity that Judy hoped one day to imitate. (Should she decide to begin wearing rouge and lipstick, that is.) Mothers tucked babies and toddlers between themselves and the backs of their drivers. She couldn't help but notice that no one else was gripping her driver so tightly. She must learn to relax with Isaak.

"How am I supposed to get around? I can't walk huge distances in the heat, and I don't understand how *matatus* work."

"You are a Caucasian woman," said Clara.

Judy, who'd been raised on the Ithacan bias that Scandinavians were the most liberal people on the planet, was shocked at Clara's Jim Crow inflection.

Clara, her earlobes turning scarlet with offense, motioned Emil over.

"Were you at least wearing a helmet, Judy?"

"I wasn't offered one."

Now they were both annoyed.

"Did you come by *boda* tonight?" Judy nodded. "The Embassy will send you home in a car."

"No need, Clara, really. You and the Ambassador have already done so much for me. I felt quite safe with Isaak and Emil."

More than safe. Wedged between Isaak's butt and Emil's groin, over a running motor, was a novel sensation. Lucky Pierre, she'd thought, recalling a filthy gay term Dave had taught her once upon a time. She was Lucky Pierrette, a Fellini starlet racing through the smoky hills of the metropolis, a headscarf shielding her hair from the dust and her heels dangling insouciantly from an upturned palm, all set to a rollicking Nino Rota melody intercut with African drums.

Clara's eyes narrowed. "He's using Isaak again?"

There was no answer for that, so Judy smiled at several white men clocking them nearby. Seeing them in a clump like that, she hadn't realized how unappealing white people looked. The Ugandan median age was an astonishing sixteen; next to Kampalans, post-thirties *muzungus,* the men especially, were wrinkled, spider-veined, pink-to-purple fleshbags who took up too much room with their bodies and their voices. You'd never catch two *muzungu* men riding the same *boda,* even if they could squeeze behind the driver.

The thought that she might look as ghastly as they did was liberating. After six weeks in the heat and the clay, and with her hand mirror neglected in a drawer, she could wave goodbye to the last of her vanity. Alice, as well as the women teachers at Good Lights, had been shocked, no, *dismayed,* to learn that Judy was childless. Even Isaak had asked her, in his terrible English, how many children she had back in her village in America. Every reply—she wasn't ready for children, or finding a husband came first, or she wasn't sure she even wanted them, or why bring another life into an overpopulated planet—was met with uncomprehending stares.

Or judgment: "*Omukyala awedde kumpaggala,*" sighed the Headmistress to Nandie and Patience one day at their tea break. The hands of both girls flew to their mouths.

"Might I have a translation, please?" asked Judy.

Headmistress made a great show of her teeth. She set down her mug, brushed crumbs from her starched ivory blouse, adjusted her head wrap in a slight clockwise direction, and stood to go. "It means you are a very independent woman, Miss Gabelson."

Nandie and Patience, eyes bugged out, didn't need to tell Judy that Headmistress was lying. *Omukyala awedde kumpaggala*—she made them write it out on the blackboard—meant a hen so old she couldn't lay eggs anymore. Miss Gabelson was an off-layer, an off-layer in a proudly fecund environment. At thirty-five, Judy should have had six children already, her girls bent over the earth, her boys swatting cattle until they were old enough to sit idling and drinking home brew with their fathers, until their sisters brought them dinner on their knees. Let them all assume she was barren; what mattered to her in the moment was that Nandie and Patience trusted her enough to rat out Headmistress.

Emil, breezy and natty in his plaid sports jacket, approached with glasses of champagne. Clara's scolding tone with Judy shifted to mildly patronizing with him. Wasn't he a scandal to send her off all by herself to *boda* through downtown Kampala? No more scandalous, Emil replied, than the Ambassador's Wife taking a night flight to Daar-es-Salaam without telling a soul. Clara laughed, drained her glass, and a shoe dropped for Judy. In a country lacking any tradition of narrative or musical theater, in a capital city recovering at a glacial pace from the actions of a brutal dictator, a city decimated by plague, desperate for a professional class and traffic lights and the return of its one rail line to Nairobi, the Swedes were allocating five million Ugandan shillings to an American-style musical about miscegenation. Footing the bill for Emil's dream could only mean that he and Clara shared a very personal history.

Watching them bend into one another like movie stars at a klieg-lit premiere, Clara's glazed chignon shining like an Easter bread—Judy realized that it might actually be Valentine's Day. The year before, she and Mark Shinner had varied their routine by having sex before dinner at Vinnie's Dockside Café, not after. Mark sometimes talked about wanting to be a father, and she'd idly supposed he'd make a good one. His Christmas bracelet was stashed in with her underwear and her mirror. Alice changed its position from time to time in the drawer to signal diligence, but Judy couldn't recall the last time she herself had opened the box to look at the bracelet. It might have occurred to her to put it on for the embassy concert, but instead, she found herself wondering what it would fetch; she could give the proceeds to Alice to send back to Bukedea to her children. Where would one sell a piece of Western jewelry in Uganda?

Returning to the matter of performance dates for *Mango Roses*, Clara asked Emil how much would be required in the way of bribes. Before he could answer, she chided him once more for not going with Judy and taking charge of things. "You really mustn't waste her time, Em."

Emil pivoted to Judy. "How many men did you speak to at the National?"

"Excuse me?

"Did you meet with the Artistic Director?" Emil had begun to flush.

"No," she replied. "No one seemed to know where he was."

"I'm sure he was waiting just behind the door that had his name on it," said Clara dryly, looking at Emil. "Palm up and out."

And that was the last of the fun for that evening. Clara sent them home in an official car. An underling gave Emil an envelope of shillings for the six men Judy had already dealt with, plus enough to motivate the Artistic Director to open his desk calendar. Judy received a handshake from Clara and a thousand-shilling note for Isaak, who had been waiting for them all evening on his *boda* in front of the embassy gates.

In the car, Judy found herself apologizing to a fuming Emil, whose pride was definitely injured by Clara's mild dressing-down, for not realizing that bribes were an essential feature of getting any business done in Uganda. "It is shameful," he said, more than once. Judy couldn't tell whether he meant the bribery, or Clara's behavior, which had also included a slight, but definite pressure at the center of his back to keep them moving through the stream of guests toward the *porte-cochère*. Judy certainly wouldn't reveal to "Em" Clara's thoughts about the non-industry of the African male, even if Emil self-identified as a citizen of the world.

The next morning Emil went to the National and secured weekend dates in early May for *Mango Roses*. Judy returned to her apartment at lunch to find Alice happily and redundantly polishing an onyx motorcycle helmet that had been messengered over, with a note on embassy stationery too expensive to curl or warp in the humidity.

There would be ten songs in *Mango Roses*, crowded for a one-act musical, but Judy, once begun, was excited, even given the after-school special limitations of the material, to discover that she had some compositional range. As with "The Matatu Song," she wrote swiftly, demonstrating, she reminded an ever-impressed Emil, either a prodigious talent or no talent at all. Nandie and Patience continued to chip in with the lyrics. For example, a free-writing exercise Judy gave Patience about her life goals led right to Jamie-Rose's anthem, "Kampala Girl." Tired of watching Alice bring Emil his meals literally on her knees, and having made no progress with either one of them on altering the custom, Judy was especially pleased with "Who Are You?" a fierce duet between Rosie and her Aunt Namayanju about the futility of female deference. The group numbers included an opening chorus of urban mothers seeking help at the Open Arms clinic and a challenge dance at a pork joint called "Come to My Village," which owed not a little to Anita and the Shark Girls singing "America" in *West Side Story*.

A pork joint was the Ugandan equivalent of an open-air barbecue pit. Every quarter mile on any commercial road, one could find a pork joint serving meat skewers to wash down with *waraji*, an eye-slitting, throat-burning local moonshine sold in little plastic bags. Everyone got blotto waiting for pork or chicken skewers and *muchumi*, a chopped tomato and onion salad. After the worst hangover of her life, which had followed a solo spin on the dance floor and a make-out session she'd initiated with Emil under a mango tree—which, between kisses, she hazily insisted was strictly for research purposes—Judy resolved to switch from *waraji* to Krest Bitter Lemons.

The cover of a mature mango tree is legendarily dense; its thick, jade leaves overlap as tightly as the scales of a pangolin. The air beneath the canopy is close and fragrant. The quiet, once inside, adds to the sorcery. Clearly the go-to umbrella and rumble seat for African millennia, the tree somehow gave her permission to transfer her exploring fingertips from the smooth trunk to the loose crook of Emil's forearm. Judy had noticed, then decided for herself, privately, that Ugandans were a unique combination of the prudish (long skirts, covered shoulders and throats) and the sexy. Their sexiness wasn't, however, overtly sexual. It flourished without comment, or gesture, or advertising dollars.

She moved her fingers up to Emil's shoulder, paused to test its strength, then tucked them inside his collar to rub his collarbone. Although Isaac and his *boda* and the ceaseless nighttime foot traffic were not five yards away, she wasn't able to hear anything but Emil's breathing. He was a good kisser, content to follow her lead; he didn't pull on parts of her or stretch her mouth or overdo with the ginned-up, presentational ardor of American men. Having never envied or imitated her friends' or her brother Cary's outdoor escapades, she now found herself aware for the first time, as with her first motorbike ride, of the appeal of sex in the wild.

She fluttered her fingers against Emil's not-quite-wavy, not-quite-curly hair. She had been wanting to feel that most of all. It was unexpected to the touch, like a soft, dry paintbrush.

Judy dropped her hands and stepped out of their embrace.

"What is the matter, Judy?"

She hadn't felt this self-conscious—Lady Off-Layer (another plum part for Katherine Hepburn) encounters the Oxford African (Sidney Poitier)—in a very long time. Was it that she had never touched a Black person's hair, or skull, or lips, in her life? Who else but a Black man was she supposed to have sex with in Africa? Was she to restrict herself to *muzungus*? The fib "I'm engaged" flew out of her mouth.

"And so?" said Emil, sounding amused.

"I'm engaged to be married."

"I am aware of the meaning of the word."

"To Mark Shinner." As if naming him made it more convincing.

"He is a lucky man, Judy Gabelson."

Now he *was* mocking her.

"I am too. Lucky."

"But if you are engaged to be married to him, why would he allow you to come be here with me?"

"Because he trusts me, Emil." And because I told him you were gay, she nearly added, another fib insofar as Mark, who did trust her, had never asked her the first thing about Emil. Had he asked, it might have led to a genuine conversation that might have kept her in Ithaca wearing his bracelet. "And I'm not here *with* you. You and I are here…together. Separate but equal."

As payment for his irritating response—a thoroughly chauvinist shrug that acknowledged the sensual license of the mango tree and the fact that she had made the first move—Judy set Emil in the middle of the *boda*, behind Isaak, and in front of her, on the ride home. Drunkenness exaggerated her umbrage, but the motor noise prevented her from delivering an addled lecture on women's rights and Valentine's Day traditions.

———

In the days to come, there was no tension, mention, follow-up, or follow-through to their bout of tonsil hockey. African Time, she wryly concluded. It was like having played Spin-the-Bottle with boys from another high school. No one need ever find out, which carried an upside and a downside.

Emil was now dividing his time between teaching and spreading the gospel of *Mango Roses* to potential singer-actor-dancers. Patience and Nandie kept refining the script. Judy's last assignment was a "prophecy song" for Namwasa, the *juju* who tells Rose and Jamie-Rose that they must attend Grandma Rose's funeral in the village. No bones through the nose, fringed shawls, or chunky beads. Judy wanted the character and the song to possess more authenticity than Bloody Mary or a Verdi fortuneteller. Emil's contrarian position about the number was that the history of European art was one of cultural appropriation, so she could write whatever she wanted. Besides, he hadn't the slightest idea where to find a good witch doctor. Judy found the notion of a *bad* witch doctor comic. They weren't heart surgeons, after all.

Alice, privy to the discussion by virtue of serving them fruit every morning, waited until Emil had gone to take his shower before addressing Judy.

"Mistress Judy, I know where famous *juju* is, please."

This was the first time Alice had initiated conversation, but still, she kept her eyes lowered. "Tell me," said Judy.

"He save my sister and my cousin many times from spells."

Judy knew Alice spent most of her free time reading her heavily inked Bible, and her nights off were spent at marathon-length shout-along revival meetings on Bugolobi Road. Judy had never met someone so literally God-fearing.

"One time, my sister was wearing a sweater with a curse on it, and she got trampled over by bull and break two legs." Alice held up two fingers.

"Did the traditional healer re-set her bones?"

Alice shook her head, as if the bones were immaterial. "The *juju* remove curse from the sweater."

Alice's healer was out west, all the way to Gayaza. Judy ignored her advice to visit the witch doctor without Emil. From the best she could understand, Alice didn't think Emil had the proper reverence with which to enter a *juju*'s hut. He was too "stubborn"—the Ugandan nuance here, Judy had learned, meant "mocking" or "jokey." They took two *bodas* because they would need an interpreter. Judy rode with Isaak, and Emil rode with a driver/translator named Sowedi.

It was a seventy-minute, glute-testing, uterus-tipping ride through some impossibly bad stretches of rutted mud and rock fragments masquerading as a highway. When they stopped to refuel the *bodas* on Ggaba Road, a commercial artery out of the city, Judy removed her safety helmet and got a blow to the heart. Just beyond the petrol stand, in an area the size of a football field, and as busy as a shipyard in wartime, was an outdoor woodshop devoted to the construction of coffins—rows of finished product standing on end wound through the space like so many surfboard necklaces. Closest to the road were the infant caskets, stacked vertically, as in the stock room of a shoe store. The air was thick with sawdust motes; in many spots, the carpenters stood ankle-deep in butter-yellow shavings. Sun slivers glinted off their tools in ceaseless motion. Public spaces in Uganda were uniformly raucous, the markets especially noisy with drumbeats and haggling, but here the only sounds were saw and hammer and plane. The few women she could spot in the silent hive were, she supposed, grieving survivors. Uganda was trying to catch up to the Reaper's demands with hundreds of caskets as fresh as the fruit on the trees.

"The slim disease?" she asked, already knowing the answer.

"They cannot make them fast enough," said Isaak, in sync with Judy's distress.

"This used to be the furniture market for all Kampala. Then Idi Amin came. Then *mukeneya*."

Although Judy had been to, and played for, and mourned at, many AIDS memorials, she had never witnessed such an intense visual correlative to the plague. While Isaak's eyes seemed too weary to water, Judy's filled as she thought first of her brothers (safe? infected?) on the other side of the planet. Then she thought of Merle Anderson, one of her closest colleagues at Slaterville High, whose parents had refused to take his body home, and then her childhood friend, Allen Widergren, a hockey star who died weighing eighty-six pounds. That September, Del and Dennis—nicknamed Chick and Chiclet—New York chorus boys and lovers from the Hangar's productions of *Damn Yankees* and *Man of La Mancha* some seasons back, had died three weeks apart.

She reached for the *boda* to steady herself before asking Isaak whether he had lost many friends to *mukeneya*.

"Too many to count," he replied.

That was said in America too.

By now, Judy had stood bareheaded long enough for a crowd of child vendors, all rags and smiles, to rush toward the *muzungu* and beseech her with offers of g-nuts, sweet bananas, pork skewers, scorched corn, dried mushrooms and fish, chicken feet, and other edibles. Even at the Ithaca

Farmer's Market, touts, especially children, could overwhelm her. At an early age, she'd been taught that there was no such thing as a free sample, so Judy was a woman who kept tight custom and bought only what she set out for. These little Ggaba Road touts pitched their wares with sharp cries—all she could make out were the "please" and "nice lady"—and insistent tugs at her arm and skirt. The Ithacans sold farm honey and scones to the brunch crowd, or sachets of lavender to freshen a powder room; these children were selling food in order to get their food for the day. She couldn't possibly favor two, or three, or even ten of them with purchases, and then turn away the rest. Growing faint in the heat and in the pressure of their needs, she wanted to scream that they should all be in school, didn't they know that education was the only way to get ahead in this world, knowing full well that she was lying, that there was no way out from subsistence living, the lowest, meanest world of all? They would die on the ground as they'd lived on the ground. She wished for a sack of coins to hurl in handfuls to draw them off and leave her be until Isaak kick-started the *boda,* and they made tracks for Gayaza. The hateful word "urchin" began beating in her head. She felt contemptible, defeated, meaner than her tormentors. She was the opposite of a nice lady— she was a selfish *muzungu* from civilized, barbaric America.

"*Tomalilo bude,*" said Isaak. The children fell back at once. Judy crossed her arms to stop their trembling and caught her breath.

"What did you just say?"

"*Tomalilo bude.*"

"What does it mean?"

"It means 'Do not waste my time.'"

"Is it a bad thing to say, or a rude thing to say?"

Isaak shook his head. "It is a serious thing to say."

"Is it wrong for a woman to say it?"

Isaak, who had once told her that all that Uganda had was time and children, considered this. She would respect his answer. No matter how high the temperature, Isaak's white Muslim *kufi*, its circumference threaded with gold, remained stiff and unstained with moisture. Most of his life was spent waiting, and he did so elegantly, like a weathervane that blew, day and night, in whichever direction she and Emil pointed. Isaak and his wife, who cooked for the Soviet Embassy, had three children.

"Would you like it if Taha said it?" she asked.

"Not to me," he said, smiling. "But to other men, yes."

She practiced the term. Emil and Sowedi returned with a bag of samosas and two orange Fantas. When Emil offered her a second samosa, she said "*tomalilo bude,*" and Sowedi busted a gut laughing.

The traditional healer, whose name she never learned, lived in a four-room cinderblock house with a complete roof and glass windows—a mansion by Ugandan standards—but maintained his practice in a circular straw hut some fifty yards into the bush, beyond an irregularly planted plot of maize and pumpkins.

Sowedi told them to take off their shoes and sit on the mat inside. (Judy assumed that Isaak's refusal to enter the hut was for religious reasons.) The interior smelled strongly of smoke, spices, and, more faintly, of fermenting leaves. Along the walls were jars of powders; a couple of spears, their points wound with cord, were leaning against the anchoring pole in the center. There were a great many baskets with dried herbs, a small fire pit in a far corner with dead coals, a sheaf of old copies of the *New Vision*, and perishables (or valuables) in plastic bags strung up on nails.

Sowedi explained to the healer that neither Emil nor Judy was suffering from physical ailments, but rather wanted to watch him at work. The healer nodded, unrolled a bark cloth blanket across his lap, and answered that since they had come all this distance, they should ask him a question anyway.

Judy, her mind saturated with coffins and urchins, didn't hesitate. She asked the healer whether her brothers were safe from *mukeneya* in America. How many brothers? Two. Older or younger. Both younger.

The *juju* unfolded an animal hide. Inside were a very large cowrie shell, a stick, several smaller cowries, a few coins, four crescent metal pieces, silver and brass, the size of fishing lures, and something that looked to Judy like a green plastic grape. He scooped everything up but the stick and the big cowrie, held his hands close to his face and whispered to the items. Then he threw them onto the hide and, in soft guttural sounds, interpreted what he saw. After a pause, he said something which Sowedi translated that her brothers were safe for now, but—to keep them safe—he rummaged deftly through his apothecary, then, with a tiny spoon of horn, scooped and folded two different powders into pieces of newspaper. She must bathe in the first powder for four mornings and mix the other in with a skin lotion and apply it to her forehead for five nights before lying down to sleep.

"Starting tonight or tomorrow," asked Emil in the disrespectful, "stubborn" tone Alice had cautioned Judy against.

Tomorrow was the *juju*'s answer. Despite having no spiritual practice of her own, Judy, elated by the news, bowed her head to the healer and pressed the packets of medicine to her chest.

Then it was Emil's turn. He winked at Judy, then asked whether *Mango Roses* would be a hit.

It took a lot of back and forth via Sowedi to make the healer understand that *Mango Roses* was a live performance with music, speech, and dance held in front of a paying crowd. Finally, he whispered to his handful of charms and threw.

This reading took longer. Twice the healer scrutinized Emil's face, then looked back to decipher the arrangement on the hide. Finally, an answer—"You must respect him first. Then love back."

"Respect who?" asked Emil.

"Your father."

Emil clenched his teeth, balled a fist, slammed it into his palm. "That's preposterous!" he shouted. Judy watched his crossed thighs strain upwards, as if he might spring at the doctor, or, since there was no *ponga* at hand, wield one of the spears, or snap the center pole of the hut and bury them all in thatch.

Emil refused the treatments the doctor offered and remained aggressively silent throughout Judy's Q & A about practical healing matters: the hide was antelope, three of the metal pieces represented the river god, the thunder god, and the lightning god, the coins were nothing special, and yes, it was a plastic grape that he found many years ago in a special place he would not reveal.

The *juju* allowed her to examine everything, just as a Western physician let patients handle blood pressure cuffs at a health fair. Eventually, she realized she was dealing with local medicine, no more special (or mystical) than her annual check-up with her doctor in Slaterville Springs.

Emil left the hut first; she heard him take in and expel great lungfuls of air. She paid for both readings and tried to communicate to the healer through Sowedi that she was sorry for how her friend had behaved. He shrugged and relayed that her friend was possessed by a bad spirit that he confused with his father, his expression conveying that daddy issues were a global ailment.

Emil even refused the jackfruit snack the doctor's wife had prepared for them. As Isaak and Sowedi dove in—jackfruit cut right from the tree was hard to acquire in the city proper—neighbors gathered at the edges of the compound to stare and smile, as ever, at the spectacle of a white lady in the bush.

Judy took her traditional meds and sent postcards to Dave and Cary with the message that "the gods of the best witch doctor in Gayaza is keeping you from all harm." Emil, evidently still affected by the *juju*'s interpretation, wouldn't offer any kind of an opinion on the song she composed for the character of Namwasa, called "River, Thunder, Lightning."

The *Mango Roses* auditions at the National Theatre the following weekend challenged additional cultural assumptions Judy had held, chief among them the belief that musical theatre was an international language, and that its aspirants were the same the world over—loud, confident, and trained. Twenty-seven young people, women slightly outnumbering men, showed up, took audition sides from Clara's eleven-year-old son, tow-headed Lars Svoboda, who was going to be their stage manager (!), and of them all, only three could read English without stumbling or constant mispronunciations. Only one among these three could be induced, despite insistent prompting, to project her voice above a whisper. When Judy tested their vocal ranges at the piano, all of them could hit and sustain notes, but not one could sight-read music. Even more alarming was their ignorance of the concept of part-singing. Before they would be able to learn Judy's harmonies—she had composed some fairly sophisticated choral numbers—she fretted that she would have to begin, kindergarten-style, by teaching them to sing "Row, Row, Row Your Boat" in rounds.

"Heinous" was the word Gavin Steeg used when Hangar auditions ran even three minutes late, or his egg salad sandwich arrived with lettuce on it; "H" (for heinous) was the letter he'd scribble on headshots when an actor was pitchy or fat or ugly or wrong for whatever reason. This is a completely heinous fiasco, thought Judy over and over, but Emil, beaming and peppy and glad-handing, didn't share her opinion. When he excused himself to take an undeserved cigarette break and told Judy and Patience to vamp until he came back by explaining the plot of *Mango Roses* to the hopefuls (Nandie wasn't able to make it to the auditions), Judy wanted to wring his neck. Although she had been tricked into writing a musical from scratch, she was proud of what she had accomplished, but now, didn't he realize that they had to *put it on, get it on, get it up, put it up, make it work*? There was going to be an audience!

The group was gravely attentive, in the manner of Ugandan pupils; some nodded in recognition to hear of "Punishment Island," and the boldest smiled when Judy explained "The Matatu Song." There was only one question when they finished: "Who will assume the character of the *muzungu*?"

Judy was confused.

"The Catholic grandmother Meaghan Braithwaite from Ohio," clarified an unusually attentive listener in the front row.

With an entirely African acting pool, who indeed?

"I think Miss Gabelson should play Auntie Braithwaite, don't you?" said Patience, pointing at Judy, as if she'd been planning this all along. "She is a beautiful singer," she added, unnecessarily, because the group was already clapping with great enthusiasm.

Judy was gobsmacked. Why hadn't she thought this through? Except for choir concerts in high school and college, she had never set foot on a stage, or even sang a solo. She wasn't about to make her stage debut in Greater Kampala. "Get me rewrite!" she wanted to shout, a tension-breaker Gavin used whenever he couldn't make something work. She and Emil could re-conceive Meaghan, or use color-blind casting, or write the character out of *Mango Roses*.

Emil suddenly returned with two drummers and before she could call a time-out to broker a solution to the casting conundrum, he bid the men to start a beat.

"Sing! Dance!" said Emil. There was a pause. The auditionees looked at one another. "Sing your village songs," he shouted over the drums through cupped hands. "Dance like you do in the village."

Members of the same tribe had already grouped themselves together, so there was no hunt for partners. In thirty seconds, the room went from utter silence to a controlled pandemonium of sound and movement and kept building from there. The collective talent was so incredible, Judy couldn't at first take it in. She closed her eyes to listen to the cascading, polyphonic chants, to rippling, harmonic cadenzas like birdcalls, to blue notes held and bent like laser beams. She opened her eyes and focused on physical undulations that matched, or, depending on the tribe, went against the drumming. Judy counted four groups; each had self-selected a pattern leader; two were led by women, two by men. No one tribe was attempting to out-sing or out-dance another. The drummers shifted their rhythm constantly, and the dancers, accepting the challenge, never missed a beat, their bodies weaving and spinning, their hands and feet and heads rolling twice as fast as the wrists, ankles, and necks they flowered from. Eventually, she saw that the leaders had begun trading places with one other in order to share their steps with the other tribes.

As the four villages merged into one, Judy thought fuck the script, fuck the songs, fuck the harmonies, fuck upstage and downstage and rehearsals and run-throughs and tech, here was the most enthralling live performance she had ever seen, and it flowed in utter spontaneity through two drums and twenty-seven bodies. Performance *was* a global language: these singer-dancers seemed to be just cutting up, the way hyperactive American chorus kids did during rehearsal breaks. After two and some hours of mostly failed attempts at connecting with them, Judy began to weep at their virtuosity, youth, beauty, and un-self-consciousness. After two and some hours of puzzled looks at the treble clef and mangled dialogue and whispered answers to basic questions, these young people who were playing in the truest sense of the word reminded Judy of why she was in the theatre. Gavin Steeg, a born cynic, once confessed to her that he had spent thirty-five years falling in love with talent. Here it was, an effortless, glorious, heavenly inferno of talent.

Emil finally signaled the drummers to stop.

"Clearly, we are going to have to hire local percussionists," Judy said, wiping her eyes while the room caught its breath. They cast all twenty-seven.

Rehearsals, which began the following week on the stage of the National, were more of the same—a surreal mix of the breathtaking and the inept. Judy taught the music by rote; they were swift learners in that department. Emil selected two older cast members to choreograph. The scenes continued to be the biggest challenge. It took some time before the actors understood that they were to commit their lines to memory and deliver them to each other and not to wherever Emil was in the house. More time after that to learn not to pursue their own conversations onstage when a scene was being played. Emil's vexed "I can't hear you!" from the back row quickly spread, such that the cast would take it up as a group chant when one of its members failed to project his or her voice sufficiently, even when they were all onstage together.

Because Judy would be playing the piano *and* conducting the singers *and* cueing the drummers, she was able to avoid playing Meaghan Braithwaite. The solution, once Clara Svoboda passed on the role with an "Are you utterly mad?" was whiteface on the oldest woman in the company. Although she knew that many African tribes used whiteface for ceremonial purposes, both the practice and the actress's wild delight at being selected to play the *muzungu,* made Judy uncomfortable. When the actress began to lord her status over her peers, Judy took Emil aside.

"She thinks hers is the most important part," said Emil, who had noticed the behavior but didn't care. Anything that served the show was okay with him.

"Because she is white?"

"No, because she solves the plot and saves the day," he said.

This was BS. "But she *doesn't* save the day, and at best, she muddies the plot. Were it up to me, Meaghan would never have been written into the show. I did it for Nandie and Patience."

His look was long and supercilious. She might have been airlifted into the presence of Dave Bailey, presently on the other side of the world using his gifts to dream up ways to increase world consumption of breaded pollock sticks. Africa would appall Dave completely. The dirt, the trash, the noise, the chaos on the streets would give him migraines. Cary, adaptable and curious, could probably make a go of it.

"Don't you like the image of white people and Black people singing together in the finale?" asked Emil.

"White *person* and Black people," she replied. "Meaghan Braithwaite is not Lady Bountiful or Harriet Beecher Stowe. That's the woman who wrote—"

"*Uncle Tom's Cabin.* The little lady who started the great, big war. Don't patronize me, Judy."

She suddenly saw that it wasn't the older actress and her silly demands for a soft cushion and a parasol that had been perturbing her. It was Emil. He had been ordering the cast around like a plantation owner, pushing them into place and barking at their mistakes, with lisping, eleven-year-old Lars, who hardly cleared five feet, as head overseer. Actors sucked up to directors, it was part of the need game, but these Ugandans had had no previous experience with the dynamic. It was ghastly to watch them take Emil's direction like a bowl of *posho* in a UNICEF ad, bowing and scraping and apologizing and thanking him for corrections and adjustments, thanking him for his mistreatment.

"Don't you patronize *me,* Emil. Or them!"

"What are you talking about?"

"They aren't children. Or workers. Or—"

"Slaves?" He'd read her mind.

"Robots!"

"I should think not. Robots are designed for efficiency."

She challenged him to tell her all their names. His perfect score enraged her.

"Then why don't you try using them for once!" she snarled in a general silence, then stomped over to the piano. Falling into her own trap, she announced to the room that yes, Mommy and Daddy were fighting. It broke the tension at Hangar rehearsals, but to the credit of the Africans, they failed to understand her stab at Freudian humor.

Two days later, when the embassy car came to pick Lars up post-rehearsal, Judy was surprised to see Clara emerge from the back seat. Mother and son shook hands; Clara air-kissed Emil, then invited Judy to lunch at the Imperial Hotel that Friday in a tone so ambiguous, Judy imagined she had done something wrong.

The Imperial was in an advanced state of decline, but nevertheless Judy was able to picture it when it was the poshest address in the British Protectorate of Uganda. A framed portrait of a twenty-something Queen Elizabeth reigned over the sweeping mahogany reception desk. The deference shown Clara Svoboda was extended to Judy, who eventually concluded that her oohs and aahs at the heavy doors, the marble and the marquetry, the Persian rugs, the enfilade of columns and the egg and dart pattern moldings, were gauche. The *maître d'* seated them by the window in the luncheon room, which the women had completely to themselves. Unlike Alice's results with the laundry, the napkins and tablecloths didn't feel to Judy's touch as if they'd been boiled in lye and fired in a kiln. Every piece of her silver matched; fork tines were pressed into the cloth like children sent to stand in a corner, and there were four crystal glasses to her place setting. Looking out at the lush, undulating lawn, she thought it amusing that this meal, her closest brush so far in life with fine European dining, would involve a trio of baboons pitching fruit husks at each other like college students with a Frisbee until a dignified boy in a turban chased them off with a gilt staff. One day she would get to Europe too. Europe would be a cakewalk after Africa.

Clara, smoking sidesaddle in her chair, athletic legs crossed at the ankle, was difficult to read, so Judy began lunch with profuse thanks for the recent script copying, the higher music bench for the piano, and the extra funds used to dress the dancers in *kitende* cloth. Clara dismissed all that with a tap of her ash in a little brass scallop shell, which was instantly replaced. Each woman had her own server.

"Lars said you told him he might be nicer to people."

Judy had done something wrong.

"That wasn't what I said." Clara arched her perfect eyebrows. "Lars was yelling at several actors to calm down—'Stop your mouths' in fact were his words—"

"There seems to be a lot of that going on at these rehearsals—"

"*I* certainly don't raise my voice to the actors. I only told Lars what I tell my students back home when they misbehave."

"Which is?"

"I told him to treat the cast members as he himself would wish to be treated."

Clara's pained sigh made it clear that the Golden Rule might not apply to her firstborn. "He is eleven years old, Judy."

"Exactly my point."

"You have been in Uganda for how long?"

"Four months, Clara, but that's hardly the issue. I mean, isn't 'Do unto others' how we're all supposed to behave?"

Clara considered this for a moment, but Judy knew from watching actors on stage that Clara was only pretending to consider this. The life of an embassy wife had to be filled with pretend moments.

"Certainly, in our nations of origin and among our peers we do—or ought to."

In Judy's flabbergasted silence, Clara picked up her menu and closed out the subject by reminding her that she was the child's mother and that Lars' moral guidance was one of her custodial powers. Judy's first impulse was to throw her napkin on the table and flee the restaurant but was forced to remind herself that she was a guest of this country within a country too.

They ordered sole *meunière* and steak *au poivre*. With the unpleasantness out of the way, Clara was prepared to be more winning.

"Will you be going on safari while you're here? You must be dying to see the animals."

Judy couldn't see how that would happen. She would only have three weeks after *Mango Roses* closed before she was to fly back to the US. The only available sights, besides a day trip to cross the literal Equator, was a drive to Jinja and a hike to the Bujigali Falls, two hours east. Cary's safari hat had saved her cheap Irish skin from sun poisoning on a daily basis, but she hadn't thought at all about elephants and lions and chimps. Africans never discussed them. She had initially wanted to visit Lake Bunyonyi and Prisoner's Island, but Emil said it was closed to foreigners.

"I thought Idi Amin had destroyed everything."

"He didn't manage to destroy the game parks, although they're frightfully mismanaged. And the roads are atrocious. It would be easier, really, for us to fly to Kenya for safari. The Kenyans had a great head start."

That sounded like an invitation, one Emil might accept, but not Judy.

Clara gestured to the empty dining room. Their waiters, misinterpreting, sped to them with comic haste. No food had appeared, so even the finest establishment in Kampala operated on AT. Good for them, thought Judy. Keep us waiting. We deserve it. To give them something to do, Judy asked for another Krest's Bitter Lemon.

"What this country needs most," sighed Clara, "is reliable leopard."

At this point, Judy was disliking Clara so intensely, she wouldn't give her the satisfaction of asking for an explanation of this clearly facetious declaration. Nor would she dig for information about what she did with Emil in bed or wonder about the state of her marriage or Swedish diplomacy or cinema or world affairs in general.

Clara, trained to bridge silences, went on: "Leopards are the most elusive and solitary animal. Entire weeks can go by at a game park or hunting lodge without a guest spotting a single leopard on safari. There's a tally kept, you see, at the entrance to the lodge where you chalk up the number of important animals you've seen on your game drive. Elephants, lions, giraffe, rhinoceri...."

"Hippos."

Clara laughed. "If you've seen one hippopotamus, Judy, you've seen a thousand, because they swarm during the day to sleep in shallow waters."

"Yes, I've seen that on television."

"At night, though, when they go feeding on land, they're a terror. Hippopotami are really very dangerous. Walt Disney should never have put them in tutus. It's false advertising."

A basket of bread arrived. With a frown, Clara nudged it toward Judy. Taking up a piece, Judy decided she would eat the entire loaf to prove a point—if only she knew what the point was going to be. She stabbed the tip of her butter knife into her individual pat.

"Have you ever seen one, Clara? A leopard."

"No." Clara laughed again, just as falsely. "They're most often found prowling about an hour before dawn near a watering hole. I can't seem to manage to get up early enough. They return at dusk, but that's cocktail hour."

Clara leaned in, an important animal on surer footing now that her guest had begun eating her food. "Tourists would pay significant sums of money if they could be guaranteed a leopard sighting on every drive."

"If the leopards were reliable, you mean."

"Exactly."

"And if Ugandan leopards were reliable, or could be trained to be, tourism would take off, and money would pour in, and the infrastructure would improve. Diseases would be eliminated, a cure for the slim disease would be found, poverty and government corruption would cease, and most important, the birth rate would drop from seven point five children per mother, to a more feasible, reasonable, and *humane* two point five."

As they looked at each other, there was a sudden chill, or rather, a rapid chilly understanding, at their elegant table, still bereft of anything sustaining but bread and butter.

"Something like that," said Clara, eyes narrowed.

"But the problem is," said Judy, "that leopards *are* reliable, but only to themselves."

"That's what makes them leopards," the women said together, in almost perfect unison.

⊢——————•——————⊣

In the rehearsal process for *Mango Roses*, it was suddenly all hands on deck. This was no different from the Hangar, except in Ithaca there were plenty of hands to pitch in, and on American time. A tree trunk needed to be built.

Emil's design solution for the *matatu*, ten chairs anchored to a wheeled platform, proved unworkable, because the stage was raked. Rather than roll into the pit, the cast would have to shake its shoulders to mime the bus ride through the bush. The floor lacked traps, so they would have to lower Grandmother Rose's body (very carefully) into the orchestra pit. Management (wisely) decided that a literal *boda* onstage would generate noise, smoke, and peril, so Meaghan Braithwaite's *deus ex machina* was initially changed to an offstage cue, but then, because the National Theatre of Uganda was even less technologically equipped than Slaterville High School, they weren't able to create a motorcycle cue on a sound system that had been stripped for parts years ago. Meaghan would just have to enter downstage left, remove her hat, wipe her brow with a handkerchief, and announce, "My, that was a frightfully long *boda* from Kampala!"

This solution cracked Judy up every time she heard it, but Emil, inexperienced at rehearsal triage, was sick about it. They argued every day about postponing the opening. The more exasperated Emil became, the calmer Judy was when putting out the daily fires. It felt familiar.

Patience Ochom, always on board as prompter and all-purpose stand-in when cast members were late or had malarial flare-ups, grew more miserably stagestruck every day. She knew—and could project—every line and lyric and had most of the choreography in her bones. That also felt familiar. When Judy was Patience's age, and had seen her first musical, a school trip to a dinner theater *Oliver!* in Oneonta, she dreamed of one day being a part of the theater and had immediately begun saving her allowance and babysitting money for trips to New York, original cast recordings, and a subscription to the Fireside Theatre Book Club. She worked build crews and played in the orchestra all through high school. Patience's hunger though, unlike Judy's, was to live *on* the stage. It would have been so easy to let Patience join the company, but Emil had said early on that Good Lights School wouldn't allow it. She believed him at the time. Now she understood that a bribe or two could change any and all policies and that Emil might have been talking out of his ass.

"I'm sorry that you couldn't be in the show," said Judy, finally broaching the subject with Patience one morning before rehearsal. They had taken up scissors, needles, and thread. All well and good to get *kitende* from Clara Svoboda for the dancers, but costumes—even the simplest of tunics—didn't sew themselves.

Patience bit her lip and said she didn't want to be in the show.

Judy finished a stitch and casually remarked, "You know, Patience, you are more important to *Mango Roses* than any actor or actress in it."

That got her attention. "Why is that, Miss Judy?"

"Because you wrote it. None of this would be happening without you and Nandie. I couldn't have written a note of music without you."

In the rush of getting the show up, Judy hadn't had the time or headspace to process how much she actually owed her two "Kampala Girls." Ten songs had poured out of her in three weeks, with scant anguish or second-guessing. They needed songs, and so Judy had written them. Who knew she could do that? And, so far, she had taught them to the cast—just as she did summers in Ithaca—without having connected the sounds they were making to the heart and ear and intelligence that had generated them. This was the sound of *her* music, and not only that, she could do it again, if she had to, or if she wanted to. Did she want to? Very likely, yes.

Judy dropped her cloth and took Patience's free hand into both of hers. "I wrote the songs for *your* characters. The melodies are mine, but your people inspired the songs, and you helped me write the lyrics. Parts of you, and your life, are in *Mango Roses,* am I correct?" Patience nodded. "So, you do live on that stage, Patience Ochom. That is what artists do when they create."

"My father thinks artists are useless, unless they are offering their gifts to Jesus."

"Yes. That is one opinion." Judy refrained from telling Patience that she thought missionaries were useless on every occasion but made a mental note to praise Patience and her gifts to the Reverend and Mrs. Ochom at the opening. *Mango Roses* would likely reveal to them more about their daughter than they might be ready to see.

"My father tells me that it is my purpose to spread the Word of God."

"But what you really want to do is to sing and to dance and to act."

Patience's hand twisted free of Judy's. "I do not live in America!"

The anguish in the girl's cry tore at Judy. Everyone wanted to be in America. Not a person to raise false hopes, Judy sidestepped the easy lie that Patience might get to America one day if she only worked hard enough or prayed to God morning, noon, and night. Those miracles weren't in the cards, or, she smiled inwardly to think of it, in the antelope hide. Judy explained instead how theater could be its own special country, or—when that seemed to make little sense to Patience—its own mission that didn't need to be in America to be important to people. She and Nandie could write a next play, or Nandie could write a play for Patience to star in, or they could write a play about life at Good Lights school and put it on there, Teacher Thompson would surely help. A play based on a famous Bible story might change her father's mind about artists and creativity. There was, in fact, a wonderful, faith-based musical called *Godspell* taken from St. Matthew. She would send Patience a cassette tape of the music over from America.

Patience nodded, less skeptically now. Judy, pulling threads off her skirt, heard Lars Svoboda tell the janitor to sweep the stage floor, a default theatre command heard the world over. Idle hands could always sweep the stage.

◆———◆———◆

Despite repeated promises, Nandie Lubangakene hadn't made it to any *Mango Roses* rehearsals. Judy pictured her digging cassava, a ball and chain on her ankle, until Patience explained that Nandie didn't have transportation money. Thus it was that when Ambassador Svoboda arranged for a mini-preview of two scenes and five songs from *Mango Roses* at the Swedish Embassy for the Ugandan Cultural Ministry, Judy and Isaak went to fetch Nandie in Matugga, a semi-rural neighborhood in the northwestern outskirts of the city.

Nandie was the eldest of the five Lubangakene children. She had two brothers, Moses and KingBonnie, and two sisters, Rami and Fiona. When they drove up, their mother, Darula, set aside her hoe and greeted Judy as the savior of the family. Judy would only concede that she had encouraged Nandie's talent for creative expression. Darula said her husband was away at work. Before Judy could ask Darula his occupation, Isaak shot her a look that meant he was off drinking *waraji*.

The elder boy, Moses, round, proud, and talkative, gave her the tour of the unfinished brick and plaster structure. There was no light inside their three rooms, or evidence of candles. The floor was dirt; the windows had no glass. There was no electricity, heat, or running water. A single jerry can for water storage, food cooked over a dirt floor fire, a pit latrine, five ramshackle pieces of furniture and a stained *ponga* for a family of seven, free-range cocks and hens and an old straw mattress in the front yard. Everywhere there was garbage and trash; rags and plastic bags were stuffed into the window bars. How was Nandie able to study in these grim surroundings? How was it that she came to school every day immaculately washed and dressed?

Judy remembered how self-conscious she was about having friends over as a girl. Her parents were an eternal embarrassment, and she hated having to explain how Dave and Cary were *foster* brothers, but Nandie, pulling homework from a suitcase filled with rotted, foul-smelling papers, was unaware of how desperate things appeared. Poverty, squalor, and desperation were Western terms shot through a Western lens when these were the blameless conditions of Nandie's life. Judy nevertheless had to remind herself of the African lesson that poverty was not a moral failing, it just *was*.

The children all vied for the attention of the first *muzungu* to visit this patch of Matugga, the boys doing handstands and Rami explaining each scrap metal charm on her knotted string bracelet, but there was something off about three-year-old Fiona. She was completely silent—no words, or cries, or even babble. She just trailed Judy with outstretched arms. She and Isaak began by taking turns. They'd pick Fiona up and rock her. When she grew too heavy, or Judy was called upon to meet yet another neighbor, or look at Nandie's old report cards, she would set Fiona down. "All better now," she'd chirp. Without changing expression, Fiona would instantly raise her arms again, pleading for contact.

Annoyance turned to fear. Judy began avoiding the look; she'd hand Fiona over more frequently to Isaak, whose own expression began to suggest that he too believed childcare was women's work. She nearly offered him a double fare if he would take Fiona and KingBonnie for a *boda* ride, but she decided that talking about the situation would mean acknowledging there was a situation, a situation she was failing.

The clock was ticking, but Judy knew that it would be bad manners for a visiting dignitary to refuse lunch. Attempting to rush things was also out of the question. The adults ate first, cross-legged on the discarded mattress in the yard. Isaak and Judy were awarded the spoons. Darula sliced hunks of *posho* with the edge of a yellow plastic plate and poured savory beans over them. Judy's compliments seemed to confuse her.

By custom, the children ate what was left over. Watching Fiona's hands scoop beans from the bowl, she racked her brain for what it could recall from her college childhood ed classes. Was it a motor disorder, or cognitive impairment, or a developmental problem, or neurological, or a combination? Could Fiona produce speech? An American child that presented this way would be observed, tested, diagnosed, perhaps sequestered and trained to function as best she could in a group living situation.

No other Lubangakene seemed aware that anything was wrong with Fiona. Finally, Judy asked Isaak what he thought.

"She wants attention." Isaak, a patient man, and a good father, according to Emil, didn't get it either. Might she be projecting a Western condition onto Fiona? If Judy grew up like this, in the bush, competing with her siblings for table scraps and the corner of a filthy mattress, would she feel like talking?

"Is it hunger?"

"She is fed."

"Is it a sickness?"

"Not one there is a name for."

Judy hoped lunch would make the girl nap, but as soon as the children finished eating, Nandie went to get dolled up for the embassy, the boys went off to play, Rami wiped the dishes clean with a filthy rag, and Fiona instantly pivoted to Judy, arms out and up.

Judy ferried the last utensils inside to Rami and, to avoid Fiona, studied a religious tract in a language she couldn't read posted on a wall. The girl stood behind her, a silent shadow. Judy then sat on the one stuffed chair in the house and blocked her lap from Fiona's hands by taking up a family photo from the dirt floor and having KingBonnie explain its provenance.

In a final attempt at escape, Judy zipped across the porch and into the pit latrine, which she did not need to use, and, struggling for poise in the stench, looked at, and attempted to see, herself. She was a thirty-five-year-old woman at the apex of the global food chain terrified of, no, *terrorized* by an obviously impaired girl with an addressable need. She thought of the very large snails she and Alice would find on her porch some mornings. Most of them were whole, but occasionally, one would have its shell busted in. That meant an even larger bird had pecked it open in the night with its razor-sharp beak and consumed its softest parts.

After a long moment, Judy turned around, not to squat, but to face the fresh air. She took in the pattern of *mtoke* fronds scraping the roof of the outhouse and the sounds of the bush. From the look of the sky, clear blue now, but with a churn of hazel and violet in the distance, she predicted that she and Isaak and Nandie would encounter an intense, twenty-minute cloudburst on the boda to the embassy. Their arms would get tired from holding banana leaves over their heads in the traffic, but it couldn't be helped.

She looked down. Under the bottom of the swinging door, there were two bare feet planted in the dirt. Fiona was not a projection. Fiona was achievable.

She took a breath, then opened the door with a bump of her knee. Before Fiona had the time to lift her arms, Judy swept her up and marched her over to cuddle on the cement threshold of the unfinished house. Nandie, through a window, warned her that Fiona still wet the bed. Fiona would in fact wet both herself and Judy before the *boda* left for the city, but that too couldn't be helped.

Cradling Fiona Lubangakene in her lap, Judy Gabelson didn't yet know that *Mango Roses* would never happen. The presentation at the embassy, for which she and Nandie would arrive ninety minutes late because of rain and traffic, and something known to all and explained away as African Time, would be a catastrophe. The musical's depiction, however muted, of female empowerment, would put the Swedish Ambassador in jeopardy. The cultural officials would begin grumbling loudly during Jamie-Rose's "Kampala Girl," then would literally turn their backs to the actresses playing Rosie and Aunt Namayanju when they sang "Who Are You (to Change a Culture)?" In an ensuing week of intense meetings, Judy would volunteer to soften the feminist slant to the lyrics—oddly, the dialogue seemed to have escaped notice—such is the power of music—but Emil would refuse to allow the alteration of a single syllable, leaving the Swedish Embassy no choice but to withdraw its patronage. Emil would vow to carry on without their support. They were so close to achieving their dream, but the National Theatre, understandably fearing government reprisal, would cancel the production. The show would not, for once, go on.

Clara would manage to prevent Emil from going to the media with a tale of censorship, or from sending a letter to President Museveni saying that Uganda couldn't make an inch of progress in a million years with such backward-thinking attitudes. Judy would suppose that the cancellation would distress the cast, but they faced the news with equanimity. The most articulate cast member, Angela Murwurwe, who played Jamie-Rose, said that *Mango Roses* felt like another example of Western aid: great guns and promises at the outset, then no follow-through.

It was also during this awful week that Judy would be privy to the revelations that Emil slept with Clara *and* Isaak (but not together), expenses for the latter contained in his monthly retainer as Emil's principal *boda* driver. Less beside the point was the news from Clara that Emil's father was an Afrikaaner tea planter who had paid for Emil's education, but had refused to make contact with his son during his boyhood. Now, the shoe was on the other foot—the father, ancient and ailing, imploring for, and the son refusing, contact. When Judy reminded Emil of the *juju*'s diagnosis—*Mango Roses* would succeed if Emil telephoned his father in Johannesburg—he would refuse to speak to her for three entire days.

But all of this was ahead of them. In the actual present, Judy was thinking about what to get first for the Lubangakenes. Water, she had been observing all afternoon, was the most essential element to the stressed household. The closest communal borehole was a half-mile off; one of the children was always trudging back and forth to re-fill the jerry can. She decided she'd come back with two more jerry cans, as well as a small cart, to triple their storage and speed the transport. Then, a rain barrel and a cover, as she'd noticed outside a couple of the other, more stable dwellings. Once the water situation improved, glass for the windows to keep out the dust and the vermin. Then she'd figure out a way to get them more bedding, and raise what bedding there was from the ground.

Closer to home, she would purchase a soccer ball for Alice to take to her sons and to all the boys in her village. And books books books books for her daughter and all the girls of Bukadea, every book she could lay her hands on, so many books that the boys would stop the ball with jealous feet and ask for a look between the covers.

Teaching was a global language too. If no school would have her, then, taking a page from the Open Arms Shelter in *Mango Roses,* she would find an NGO—or start one—that promoted family planning, a Sisyphean sell in this country, but worth the effort. Life in Kampala was so cheap, and so rich. If an emergency arose and she had to get back to the States, she could have Clara Svoboda fence Mark's tennis bracelet. But before she could set anything in motion, she and Isaak, currently leaning against his livelihood in the nearby shade, would have to take the *boda,* and a pocketful of bribes, down to the American Embassy on Ggaba Road where she could register her whereabouts and renew her Ugandan visa.

As if sensing Judy's straying focus, Fiona Lubangakene re-claimed her attention by digging deeper into her arms. Judy smiled and thought "*tomalilo bude.*" Should she be able to remain this fortunate, her time need never be wasted again.

Part Four

Mark Shinner

1990

Where the apple reddens, never pry—
Lest we lose our Edens, Eve and I.

~ Robert Browning

Standing in the middle of the dining room, Mark Shinner finished a second pilsner but, typically, didn't know where to put down his empty beer glass. Placing it by his plate would mar the symmetry of the table setting. During meal prep, Cary Dunkler's kitchen was off-limits to guests, even to pitch a napkin in the trash. There was a candle stand at the foot of the staircase, but Mark might forget he'd left it there and leave it for Cary to clean up. But wouldn't Cary be cleaning everything up in any case? Even in a space he visited frequently—Cary shared his house with Mark's younger brother, Edgar— hospitality questions flummoxed Mark Shinner.

That evening Cary's face was the gray of a vacuum cleaner bag, and he was moving at an old man's pace. His brother, Dave, had been in the ground for three weeks. No one in Ithaca could recall a more senseless death. It had been close to two in the morning when a semi driver cut Dave and his partner, Gavin Steeg, off on too sharp a turn at Bessemer Hill Road on 79 East. Dave had been thrown fifty feet from the passenger seat. Some wishful thinkers, especially his adoptive mother, still clung to the notion that the extra time it had taken to find him in the dark was what had cost him his life. Mark Shinner, who worked in the billing department at Tompkins County Hospital, had access to death reports and knew better. Dave and Gavin had been going eighty miles an hour at the moment of impact. Gavin was saved by his seat belt. Dave lasted four days on life support.

The pair had made the trip dozens of times, so no one suggested they get a fresher start in the morning. The Hangar season was over, and Gavin lived by the stage bromide, "Always leave 'em wanting more." Dave was itchy after two August weeks upstate to get back to real life in the city. Ithaca was Gavin's gig, not his. They'd waved farewell to Hangar staff and trustees and interns and had jumped in the packed car before the kegs were drained and the industrial barbecue grill was scraped clean. Cary had been tossing the last of the trash bags into the Cass Park dumpster when word came that there had been an accident.

Dave's mother, Leigh Bailey, had always resented Gavin Steeg for stealing him away from Ithaca, from scholarship, and from her. Death provided her the opportunity to take him back. On day five, she stopped life support before Gavin had graduated from critical care. In further revenge, she had had Dave buried in Lake View Cemetery without Gavin's input. Because the plague still raged, gay men were in the habit of making posthumous plans, but not Dave. Leigh's maternal claim gave her the right to dispose of the body however she saw fit.

There had been so many AIDS funerals and memorials that it was easy for Ithaca to forget that Dave Bailey had not died of it. Whether that comforted Leigh Bailey was beyond knowing, but, with Gavin still in the hospital, mentions of Dave's personal life were conspicuously absent in the tone-deaf hagiography given by a religious studies professor known only to her. The service focused on Dave's storied undergraduate career at Cornell; of his magnetism and his way with words, so helpful to several of Ogilvy & Mather's global accounts, much was said; of his ACT-UP advocacy and his decade of domestic partnership with a man twenty-five years his senior, nothing.

Given their bad blood, Leigh hadn't allowed Cary to speak or read at the service. When Dave was in the sixth grade, Leigh had removed him from his foster parents, Hugh and Mary Gabelson, (and Cary), and legally adopted him. When Dave came out of the closet, Leigh blamed Cary, coincidentally gay, and to her thinking, an eternal negative influence.

Fretting by the window, where the sky was signaling a September cloudburst, Mark rejected setting his beer glass on the sill. Edgar's wheelchair might brush it off. Mark supposed that Leigh, an Ivy League professor of *sociology*, suspiciously single herself, would have worked through her abhorrence to Dave's sexual identity to the point of recognizing it as baseless prejudice. But then—as he always did—Mark Shinner, who was also trained as a social scientist, checked his biases. What did he know about it? Neither a mother nor a father, he couldn't claim bad blood with anybody ever. He was a man who had failed his entire life to ignite passion in others. Mark's dissertation advisor hadn't been able to drum up the energy to tell him that permission for another extension had been denied him and, moreover, that he had retired. The official heave-ho had come over the telephone from the department secretary.

Call it magnetism, call it charisma, call it musk, but certain men were innate charmers. Gavin Steeg and Dave Bailey, before his death at thirty-one, were born-with-it leaders. Edgar Shinner, in a wheelchair since 1966, had been voted Dean of the Year at Ithaca College five years running and got mash notes from every campus stratum. A graffito in a handicapped stall in the admissions building called him Gregory Peck in a neck brace.

Their uncle, Solomon "Sharky" Shinner, a diamond cutter on Jewelers Row in Philadelphia, had told Edgar and Mark as they were nearing puberty, "In every love relationship, boys, someone is the jewel, and someone is the setting." Demonstrating with the topaz on his pinkie ring, he'd say, "Never pretend to be a jewel if you're not a jewel, or a setting if you're not a setting." Sharky, who had fled the Cossacks with four brothers, three beets, and a sickle, hadn't needed to classify them. Edgar Shinner's spinal injury in his teens had only lent additional sparkle to the original multi-faceted jewel, while Mark Shinner was a classic, and primarily empty, setting.

That night Mark would have welcomed Sharky's opinion on his latest quest for a jewel to call his own. Edgar had been appalled when, during cocktail hour, Mark had shown him the brochure from *Jana's Daisy Bride: International Marriage Agency*.

"This means you've given up," Edgar had said to him. "I don't accept that."

"I am forty-three years old."

Cary was inspecting the mailing envelope. "Gorbachev?" he asked, meaning the stamps.

Edgar, flipping pages, began mocking the ads. "'My name is Tati, and I like scubadivesing.' 'I am Lenka; fast cars make me horny.'"

"She does not say that," said Mark.

"'Okay, fast cars make me happy.' It's not a good sign that you've already memorized Lenka's specs."

Cary caught Mark's eye and took the booklet from Edgar. Both were sad settings, or more precisely, Mark was lonely, while Cary bore a core of melancholy that not all of his professional success with Clever Hans or his life with Edgar could conceal. Edgar had said that Cary had been utterly silent in his suffering over Dave, had not teared up once since the accident. Offered sometimes as a dinner party joke, it was Edgar's belief that Cary had never sufficiently processed having been picked second—after Dave—by the Gabelsons in a "Two-for-One Orphan Deal" up at Cornell in 1964. Cary would dismiss this "wound to end all wounds" with an offer of more wine or, if there weren't candles on the table, a swift dimming of the overhead lights.

Mark once asked Cary why he and Edgar wouldn't move to a rancher; a wheelchair for each floor seemed cumbersome. Cary had said he liked nothing better than to carry his man up and down the stairs all day long—it kept him fit.

It kept them close, too, and Mark envied it, envied all intimacy. The closest he had ever gotten to such closeness in his years in Ithaca had been with Cary's foster sister, Judy Gabelson. To Mark, it had felt that he and Judy had been married for ten years—a good feeling—even if Uncle Sharky would have deemed Judy as another setting and said, as he always did, "Don't bother with identicals boys they never work."

Mark would never have thought to carry Judy upstairs in his arms, certainly not in her own house. Three years ago, she'd left for Uganda on a whim, and now, having sold her house on Titus Street to Cary for a song, clearly wasn't coming back.

All who knew Judy were happy she had found a calling. Her "Book Drive for the Bush" netted thousands of volumes every spring; schools and libraries all over Tompkins County outdid each other in shedding excess inventory. The Cornell Law School sprang for the postage and shipping. It was Ithaca at its communitarian best.

Cary served the quiche and Mark asked the table if Judy had sent any word. Judy Gabelson had no phone number or street address in Kampala. She had *locations*.

Cary shook his head.

"The consulate has put out the word on Dave's death to her known checkpoints," said Edgar.

"As if she really were a spy," said Mark. The thought had crossed all their minds since her vanishing act.

"Like your bombshells from Jana's Daisy Bride," said Edgar.

At that, an irritated Mark missed his quiche with too heavy a hand, such that his fork scraped loudly on the plate. Lay off, he wanted to say. No need reminding him he was boring, flabby, balding, ABD, and neither fun nor funny. In his defense, however, he didn't collect *Star Trek* figures or vintage license plates or haunt stripper bars or carve duck decoys in his basement. Every woman he had ever dated praised him, usually during the brush-off, for his listening skills. He owned his own home at the corner of Utica and Yates, had socked money away for retirement and the Big Sleep expenses, and would welcome children, so why couldn't he be allowed to help a woman seeking a better life to escape The Ukraine?

Cary, the sturdiest of solid platinum settings, understood. "What's your beef, Edgar? Everyone deserves a decent partner. Everyone who wants one."

"Through the mails?"

"Call it reciprocal desperation," said Mark. "Something Tati and I can share while we scubadivesing." This failed to lighten the mood. Mark had been Edgar's caretaker before Cary. Because he required so much physical assistance, Mark privately thought that baldly expressed emotional needs freaked his brother out.

"You're desperate enough to buy yourself a bride? This isn't Sacramento in the Gold Rush."

"I'm not buying a bride, Edgar. I'm paying a finder's fee. For Christ's sake, our great-grandfathers used matchmakers."

Edgar let that pass in favor of another irritating idea. "If you're really in the marriage market, I've heard Asian women make the most grateful wives." He paused. "So much for my cultural sensitivity."

"And a migrant worker at Lucas Vineyards would be free," said Mark, nearly snuffing a candle with his shout. "Believe me, if I thought the right woman for me was picking grapes up in Interlaken, I'd be there behind her, holding her gunny sack!"

A crack of thunder supported Mark's anger, then the hissing sound of a heavy rain came through the screens. Ithaca is as steamy as the Carolinas from July through September. Cary looked in his lap at his hands, which he did when there was an upset. With the timing of a born leader, Edgar paused, and then, a fake sob in his throat, said, "I just don't want to see my big brother getting hurt."

It was the truth, but it also got a big, tension-breaking laugh.

Mark cleared; Cary prepped dessert; and Edgar reported that Gavin, who was rehabbing his shattered arm and shoulder in New York, had fired his "mother-in-law" from the Hangar board. (The adage about keeping your enemies closer to you than your friends explains why Leigh Bailey had served as a trustee on Dave's "despoiler's" arts organization.) Edgar was board Vice-President and served as the theater's liaison to Ithaca College.

"I'm sure that was devastating," said Cary from the kitchen, where he was tipping a shot of rum into the whipping cream.

"I don't know about that," said Edgar, "but the business manager has resigned in protest."

"You mean Leigh's dykey best friend, Nancy Norris, has resigned in protest," said Cary.

"We'll be losing both of their annual gifts. And Leigh's five spare bedrooms for visiting artists." The Hangar ran on a shoestring. Gavin Steeg was famous (and lovingly mocked by staff) for the hammy fundraising pitches he gave to the audience before every single performance.

The rain had picked up and was blowing sideways, wetting the sheers in the living room. It was dusk now. Mark shut the windows. Out of habit, he scanned the lawn for raccoons to emerge from under the porch the way they had when Judy lived there, but, concluding that woodland creatures probably enjoyed a surprise shower about as much as humans did, he walked over to Cary to take the beater he was holding out.

"Walnut cake?" he guessed. Cary nodded. "You're the best."

"He knew you were coming, so he baked a cake," sang Edgar. The song had been a childhood favorite. Before her marriage, their mother, Penny Purdum, had toured New England for two summers as a band singer. When they were little boys, she'd serenade them just before bedtime.

Edgar was licking the second beater. "So, the Hangar is going to need a new business manager. Very part-time, of course."

"Are you looking at me?" asked Mark.

"I am. The cake is a bribe."

"Only if I eat it."

Mark, something of a movie buff, preferred *film noir* and classic rock to live theater, but he knew that the Hangar added value to an Ithaca summer, and he could handle a spreadsheet. His co-workers at the hospital thought he needed to get out more, and volunteering was as essential to the sprouty culture of the town as the Farmer's Market. Mark agreed to pitch in as interim bookkeeper and financial advisor until they could replace Nancy Norris.

He scheduled two three-hour lunch shifts a week in the tiny Hangar office on the second floor of the Dewitt Mall. When the season started, operations would move to the actual theatre next to Cass Park; for now, weekday shifts were just Mark and Doris Littauer, a retired German teacher from Ithaca High famously deaf to select pitches. When Doris couldn't follow what you were saying—and this might happen with any sentence—she would tap an index finger against the temple piece of her eyeglasses until you adjusted your voice to a tone, higher or lower, that she could hear. Although curious to learn the etiology of her quirk, Mark never asked Doris for details, afraid she would tell him that it had happened in a camp. He wouldn't know how to have that conversation. A fair number of Jews had come to Ithaca after the liberation of the camps. The Jewish branch of the Shinner family had arrived through Locust Point, Maryland, long before the Third Reich.

Doris kept fruit waiting for Mark. She had a gift for selecting perfectly ripe pears and was an expert on apple varieties, a connoisseurship both German and Ithacan. She answered the phone and opened the mail, and Mark dealt with the payables still trickling in from the final show that season, *Crimes of the Heart,* an aggressively wacky Pulitzer Prize comedy about three Southern sisters that hadn't been anyone's favorite.

Until Gavin announced the five-play 1991 season at the beginning of October, there would be little to do. That's when Doris, who had been an apprentice stage designer for one of Max Reinhardt's Berlin theaters back in the day (Edgar cued Mark about what a huge deal this was.), would go into overdrive—reading the plays, devising their blurbs, creating a brochure, developing production budgets and casting breakdowns, crafting individual and corporate fundraising appeals, press releases, and re-lighting a fire under the board members, most of whom, she would sniff, would prefer to forget about their responsibilities and just hibernate until the kick-off cocktail party in March. Doris had zero tolerance for rich people and shirkers. When Mark asked Doris why she hadn't been made managing director, she'd said, oh no, she loved the theater too much to get paid for it.

One Tuesday, Mark came to the office with a thermos of soup and a wax paper bag of carrot sticks. He had been trying to lose thirty pounds for thirty years; this time was the cabbage soup diet. Under a handful of fresh figs and a bar coaster, Doris had placed an opened letter for him.

September 20, 1990

Dear Gavin Steeg:

Hello! My name is Hannah Habecker, and I'm a brand-new MFA director from the University of Minnesota. I'm writing you today because once upon a time, I worked for David Bailey at Ogilvy & Mather. I so wasn't right for the advertising world. Dave knew that and cut me slack on many occasions. He always encouraged me to pursue my dream, which was and is making theater. He even went so far as to write a positive letter of recommendation for graduate school.

Dave often spoke about your life together and the summer theater you ran upstate. I attended a couple of your productions in New York, but I was too shy to approach you, despite Dave's encouragement to do so. Your incisive Men in White at the WPA impressed me particularly.

Cut to the chase: post-graduation, I'm looking for work. As you can see from my resumé, I've directed a wide range of plays, from Shakespeare to Christopher Durang. My thesis show was my original adaptation of Virginia Woolf's experimental novel, The Waves (1931). Heady stuff, I know, right? We killed ourselves getting it on, but it was a success, and I'm very proud of it.

From my research, I see that the Hangar continues to thrive under your stewardship. Your commitment to including new work in every season is laudatory.

Cut again to the chase: I am moving back to New York next month, and I would love to meet with you at your earliest convenience to discuss next steps for my career. I would love to be considered for an assistant director position at the Hangar next summer. Barring that, I am certain you will have ideas for other pavements I should pound when I hit the streets (overworked metaphor).

I won't have an address for a while, so please feel free to leave a message with my parents in California. Their number is (408) 662-6572. I'll be checking in regularly.

I hope I have not been overly importunate with my request. Dave always said you were a most approachable man. Please give him my regards and tell him I can't wait to catch up with him soon. Tell him he was my favorite "real" boss ever.

I look forward to hearing from you at your earliest convenience.

Respectfully yours,

Hannah Habecker

For a moment, Dave Bailey was alive again. Dave spitballing with his creatives about how to get a heated shaving cream dispenser onto every upstairs bathroom counter in America, Dave getting arrested in Washington for helping close down the FDA, Dave making them howl with laughter at five-hour dinners with Cary, Edgar, Gavin, and Mark on hand as the token breeder, Dave walking through a shower of confetti wherever he went. Then Mark saw the pallbearers wheeling his casket on the sidewalk, their black wool suits sticking to their frames in the September heat, Cary, stoic, hair wild, mute with grief, and later, Leigh Bailey keening like a banshee over the hole in the earth.

Mark folded Ms. Habecker's materials back into their envelope and regrouped.

"Very professional," he said to Doris, who was spritzing the receiver with distilled water, unaware that no one else's germs got on the telephone in the off-season. "She gets points for 'laudatory' and 'importunate.' And 'stewardship.'"

"She gets points for *chutzpah*," replied Doris.

"Does Gavin get many letters like this?"

"All the time. Playwrights, designers, actors, actresses' bosoms falling out of their undershirts in their pictures, but not," she said, making a face, "from women directors. Women can design, act, write, but they cannot direct."

Mark thought about bringing up the Kitchen, a feminist theater collective in town known for its edgy political work but decided not to rebut the opinion of someone who had once taken notes from Max Reinhardt. He also believed in respecting one's elders. "What should we do?"

"You should call Gavin."

Doris, a terror to many, was terrified of Gavin. From his years of team management at the hospital, Mark noticed that a certain type of person will choose to fear the boss as a way to generate their best work.

"This letter will make him cry, Doris."

"There are worse things," Doris replied. "Do you want to call the parents in California and tell them to tell her that David is dead?"

Either way, Mark was making the call.

When they were dating, Judy Gabelson used to say to Mark that Gavin drove her nuts on a daily basis—she had been his musical director for several seasons—but then in the next breath insist she'd walk through fire for him. Even in mourning, the man was charismatic. When Mark told him about Hannah Habecker's letter, Gavin insisted he drive to the city to discuss it. As that seemed unnecessary, and time-consuming, Mark read the letter over the phone. Gavin then commanded he come down...since *he couldn't yet get behind the wheel.*

The car reference guilted Mark out. He left at six a.m. that Saturday. Doris had given him a bag of fruit, a folder of correspondence, and told him not to bother coming back to Ithaca without Gavin's list of plays for the next season. Mark swung by Titus Street. Cary kept baker's hours and had left in the front hall a bag of Gavin's favorites from Clever Hans. There was also a condolence letter from Judy Gabelson postmarked Mbarara Uganda. Its envelope was greasy to the touch, and it smelled like insect repellent. As Mark was leaving the house, Edgar called down to Mark from their bedroom window, "Remember, no glove, no love!" a safe sex mantra the IC kids were saying that semester.

Mark stowed the Clever Hans in the trunk, so he wouldn't be tempted to raid it. He couldn't recall the last time he'd seen his box of condoms. He visualized where they might be. Had they migrated from the nightstand drawer to a position next to a dried-out Airwick Solid under the bathroom sink? If so, then he was in even worse shape than he'd been supposing. That grim thought, plus the crisp, sunny day, made him smile. Nowhere to go but up, he thought.

After six weeks, the tire marks from the crash still hadn't faded on 79. The skid felt the length of a football field. He wondered whether Gavin had done anything yet with Dave's personal effects. All that would be left of Mark when his number was up was a contact lens boiler and four of the five projected chapters of his dissertation, "Land Use in Old Massachusetts Bay: Hingham and Weymouth 1650-1700," cause for another grim smile.

Mark's father believed Mark wouldn't get married until he finished his dissertation, unaware that the expiration date had passed. Ever since *Ordinary People,* his mother's theory was that he would remain single until he sought treatment for his survivor syndrome. To this, Mark would reply, with as much calm as he could muster, that he hadn't been in the same zip code, much less the same sailboat when Edgar had fallen into the empty swimming pool. Mark had been two towns over, taking tickets and sweeping popcorn at the Elwyn Cinema. Not to mention, unlike the brother in *Ordinary People,* Edgar was still alive.

The Shinners tended to forget that Mark had lived conjugally with Valerie Miner through four years of graduate school. They didn't know he would have proposed marriage, except Val had finished her PhD and already landed a big job at Vanderbilt. At the time, Mark thought he hadn't wanted to clip her wings or cloud her decision-making. Now, he knew, deep down, that she would have rejected his suit. Val was still in Tennessee, a full professor and a mother of three.

Ithaca to Manhattan was a pretty drive; certain bends in the pristine hills around the Delaware Water Gap made him feel like he'd been thrown back to the days of Johnny Appleseed. He sped past the exit for the Roscoe Diner and its legendary pastrami and made it to the George Washington Bridge in record time. He'd given himself plenty of leeway to find parking in the Village and to pick up the most somber bouquet he could find at the Gristede's grocery store around the corner from Morton Street.

A bigger apartment had been a running argument between Dave and Gavin. Older New Yorkers, especially those who had migrated in from the boroughs as Gavin had from Queens in the early fifties, hung onto their original claims like Fred Dobbs in *The Treasure of the Sierra Madre.* A second bathroom and a guest room had become non-negotiables for Dave, who'd been earning, as he put it, stupid money at the agency. Winded doing the three flights of stairs, Mark would have started with an elevator building.

Gavin opened the door. Mark spotted another guest sobbing on the corduroy foldout. A framed photograph of Dave chanting at the first ACT-UP action on Wall Street in 1984 stood on the cushion beside her.

"This is Hannah Habecker," said Gavin, limping into the cul-de-sac kitchen with Mark's flowers teetering on the arm of his shoulder cast.

Hannah, whose hair was the nearly white blonde of several Ukrainian mail-order brides, was a wreck. Her hand shook on his introduction, and her words of apology were indistinct. Accustomed at work to people in extremis, Mark reached over and pulled some Kleenex for her from an end table. Gavin returned with a tray of iced teas and shot him a "Thank God you're here" look.

Hannah Habecker wasn't a Beach Boys kind of California girl. Gavin would eventually dub her the Little Match Girl for the multiple, drifty layers of skirts she wore, and for her distracted self-presentation. What Hannah was, though, was adamantly *alive*. Once she began talking about Dave, her recollections of the office culture he'd created were laser-like. She described his ties and cufflinks, his gestures, his catchphrases (a couple of which Gavin chimed in with), his brand of gin, his dismissive side-eying when irked, his triumphs, peeves, and disappointments. There was a pulse to her storytelling that put Mark in mind of Roman orators and the Puritan pulpit. During pauses, Hannah would rapidly tap four fingers against her upper lip. When the next thought arrived, she would open the hand like a flower as if to speed it to them. Mark checked Gavin to gauge whether they needed to get off this sad subject, but he was beaming like a king receiving glad tidings from afar.

They turned to Hannah's ambitions on the second glass of iced tea; Mark was safe to zone out while they threw around play titles and traded violent opinions about the current New York scene. Part of Gavin's success was the ability to take good ideas from anybody, so he was interested in Hannah's opinions of his season choices. (These were the kind of shop conversations that used to drive Dave to the bedroom television. Though supportive of his career and resigned to Gavin's four-month commitment to Ithaca, Dave had never loved the theater the way Gavin had wanted him to.)

Mark re-focused when the pulse in Hannah's voice returned to describe the richness and profundity of *The Waves*. She made him feel he'd missed out on the greatest novel of the 20th century. She pulled a paperback copy from her bag to Gavin and apologized to Mark for not having an extra.

Mark smiled. "You weren't expecting to meet me, I know. I read the ledgers and count the beans."

"Nonsense, Mark," said Gavin. "You've been a member of the Hangar family for years now."

"Only by marriage," he said to Hannah. He was the older brother of the late David Bailey's foster brother's lover. Would that make him a brother-in-law once removed?

Hannah smiled and turned to Gavin. "I hope I've made it clear that I'd like to become a part of the Hangar family."

"Abundantly so," said Gavin. "You're hired."

"No! Now?"

"Absolutely."

"As your assistant?"

"For the whole summer. 'My first impressions of people are never wrong,'" he said with a British accent.

"Oh God! I'm dying to direct *Earnest* one day."

"Mark will send you a contract."

Their hug was genuine, if cumbersome, because of Gavin's cast, the kind of spontaneous "show people" gesture that made Mark uncomfortable. Judy Gabelson had said one eventually grew accustomed to them.

To put the final icing on the cake, Gavin asked her to send him her adaptation of *The Waves*. There had to be a new work in every Hangar season, and he loved the gestalt of her vision. Hannah, looking like she would pass out, babbled that she had considered bringing a copy of it with her, but she didn't want to presume, or come off as too pushy, or jinx the interview.

After she left, the men ate Cary's goodies and went through Doris' pile of papers. Gavin set Judy's note of condolence aside for later. As his painkillers wore off, he seemed to age three decades, but strove to stay chipper. But, like Cary, he wasn't giving sorrow an in, and Mark felt it wasn't his place to open the door to it.

Before Mark left, a scribbled list of four plays and a TBA in his wallet for Doris, he felt bound, in his capacity as interim bookkeeper, to tell Gavin that there was no salary line in the Hangar budget for an assistant director.

Gavin pierced Mark with a leader's gaze, and said, "Then you're going to have to create one." Mark had cleared a first landing in the stairs when Gavin called him back to give him the copy of *The Waves*. "Here. You read this."

"But—."

"I don't have time."

"It's none of my business, Gavin, but the project sounds a little experimental for the Hangar."

"Only a *little?*" He winked. "I think Ithaca is safe from Woolf's high modernism for the time being. She's a smart girl, but she'll never get the rights." He meant Hannah Habecker.

———————————

"Her Most Experimental Novel!" read the jacket line on the back cover, and even Mark Shinner knew that was saying a lot. His most vivid memory of Virginia Woolf was the sad spectacle of his housemate, red-headed Liz Rosdeitcher, sitting at the kitchen table their senior year, head in her hands, a bottle of bourbon to the left, a box of Cap'n Crunch to the right, an IBM Selectric in front of her, moaning over and over, "I can't write my paper."

If Liz had been writing about *The Waves,* and not *To the Lighthouse,* then she had Mark's retrospective sympathy. It's not that he couldn't make heads or tails of *The Waves*; it was more like, after forty-some pages, he didn't *care* to. In alternating soliloquies of purple, unpunctuated prose, six different narrators grow from childhood to middle age, interspersed with scenes that describe a beach from sunrise to sunset. All six refer to a friend named Percival. *The Waves* made Mark feel stupid, and stupidly male. Halfway through the book, he went to the town library for facts. As he'd begun to expect, Percival, like the Messiah, is a no-show. An article he skimmed revealed plot points that showed he wasn't missing out on *everything,* so he felt capable enough to finish the book. Still, if he were ushering at *The Waves,* he'd be tempted to offer ticket holders a choice of caffeine pills or earplugs.

But producing *The Waves* wasn't his bailiwick, and the Hangar was facing more pressing issues. By October, the newspapers had announced that the longest peacetime economic expansion in U.S. history had ended that July. Moreover, the economy had been weakening for more than a year, because of what pundits believed was an overly restrictive monetary policy. On top of that, the price of gas had doubled after Iraq invaded Kuwait in August, a systemic shock which had led to a swift, significant drop in consumer and business confidence and the loss of tens of thousands of jobs.

That was the macro. At the microeconomic level, it meant that the Hangar's high-rolling donors were late with their annual contributions, or they reduced them. Some, like rich gay undertaker J.M. Dondher, took a pass altogether. "'Tapped out'," Doris would sneer into the receiver after hanging up with another piker, "'Tapped out' *ist Scheiße.* In bad times, you must make theater. That is what art is for."

On the expenses side, the printing company was demanding larger deposits for the brochures; ad buys, and rental reserves were pricier; worst of all, the Early Bird Campaign was tanking. "Early Birds" were subscribers who paid upfront for their season tickets at the first opportunity, and at a decent savings. Fewer Early Birds meant less money in the bank, slower cash flow, and additional pressure in an ever-tightening lending climate.

During lunch on one of Mark's Hangar days, Edgar outlined for his brother Gavin's biggest worry—a deficit. Starting the season in a deficit position would leave the Hangar open to unwanted influence from Cornell and Ithaca College, who would be happy to close financial gaps in exchange for more student and faculty participation on stage. It had happened in the past, and Gavin loathed being beholden to the university theatre programs, whose leading citizens he found snooty and unjustifiably impressed with themselves.

"Why are you telling me all this?" Mark asked.

"I thought you should keep this in mind when you ask Kristy Schroyer for an emergency contribution to the operating budget."

Mark's gorge rose instantly. He pushed away his bowl of soup. Just hearing Kristy's name roiled his stomach. In the summer and fall of 1982, she had been a big romantic mistake, his biggest in this town, his biggest ever.

"I can't go to Kristy. You call and ask her for money."

"I don't know her the way you do."

"*Did* know her. I am a *volunteer,* Edgar."

"We're all volunteers."

"I have a real job."

"As do we all."

"Send Cary. He was her best friend."

"He's not invested in the Hangar the way we are."

"The way you are."

"The past is past."

"If you're trying to send me on some Joseph Campbell quest, I'd rather poke my eye out with this spoon."

Edgar maintained his composure. They had had massive blinking contests as kids.

"I haven't spoken to Kristy in eight years."

"She came to you for help once."

"You just had to bring that up, didn't you?"

Cripples—Edgar's term—didn't fight fair, or the one Mark had grown up with didn't and never had.

On the way to Kristy's house, Cary, who was plenty pissed at her for not showing up to Dave's funeral, provided Mark with the latest intelligence. She lived in a modern house designed by a famous architecture professor just north of Esty Point on the lake. Her youngest, Penny, was a rising sophomore at Vassar. Darcie lived in Los Angeles. Only Jan, now twenty-four, had had trouble adjusting to the windfall of Darcie's TV money. Their family therapist had said that Janice, the eldest, was the most strongly identified of the three girls with her complicated father. ("You mean 'dirtbag dad,'" interjected Mark.) Wayne Schroyer had left town for good in 1986. The last time Cary and Kristy had spoken, Kristy was worried that Wayne was bleeding Darcie for living expenses but *wasn't allowed to* ask about it—therapist's orders.

Cary had Mark park fifty yards south of her driveway on Blackchin Boulevard, then, as they were creeping along a stand of sumacs, confessed that she didn't know they were coming. Before Mark could object to the ambush, Cary whisked the car keys out of his hand.

They buzzed three times before they heard footsteps. Mark held to the side of the front door to let Cary step through first. At the sight of him, Kristy scrunched up her face, and, throwing her arms about him, began to cry. "I'm just sick about Dave. I really am."

When she saw Mark, it was like Julia Adams seeing the Gill-Man in *Creature from the Black Lagoon*. She dropped her arms and started backing up. "Mark Shinner?" Her elbow knocked something over on a little shelf under the front hall mirror.

"Hello, Kristy," said Mark. "It's nice to see you again."

"Am I in some kind of trouble?" she asked, looking wildly from Cary to Mark. Her face clouded up. "Wait a minute. Did Penny send you up here?"

Strung out on something, she began sliding along the wall towards an arched doorway. Beyond it, Mark could see Lake Cayuga sparkling through a floor-to-ceiling expanse of windows smeary with handprints.

"No, no," Cary said gently. "We were just in the neighborhood—"

"Bullshit," she said, cutting off the cliché. "Penny sent you."

Cary was inching closer. "I swear to you she didn't, Kristy. Is Penny down at school?"

"Damn straight," she said proudly. "Thirty grand a year it cost me."

"That's an awful lot of money."

Suddenly sweetness itself, Kristy raised her palms up and out in a prayerful position. "I know. Can you believe it? I mean, can you believe it?"

Mark counted four colors to her hair, which she'd hacked to her ears every which way. "I think it's great, Kristy," he said. The sound of his voice sent her racing through the doorway. They followed her in.

Her living room looked one corpse short of a crime scene. After a slow pan through the mess of papers, rags, dirty dishes, pillows, pizza boxes, loose VHS tapes, wine and soda and tanning lotion and sunscreen bottles, beer cans, overstuffed ashtrays, flip-flops, cosmetics, hair implements, sandals, long-soured beach towels, two overturned chairs, and improbably, a giant blue exercise ball, Mark turned to Cary and mouthed the word "Wayne." He had to be around somewhere. There was no other explanation for the squalor. Cary shook his head no.

The sprint from the hall knocked the wind out of Kristy, who sat, glassy-eyed, sprawled on a costly suede couch. She kept rubbing her dirty heels against one of the arms. It was October, but she was dressed for the beach in short shorts and a spaghetti strap T-shirt. Despite the crazy hair, Kristy was still beautiful, and still too skinny. She made Mark think of Edie Sedgwick, the Boston Brahmin destroyed by the Andy Warhol and his Superstars.

"I think I'll make some coffee," said Cary. "Would you like a cup of coffee, Kristy?" Ignoring Mark's signals of discomfort, Cary disappeared to process his own reaction to her transformation.

The thought of asking Kristy for money for the Hangar struck Mark as so absurd, he wanted to laugh. It would be more productive for them to call county services and Merry Maids.

It was time to say something. On a far wall hung a giant canvas of two racehorses by a painter whose work Mark recognized from barbershop magazines. "Is that a LeRoy Neiman?"

This time, his voice started Kristy on a talking jag.

"Absofuckinglutely. I have a painting of an Olympic high jumper that's worth even more. Are you still single? I'll bet you are; my sister Sheila has been divorced now for three years she's always looking for a man, but she's a total bitch, I almost said 'cunt,' Penny and Darcie hate it when I use that word, but that's what Sheila is, get over it, Jan's okay with the 'c' word, uses it all the time, wherever she is, guess she takes after me after all, ha!"

Speed? Freebasing? Mark was bad at sussing out drug reactions.

She took a breath. "Well?"

"Well, what?"

"Do you want me to fix you up with my sister Sheila?"

"That's kind of you, Kristy, but no."

Her eyes turned to slits, and she made a face like he'd farted.

"You're doing it again, Mark."

"Doing what, Kristy?" he said patiently.

"Patronizing me. 'That's kind of you, Kristy, but noo-oh.' You haven't changed a bit, not one little goddam bit."

The idea of his character stasis so amused her, she began to laugh, which led to symphonic coughing, which led to a frantic search for cigarettes. Mark, happy to help at anything, located a pack of Virginia Slims in a sticky, near-empty Purity ice cream container. It made him sad that after eight years, Kristy still confused politeness with patronization. He asked after the girls.

"Doing very well, thank you. Darcie, as you probably know, has won two Emmy Awards, one for daytime and one for nighttime, and Demme's people, *Jonathan* Demme's people have recently contacted her agent about a role in his next film, could you just die?" Now she sounded as if she were chatting up an old acquaintance at a salad bar. "I worry sometimes that Penny works too hard at school and doesn't do enough things that make her happy. You're only young once, I try and tell her. That's just what my mother always said to me. You remember my mother, Louise." Kristy took a very long drag and coughed. "I miss that woman every single day of my life."

"I'm sorry I never got to meet her."

"That's right—she died the summer I—."

"The summer you and I met."

They were veering into dangerous territory. Kristy's face began clouding up again. Unfit to play mad scenes, Mark was ready to run and grab Cary but was saved by her abrupt exit down a half-flight of stairs. Cary returned in her absence, bug-eyed, and slid some debris off the coffee table with his foot to make room for his tray.

Her entrance with combed hair, long pants, and a Vassar sweatshirt gave Cary the opening to reminisce about their years selling college memorabilia at the Army-Navy on the Commons. Cary had always been able to relax her.

Mark sipped his coffee and watched her the way he had back in the day. She was the prettiest jewel he had ever dated. Her second job then had been waitressing at Simeon's. He would overeat there over often, just for glimpses. Too bashful to bribe his way into her section, he was happy just to watch Kristy putter to other tables, hands flying, hips and heels rocking, and sail through the kitchen door, a heavy tray raised on her palm like Lady Liberty's torch. She never wasted a single motion. Leroy Neiman could have painted her.

When he got one of her tables, Mark would over-tip, but she had paid him no attention until Penny sustained an eye injury and Kristy had come to his office unable to pay the bill. In asking her straightaway for a date, he had seized his chance the way a leading man might. But then, like a pimply juvenile, he took three showers the day they went out to the Rongovian Embassy.

Following the tumble of her words with Cary on the couch, Mark remembered how jealous he used to be of their "straight girl + gay best friend" dynamic, but now, it was a forgiving balm that might, in a blue moon, wend its way to him. There had been one crazy summer day when Cary and Kristy took him to the Triphammer Mall to get a new pair of eyeglasses. He'd wound up buying contact lenses, two belts, three pairs of pants, two sport shirts, a bar cart, and a volleyball net. After the spree, they had laughed themselves sick at Friendly's Restaurant by repeating over and over, "I'd like a hot Fudgeana, please," until patrons finally sent the manager over. They had sex for the first time that night. Sex that felt, to Mark at least, important. "Hot Fudgeana" and endless silly variations remained a password for the seventeen weeks Kristy and Mark spent as a couple. If anyone ever cared enough to ask, he would tell them that that day at Triphammer Mall was the happiest of his life.

Kristy walked them back to Mark's car and made a plan to visit Dave's grave. She had not asked again why they had come, nor did she say that they, meaning both of them, couldn't come for another visit.

Mark put the car in gear.

"Jesus," said Cary. "Let's get a drink."

"Let's get five," said Mark. They were the strung out ones now.

Through Kristy, Mark had met Cary. Through Mark, Cary would meet Edgar, so something positive had emerged from their personal disaster. The experience of seeing her again hadn't made him feel miserable or nauseated as he'd been when Edgar brought up her name. At one point, he'd heard her say "I've missed you." She was talking to Cary, but he could pretend she'd meant him too all the way into town.

⊢————•————⊣

By the end of October, Gavin had finished with home PT and had cabin fever. Sick of relying on friends to get his groceries, he'd begun moving around the neighborhood. This proved to be too soon, and so, shopping for his favorite *babka* on Bleecker Street, had a mild heart attack. During this second recovery, he wouldn't be able to come up, fire his base, and shake the trees for money. Early Birds for the 1991 season, *The Little Foxes, Grease, Candida, Love Letters,* and *TBA* had trickled to nothing, a troubling long-term situation. Over eleven years, Gavin's super-charged enthusiasm had grown the Hangar from a money-losing fiefdom fought over by Cornell and Ithaca College into a vibrant summer destination for audiences and artists. In light of Dave's death and the cardiac scare, how long could he, and it, last?

Cary, in the meantime, had found out more of Kristy's story by calling Penny at Vassar. Eight years after Darcie hit the American jackpot, Ithaca's busiest woman hadn't figured out what to do with herself. She had chaperoned Darcie until she grew to hate show business and its practitioners and resent the money that had saved the family. Darcie moved to Los Angeles as soon as she could get herself killed off in her soap opera. Naming Wayne as her legal guardian was what, Penny was sure, sent Kristy off the rails. Any plans about going back to school to pursue a nursing degree stopped, and the partying began. She blew through money, took up with marginally improved versions of Wayne, snorted black beauties, and got hooked, on and off, on Dexedrine, speed, and Quaaludes. Only a fear of needles kept her from injectables, and the only *nouveau riche* vice she would not entertain was plastic surgery. The crazy hair was the work of her latest squeeze, "Shad," a

165

twentysomething stylist who sold weed and lived in his mother's basement in Watkins Glen. Penny could only devote so much time to worrying about Kristy. She was there for crisis management; Darcie sent money; Jan was following her bliss somewhere on Cape Ann. The sisters, never in the same physical or emotional place for a rational discussion, couldn't reach a consensus about what to do with her.

Famous alumna Darcie Schroyer—a production shot of her as Dinah Lord in *The Philadelphia Story* had been in every promotional piece since 1982—got the Hangar through the New Year. Penny tipped her off, and Darcie sent a no-strings check the next day for twenty thousand dollars. Moreover, she drafted a personal holiday appeal to mail to all subscribers, donors, and single-seat buyers. Its success set Gavin to fresh plotting. Finally, on January 10th, he was able to announce to the press that Emmy-winning television star Darcie Schroyer was going to return to the Hangar Theatre and open the 1991 season as Alexandra Giddens, the moral conscience of Lillian Hellman's *The Little Foxes,* in a production helmed by Gavin Steeg.

The newsflash kept Doris on the phone for the rest of the month, spiked subscription sales, and boosted morale. Things were looking so optimistic that Gavin announced *The Waves* as the August *TBA*. Hannah Habecker had miraculously secured the rights from the Woolf estate. This positive omen enabled Gavin to dictate copy to Doris that had initially included the redundant "global world premiere." By the time Gavin returned to rally the troops at the cocktail kick-off in early March, Mark Shinner had fully been sucked into the Hangar diaspora, spending longer lunch hours and weekend days in the office, and using "we" in discussions with Doris and his brother. No one mentioned finding a new business manager. Mark was the one who braved a call to Leigh Bailey to see whether she'd open her house to resident artists that summer. Her acid "no" didn't faze him; he just dialed the next number. With Gavin, he had slipped into Judy Gabelson's old role as advisor/helpmate—clearing paths, smoothing feathers, following through on his good ideas, and steering him away from unworkable brainstorms.

Doris continued to give the stinkeye to the concept of women directors, so Mark, whose frame house had three bedrooms, put Hannah up for the launch trip. Other than his sister Leslie and his nephews, no one had ever used his guestroom. He scrubbed out the tub/shower, vacuumed the dead flies out of all the windowsills, and overbought on cold cuts and granola. He obsessed about whether to place the matched set of lime green towels—the foot of the bed?—on the suitcase rack?—on the actual towel bars in the guest bath?—until he was able to pinpoint the source of his jitters: Hannah

Habecker's observational powers. Eventually, however, he reassured himself that he was too old and dull to be worth the scrutiny Hannah had once lavished on Dave Bailey.

The authentic Stickley furniture in J.M. Dondher's living room made the perfect environment with which to pitch *The Waves* to the Hangar crowd. Hannah began by expertly vaselining Edgar and the rest of the board with an outsider's perspective; the theatre had become an important place for emerging artists and recent graduates to test their training. Older actors could stretch their talents in roles they would never be offered in Manhattan. Ithaca College's BFA theater program had had a 40% rise in applications over the eleven years Gavin had been running the theater. The Chamber of Commerce had estimated that the Hangar and its activities added two million dollars of income to the city coffers every summer.

Done with the facts and figures, she moved on to the more personal matter of Dave Bailey. He had encouraged her, an artistically minded twenty-three-year-old, to pursue her dream. Every single one of the supporters in the room was duplicating Dave's encouragement with their dollars, bedrooms and spare vehicles; their volunteer hours, phone calls and in-kind services kept artistic dreams alive and allowed the public to bear witness to the timeless issues facing humanity on the living stage. In a nation tragically resistant to creative expression, their patronage was as essential as that of the Medici family to Renaissance Florence. Who knew whether the next Lorraine Hansberry or Tennessee Williams might one day incubate his or her talents at the Hangar?

Hannah was on fire. Cary Dunkler, tending bar in front of a poster of J.M. Dondher on the ice in the 1972 Winter Olympics, looked up from his hands and seemed to be listening for the first time in months. Then she dimmed the lights, told everyone to close their eyes, and recited the opening paragraph of *The Waves*:

The sun had not yet risen. The sea was indistinguishable from the sky, except that the sea was slightly creased as if a cloth had wrinkles in it. Gradually as the sky whitened a dark line lay on the horizon dividing the sea from the sky and the grey cloth became barred with thick strokes moving, one after another, beneath the surface, following each other, pursuing each other, perpetually.

She asked for six volunteers to raise their hands. Each would get a speech from her adaptation to read aloud, one for each character, and they must not think of rushing Woolf's prose. More than a few guests were trial lawyers or academics accustomed to public speaking, but it was a surprise nonetheless to hear, after a crackling silence, retired Cornell Provost Laverne Tompos read a passage about making her entrance at a dinner party and stilling the restaurant with her beauty. Just as surprising was the dry, Teutonic accent of Doris Littauer walking down Oxford Street, describing a world she had imagined destroyed by lightning. J.M. Dondher went last: while merely staring into the mirror during a morning shave, he understands that he has lost his youth. J.M. had given up his skating career to take over the family funeral home; his facial wasting meant he was living on borrowed time with the virus and compounded the poignancy of the speech.

Hannah took up the thread again. She read the final paragraph of the novel in which Bernard rides unvanquished toward the final enemy. Then she told everyone to open their eyes. Blinking at the light, their arms shivery with goose bumps, the gathering listened to Woolf's final line: "The waves broke on the shore."

Death was coming for them all.

It was theatre, but then the room snapped back to real life, and in a trice, Hannah Habecker went from master magician to a goofy, distracted young woman, unaware of the spell she'd just cast. Gavin jumped in with, "World premiere opening August 6th at the Hangar Theater, ladies and gentlemen."

Mark had hoped that he was beneath Hannah's notice, but the bowls they smoked of her hashish after the cocktail party would turn out to be the truth serum he needed for his first-ever therapy session.

They were already drunk, and stuffed, when they got back to Utica Street, but took bags of chips and a six-pack into the living room anyway. Hannah offered her smoke and, as they mellowed out on the sectionals, the excited thrum in her voice lowered to a conversational pitch as she explained some of the finer points of *The Waves*. She asked him which of the six characters felt closest to whom he thought he was. Mark said Louis, the businessman who doesn't go to university.

"Why Louis?" she asked.

"He strikes me as the outsider of the group."

Hannah nodded in agreement.

"And he tries so hard to be accepted." Mark chugged some beer to hide his face with the bottle. "I think Louis tries too hard."

His stomach had taken a dive for his feet. Mark woozily strode to the window, hoping that the predicted snow had started, so they could talk about the weather, but Hannah was merciful—or merciless.

"Do you try too hard, Mark?" she asked.

"All my life," he gasped. He had never said anything close to this before. Now he was fighting tears. The words "Tell me" hung in the pungent smoke, and even though Mark was usually the listener, he took Hannah's direction and revealed the scariest parts of himself. First, Edgar and his accident came up, then his unfinished dissertation, and then, once it was broached, the Kristy Schroyer debacle of 1982 had to be talked through to the end.

Mark and Kristy had been dating only a few weeks when she discovered that Wayne, who was living by himself that summer, was screwing the *au pair* she'd hired for the girls, an Ithaca College theater major named Isa Vass. After years of on-again/off-again madness, Kristy decided that this betrayal with someone only four years older than Jan was the final last straw. She served Wayne papers for divorce and full custody that September. Mark had stood by her, did the best he could, held her hand as the court date approached and she began to waffle.

Some men are a drug. Thanksgiving Week he hadn't heard from her, and she'd missed their standard Tuesday happy hour at the Chanticleer. She wouldn't answer his messages; the girls wouldn't, or didn't, pick up the phone; she'd called in sick at both jobs. Mark knew Wayne lived in a third-floor studio over the Danskin store on the Commons.

It was a short wait. On the morning of day eight, Kristy came out of Wayne's building, as bouncy as a Disney sprite, carrying two full pillowcases. Mark discreetly followed, too humiliated to confront her, his mind ablaze with the thought that she was going home to do his laundry.

It took him no time to find out where Wayne grew his pot, but it was a gross miscalculation to notify not the Tompkins County police, but the State Bureau of Narcotic Enforcement. They threw the book at Wayne, but the team of men and dogs also arrested Kristy with a hoe in her hand. It hadn't entered Mark's mind that she could be up there with him on their sting. As it was a state, and not a county, case, all the testimonials in the world for Kristy's character couldn't prevent her from getting six months at the Elmira Correctional Facility. She was out in three, but the damage was done. Mark never denied his involvement. As for the town, the Carrie Nations and Nancy Reagans of the era found him heroic, but now, the hippies and the libertarians, if they remembered the case, would still feel he had been as ludicrous as the high school principal in *Reefer Madness*.

As they say in the hospital biz, these were unexpected outcomes.

When Mark finished his story, Hannah came over to the sectional and put her arm around him. They smoked a little more and sat and waited for the snow to fall. Mark ached to tell her that he felt as if the wave of Kristy had broken on the shore, but assumed she'd laugh at his Woolfian overreach.

In the morning, Hannah came into the kitchen and asked whether she should have made the bed or not. With her youth, her wet hair, and a tangle of army knapsack straps slipping down her arm, she looked so vulnerable that Mark noticed, for the first time, that the nails on those fingers Hannah tapped against her upper lip were chewed to the quick.

For once, Mark had a ready answer for a pesky hospitality question.

"In the great pattern of life we weave, Hannah, how can that possibly matter?"

Hearing her giggle made him very happy.

———•———

The April crisis: Darcie booked a beach comedy set to start shooting in Barbados during the second week of *Little Foxes* rehearsals. Having not signed her Hangar contract, she could have walked, but that wasn't Darcie. She agonized over the offer, offered to join the *Grease* company, even though she didn't sing, or the Shaw play. But neither role in *Candida* was right for a literal ingénue of twenty. Other Shaw comedies with suitable roles for her required additional actors, which would blow the budget. The week of back-and-forth to the West Coast was intense. The time difference, combined with Darcie's schedule, meant missed calls until Gavin, Doris, and Mark took shifts, staring at the desk telephone and willing it to ring with the concentration of a Preston Sturges stooge.

Mark had relayed several messages through Darcie's assistant without giving his name, but one night on the graveyard shift Darcie herself asked to whom she was speaking.

"This is Mark Shinner."

Her pause was definite.

"Didn't you used to date my mother?"

"I did. We did."

A longer pause.

"What are you doing at the Hangar, Mark?"

"I'm a volunteer helping out with situations."

This, he knew, was a ghastly reply, since the last time he'd helped out a situation, he'd sent both of her parents to jail.

"You are so great on your show, Darcie," he lied. He hadn't seen it.

"Thank you, Mark."

"What did you want me to tell Gavin?"

She sighed.

"My new set of film agents will drop me if I do *The Little Foxes*. It's my best shot so far to get out of television, and Alexandra is a thankless role."

"I've read the play," he said.

"So, you know what I'm talking about."

"Alexandra gets the final curtain line."

That made her laugh. "Tell Gavin that what I can do for the Hangar is make a special appearance just before I fly to Barbados. I'll read Shakespeare, I'll talk about my wildly fascinating Ithaca childhood, bring shame on all the teachers who thought I was retarded, do a Q & A about the business, sign autographs."

"'A Night with Darcie Schroyer.'"

That brought her up short. "Scratch that, Mark. I never said it."

"I think it's a good idea."

"No. You can't sell tickets to me shooting the shit, not when I don't have an hour of material, don't sing, and dance like a spaz. Plus, I've blown every joke I've ever tried to tell. Even by Hollywood standards, I am one fucking lucky Junior Miss. The thing is, I really should get back onstage. I miss it."

In the silence, listening to the lonesome, late-night flush of a toilet down the hall—the Dewitt Mall had begun life as a boy's school—Mark got another idea.

"Don't do it alone then. You could emcee an evening with other Hangar people up there with you. It could be a variety show…."

"Now that I can get behind," she said.

By the time they hung up, they'd drawn up a list of alums to contact for "Darcie and Company." Given Gavin's response to the brainstorm, which he renamed the next morning into "The Hangar's Dozen Gala, featuring Ithaca's Star Sweetheart, Darcie Schroyer!" one would have thought Mark had found the cure for malaria. (The "dozen" referred to Gavin's twelfth season.) It certainly made him King for a Day. Then, with little thought, Mark solved the *Little Foxes* crux; the answer was in plain view on the master calendar taped up next to a poster of Raul Julia in *The Threepenny Opera*. Open the season with *The Waves* and close it with Darcie in *The Little Foxes*. Switch shows. It took Gavin all of three seconds to shout, "We'll do it!" and whisk Mark off for a free lunch.

The swap freaked Hannah Habecker out; now she had less than a month's scramble to put together a cast and get her designs in, but she couldn't refuse such a huge break. Mark contacted alums about their availability, drafted a press release explaining the exciting change of plans—"Make Everything a Positive" was a Gavin Steeg watch cry—and began pressing vendors for freebies for the Hangar's first-ever fundraising gala.

"Don't you want to get in on the ground floor?" he'd say. "This party will get bigger and better every season." This was conjecture. "You'll get a free page in the Gala program, a title card in the lobby, and a special mention in a curtain speech." This was vaseline. "Clever Hans Bakery is whipping up a dozen special desserts." This was true.

Cary Dunkler then applied leverage to a new caterer in town trying to get traction in the down economy, and there suddenly was a menu. Mark played the local vineyards off one another and got cases of wine from all of them. Ditto the cheesemakers. Ditto the florists. Ditto Cornell and Ithaca College for chairs, tables, linens, plates, glasses, and silver. Dinner for four on Utica Street exceeded his hosting capabilities, but an offsite party for two hundred was a mountain worth scaling. Who knew there was such a salesman inside him?

Any less than paternal feelings Mark might have had toward Hannah were dispelled when she arrived in Ithaca to bunk in his guestroom with Rachelle, the stage manager for *The Waves*. Rachelle had grown up in a diplomatic family in Bucharest. She had an oval face with the color and the finish of a new magnolia; intense, rectangular eyebrows like black piano keys; cobalt eyes; and jet hair that fell straight as a waterfall to her shoulders. From experience, Mark knew that lesbians didn't jolly men along with facial and vocal affirmations. What he didn't know was that a good stage manager wouldn't show emotion in a five-alarm fire. Add clipped, even speech, an

Iron Curtain lack of affect, and—that was Rachelle Ciobanu. She spooked Mark. He couldn't follow her sense of humor, but he appreciated her knack at making Hannah giggle. Hannah had a quiet, high-pitched "hee hee hee" at odds with her aura of gravitas.

The three shared a special night in the first week of *Waves* rehearsals. Mark had come home from a long day of pre-audit craziness at the hospital, and an hour of gala-wrangling on the phone. He paused at the top of the porch steps and swiveled towards his side yard to take some calming breaths. Rochester has an official Lilac Festival, but Ithaca in May is just as steeped in their perfume, so rich and heavy that, bottled, he would pour it over ice cream.

He turned to go inside, and there was Rachelle, motionless in the glider at the far end of the porch. She put a finger to her lips. Mark pointed to the front door. She shook her head and motioned for him to sit. Scared to sit alone with her in a contraption designed for romance, Mark set his briefcase against the railing and sat on the porch with his feet on the second stair step. Rachelle nodded, then cupped her ear, instructing him to listen.

Through the parlor window screen, he heard Hannah working with Jim Tate, the actor playing Neville in *The Waves*. Jim was local, and from what Mark had picked up at breakfast, he was the weak link in the cast. In the novel, Neville, who is presumably based on aesthete Lytton Strachey, is in love with no-show Percival.

Hannah was listening to Jim/Neville soliloquize about waiting for his friends to come to a dinner at a fancy London restaurant. "It is now five minutes to eight. I have come early. I have taken my place at the table ten minutes before the time in order to taste every moment of anticipation. I have seen the door open and shut twenty times already; each time the suspense sharpens."

Even to Mark's ears, Jim sounded stiff. Hannah kept stopping Jim at the end of that fourth sentence and made him begin again, coaxing him to be natural, to be himself, to just talk to her, to just look at her and talk, Jim to Hannah, to say it in his own words, to tell it like a story to his best friend, to share it like a secret, to tell it like a prayer, to tell it like a joke, to tell it on a deathbed, to preach it like a sermon, to throw everything away and just say it; to not even think about it and say it, to change the order of the sentences and say it.

She might as well have been coaxing a squirrel to eat from her hand, there was so little variety to Jim's delivery, but from Hannah's side, no sign of losing patience, or giving up, or taking a break. Mark thought if this is what directing plays was like, leave them to it.

But then, on the umpteenth take, like Eliza Doolittle and the rainy Spanish plain, something clicked. Woolf's formal language suddenly belonged in Jim's mouth, and Neville was talking to her, to Mark and to Rachelle. Jim paused after, "and the suspense sharpens," but Hannah murmured, "Keep going." There was a silence in the parlor and goose bumps on the porch when he'd finished.

"Did you hear that, Jim?" Hannah's voice was quiet.

"I did."

"Did you feel it?"

"I did. I totally did."

"Can you try it again?"

"I was afraid you'd say that."

Jim's next attempt zigzagged from stilted to natural, but his third time around was even better than his first success. As was the fourth.

Jim thanked her, awe in his voice, saying, "I hope I can repeat this."

"You will, Jim. I know you will. Now get some sleep."

Her charge practically skipped down the sidewalk. A spent Hannah Henry Higgins fell into Rachelle's embrace. Mark, who couldn't wait to tell Doris that women most definitely could direct, went inside to empty his aching bladder and to give them privacy.

To celebrate Neville's breakthrough, they pulled out the bourbon, the beer, the hash, and the Clever Hans, the three of them getting so fucked up that, on Hannah and Rachelle's dare, they went into the back yard where Mark set four yellowing chapters of "Land Use in Old Massachusetts Bay: Hingham and Weymouth 1650-1700" on fire in an old tin tub. They danced around it like baby satyrs. The pages didn't burn completely, and there was an undisclosed second copy in his freezer, but, as Rachelle put it, with the tiniest hint of humor in her voice, their spur-of-the-moment ritual was "the theatre of his life."

—————————

Jim Tate did repeat; he and the rest of the cast killed it in the final dress of *The Waves*. The stage floor was white; the set, a simple blue cyclorama hung at the back and six antique chairs. The soundscape was birdcalls and breaking waves, simple effects that permitted Woolf's language to be the spectacle. The actors wore period costumes culled from Ithaca College stock and embroidered carpet slippers so they could glide noiselessly about.

It was a dance and a poem. It didn't push or shout. It was tiny and vast. It walked a tightrope of the poetic and the prosaic. Mark, who had never seen anything like it on any stage, likened it to a spider web made out of titanium. It wouldn't set the box office on fire, but it was the right thing for the Hangar to do. "I thought I didn't really like theatre," he said to Hannah when the stage had emptied and she was moving up the aisle to Gavin, and then he repeated it to anyone who would listen.

Because of Darcie Schroyer's shooting schedule, the final dress of *The Waves* finished three hours before the start of *The Hangar's Dozen Gala*. Wiped out, Hannah and Rachelle went back to Mark's house, saying they'd shower and return for the party, but he could tell that was a ruse. He went to the parking lot and started unfolding chairs and tables under the tent that had been delivered while they were watching the run-through. He had overheard Hannah say to Gavin that she had taken one hundred and seventeen notes. Mark couldn't conceive of one single thing to improve in the magic he had just experienced. Cary and the caterers were set up around the corner in a smaller tent. The scene was as focused as an emergency room, but Doris and Mark had planned the event like master "*Feldmarshälle*." The changeover crew managed to beat the clock by fourteen minutes.

The dress was Ithaca summer casual, which meant anything from black tie to tie-dyed with acorns in the hair. After cocktails and *hors d'oeuvres* in a lobby plastered with "Donated by..." placards that Doris had hand-calligraphed, the theme song from Darcie's sitcom came over the sound system, and the crowd buzzed into the theater.

Larry Brownstein, whose adaptation of Twain's *Pudd'nhead Wilson* had been the first new work produced by the Hangar a full decade ago, performed a hilarious send-up of a Gavin Steeg curtain speech. Then Isa Vass, the IC theater major (and inappropriate *au pair*) who had suggested Darcie as an emergency replacement in *The Philadelphia Story* in 1982, introduced their star by singing, "If I Knew You Were Coming, I'd Have Baked a Cake." Over the applause, Darcie walked in from one of the voms dressed as Cher, in a creation made from four rolls of tinfoil and a black wig down to her butt. The audience went wild. Isa threw on a Sonny Bono wig, and the two sang "I Got You, Babe." Isa then spun Darcie out of her tinfoil. Dressed now as a pre-teen in a pinafore, they acted out a parent-teacher conference sketch with

Doris Littauer. Isa played Kristy, Doris, the teacher bewildered by her student's nutty behavior, and Darcie, as a space cadet version of her earlier self. It was funny. There was a spoofy mix-up of *Jesus Christ Superstar* and *Cabaret*. Gavin got out of his seat for his legendary rendition of Noël Coward's "Don't Put Your Daughter on the Stage, Mrs. Worthington," which he sang directly to Darcie. The movement and mime professor from Ithaca College bombed, but what can one hope from a mime?

Late in the show, Darcie got serious and talked about how being in those four performances of *The Philadelphia Story* when she was twelve years old not only saved her life, it also saved the lives of her mother and sisters. She talked about the existential tension it required to remain focused and disciplined on stage while at the same time staying in the present moment and ready to play with the other actors. Committing to just that—disciplined play—took a lifetime for the stage actor to achieve. She had only just begun her path and looked forward to coming back in *The Little Foxes*.

Then, in an unscripted surprise, Darcie announced that she was founding the Gavin Steeg Fellowship for two young Ithacans to work at the Hangar every summer in the theatrical discipline of their choice. The cheers were loud and long; from where Mark sat, he saw Kristy and Penny sobbing in each other's arms.

Then, a piano began to play "Whatever Lola Wants." One by one, the six chorus boys they'd been able to locate from the Hangar *Damn Yankees*, Gavin's first smash hit in 1980, came out wearing Washington Senators caps and carrying baseball bats. Of the missing three, two were lovers who had died of AIDS ten months apart.

"Oh no!" Gavin shouted from the center section.

"Oh yes!" cried Darcie, crossing left to give the boys room.

When they had found their marks, the pianist segued to "Heart," Gavin's favorite song from his favorite Broadway musical. It had been ten years, but the boys—men now, indisputably men, some balding, two with bellies—remembered the lyrics, if not all the steps to their old soft shoe. Mark hadn't seen *Damn Yankees*, as he had yet to move to Ithaca, but Cary often mentioned how proud he was to have been in it, and how he never once during the run dropped his bat in the "Heart" reprise. Because time doesn't stand still, not really and truly, Cary dropped his bat. So did the rest, and as they danced on, the crowd loved them all the more for the flubs.

Gavin came down from the audience to a standing ovation. The Senators mobbed him like they'd won the actual World Series. Wiping his eyes, he took Darcie's microphone and made an (atypically) brief, three-pointed speech. One: *The Hangar's Dozen* had grossed, and he milked the moment by reminding them of the difference between gross versus net, *The Hangar's Dozen* had grossed, in this terrible down economy, yet why does art exist except to see man through terrible times, he said, milking, milking, milking, *The Hangar's Dozen* had grossed...one hundred and seventeen thousand dollars. In the gasp and applause, he announced that Two: he would be stepping down as Artistic Director after the 1991 season. Always leave 'em wanting more. Then, in the stunned silence, he announced Three: the theater, and the board of trustees, and the search committee to be formed for his successor, would be in the capable and dedicated hands of the first-ever, paid Managing Director of the Hangar Theater. He milked this announcement with a final pause, and then he said Mark Shinner.

Mark waved from his seat, but that wasn't dramatic enough for Gavin. He made him stand up and asked him if he had anything to say.

"Yes, Gavin, I do have something to say," he shouted back.

"Make it short, Mark."

"I will, Gavin. Dinner is served."

⊢——•——⊣

The next morning, twenty minutes after Hannah and Rachelle had left for the theater, phones rang all over town. Gavin, Doris, Edgar and Cary, J.M., Isa, Darcie, Mark, everyone whom Rachelle could reach was told to get his or her ass over to the theater double time.

Clustered in twos and threes in the vomitoria they gasped at the stage. Everyone should have seen it coming, but no one, not even Gavin, saw it coming as they stumbled out of the gala long after midnight. Dinner and dessert had been outside. The dancing had been inside. Marks, swipes, skids, and spots from dozens of stomping wingtips and stiletto heels and cowboy boots and wedgies and huaraches had turned the pristine floor that Rachelle and her assistant had left swept and tidy at five p.m. into a black-and-white Keith Haring drawing. Or a rendering of a zebra hide painted by an artist on mushrooms.

It wasn't a catastrophe; it wasn't a highway fatality, but it was an emergency.

Doris Littauer broke the silence with what sounded like a quote from her first teacher, the legendary Max Reinhardt, dilating from sixty years in the past on the other side of the Atlantic. "The maintenance of white is a difficult proposal."

Forget mops and buckets. They were going to have to re-paint.

A quick and by no means calm conference between Gavin and Hannah ensued. Gavin overruled Hannah's insistence on the same white in favor of the lightest gray that could cover the black marks with one coat. There wouldn't be drying time for two coats of white. It was either a light gray patch-up or cancel the first performance, red ink the theater couldn't afford.

Hannah sped to Soukup's Hardware with Gavin's Visa card. Cary dragged the thirty-cup coffee pot out of the house management closet and set it brewing. Doris removed her wig and rolled up her trouser cuffs. Mark watched Kristy, standing in the opposite vom with Darcie, pitch her diamond wristwatch into a satchel and set it in a front row seat. She slid out of her flats and, without taking aim, tossed them in the woven bag with her old, bewitching economy of movement. Remembering how much she'd (secretly) loved fixing work crises at Harold's Army-Navy and Simeon's, he broke into a smile. Then, twisting sideways and down to pull off a sock, she caught him watching her. After she'd rolled her socks and scored another basket with them, instead of heading to Rachelle, who was handing out brushes, rollers, and kneepads stage right, she marched over to Mark.

"Why did you do it?" she asked.

Mark, who had steered clear of her at the gala, had staged this conversation in his mind for years. His first line, "I wanted to save you from Wayne," was the easy part. Much harder to say, but still, he admitted it to her was, "And I wanted to keep you for myself."

Kristy waved her hand as if swatting a mosquito. Working from her own timetable, she said, "Not that, dumbbell. I know *that*. I want to know why you paid Penny's hospital bill?"

He tried to cover. "What are you talking about?" He had never expected her to find out.

"When Penny got her eye stitched up, I came to you with two hundred and sixty dollars. It was every last cent I had for a twenty-three-hundred-dollar bill, and you told me that the hospital would forgive the rest. That was a little over two grand you forked out of your own pocket for someone you'd never said boo to."

Mark hoped she couldn't see the blush climbing his neck. "How did you find out?" he asked.

She sucked her teeth. "That doesn't matter, Mark."

He looked at his hands. How *had* he justified the expenditure, and the lie?

Her cupboard was bare, and he had more than enough money to cover her debt. That was one answer. The second, more accurate answer, it turned out, was easy to admit. "You were the prettiest woman I had ever seen."

Kristy folded her arms to think about it. The date she'd brought to the opening was too old to be her pothead hairdresser. Cary said the guy was a grocery scale salesman from Syracuse. If Kristy stayed cleaned up, he would be a lucky man. After a moment she put her hands to her hips, and, shaking her head like a mother chiding her child for a fib, said to him, with a kind intention underneath, "What a chump."

"Tell me something I don't know," he said.

There was a sudden shout—"Paint's here!"—as if it were the start of a race. And it would be. The floor had to be actor-ready by 7:30 p.m. Because his wheelchair couldn't roll backstage to the stage manager's office, Edgar was at the lobby payphone with a cupful of dimes, tracking down industrial dryers. President Bush had signed the Americans with Disabilities Act the previous July. Mark looked around the lobby in his new capacity as Managing Director and made mental notes for the spots where the Hangar would need to improve patron access. He and Doris could work on a grant for that.

They fell to work. Eight of them, two to a bucket, worked from the center of the stage. From above, as if through a crane shot, they were a painting octopus, creeping outward to the edges with their brushes and rollers. Mark shared with Darcie. Cary shared with Isa. Gavin shared with Kristy. Doris shared with Rachelle. Edgar remained in the left lobby with the pot of coffee and the leftover Clever Hans from the gala.

They had only started when the actors arrived for their call. Troupers all, they wanted to pitch in, but Hannah ordered them to get their scripts and head over to a picnic table behind a stand of trees near the lake; she had a shit-ton of notes for them.

Rachelle's assistant put the cast recording of *Camelot* over the sound system. Gavin groaned: a tone-deaf Lancelot from New Jersey had pretty much sunk his production the season before, but before long, those who knew the words were singing or humming along while they painted. After *Camelot*, Cary asked for *Damn Yankees*. That summer of 1980 had been a peak time; Cary would always claim that his life before the Hangar gig had just been vamping until ready.

Mark stopped to push his glasses up—in the early morning panic, he had forgotten his contact lenses—and noticed that Isa Vass was painting beside him now, instead of Darcie. Doris, who was given the smallest brush because of her age, was still to his right. Mark knew her well enough by now to know how much the gesture offended her.

"How did you get here?" Mark asked.

"Oh," Isa said in a breezy tone, "I switched with Cary, then I switched with Darcie."

"Why so?"

"A little bird told me you liked my way with a song."

"What little bird?"

"Edgar. He told me to come over and tell you myself."

Isa Vass, the *au pair* who'd fucked Wayne Schroyer once upon a time, was flirting with Mark. Would it be his fate that every woman he knew had Wayne Schroyer in her past? But he calculated that Isa had then been the age Darcie was now. What better time to mess up with all the Waynes in the way? "Shave shave shave," says Bernard in *The Waves* to the mirror on the morning he realizes that his youth has fled. "Go on shaving." Mess up and move on. It wasn't the worst thing in the world.

Mark told Isa that "If I Knew You Were Coming, I'd Have Baked a Cake" was one of the songs their mother used to calm her boys down with. Just to get her to sing, Mark would sometimes punch or trip Edgar and start a fight. Then he said he had loved her way with his favorite song, and she kissed him.

Off his puzzled look, Isa said, "I've been wanting to do that since I saw you again last night."

"So, you remember me?"

"Of course I do."

"Do it again then," he said. "I dare you."

She did, and they did.

Hannah, meanwhile, had finished notes and replaced Doris in the circle. Brush in hand, she was beaming at him. Had she planned this reunion? Had she and Isa planned it together?

Heart pumping, Mark asked Hannah what show she wanted to direct the following summer.

"What?"

"Gavin and the board will give you a slot."

"How do you know?"

"Because as the brand-new Managing Director of the Hangar Theatre, I'll tell them they have to hire you."

"New *what*?"

"If you'd come to the gala, Hannah, you'd have heard all about my new job."

"If I'd come to the gala, we wouldn't all be on our hands and knees painting this goddamn deck."

"Point taken," laughed Isa.

Hannah drummed her four fingers against her upper lip to think about it. "*The Rover* or *Cloud 9.*"

Both titles were unfamiliar. "Who are they by?" Mark asked.

"Aphra Behn wrote *The Rover* in 1677. Caryl Churchill, the best playwright in the English-speaking world today, wrote *Cloud 9* about gender politics and British Imperialism. It's very Brechtian."

"Women are not playwrights," Mark said in his best Doris Littauer imitation. From the corner of his eye, he saw Doris, clock-watching, fretting at their pace, and munching a mini-Linzer tart. When the season ended in August, it would just be him, Doris, and Raul Julia in the office. His first business purchase would be a second phone.

"Tell that to Lillian Hellman," said Isa, who had begun to laugh.

"It's about time the Hangar produced women playwrights," said Hannah.

"Tell that to Lillian Hellman," Mark repeated.

Isa laughed harder, so much so that her bun came undone, and her wild, gorgeous Greek girl hair covered her face.

"What's so funny?" asked Hannah.

Isa sat up on her heels. God, she was pretty, he thought. All women were pretty.

"Caryl Churchill or *The Rover?* Start with something hard, why don't you? Maybe *Troilus & Cressida?* Or *The Bacchae,* while you're at it."

Hannah saw the humor and began giggling her contagious hee hee hee. Before long, the women were laughing hysterically, dripping paint on themselves, as they topped one another with play titles, none of which Mark recognized. Shoptalk. Still on all fours, he grabbed a third kiss from Isa, longer this time, a kiss to remind her he was there, a kiss with promise to it, and anticipation to spare, then let them be. He was not yet the kind of man who could recite lyrics out loud to a woman who'd kissed him, much less sing them to her, but, he hoped, he would be someday.

He picked up his brush. Just for now, Mark Shinner, a man who took direction, hummed the words to himself, "Now I don't know where you came from, cause I don't know where you've been, But it really doesn't matter, grab a chair and fill your platter and dig dig dig right in."

Part Five

Cary Dunkler

1992

You've gotta have heart; miles 'n miles 'n miles of heart...

~Damn Yankees

There *is* such a thing as bad publicity. Last month Darcie was a cover story on *Parade*, that doofus "magazine" they slip into Sunday papers all over the country. (One of its running features is "Ask Marilyn," in which the designated smartest woman on the planet, Marilyn vos Savant, answers tough questions about prime numbers and tidal patterns.) According to her mother, Darcie's handlers have been trying to ramp up Oscar nomination interest for her latest release, *In Our Stars*, a tearjerker about an astronaut who gets trapped in orbit, leaving his young wife (Darcie) to care for their children and for his father, a retired five-star general suffering from emphysema. One day she discovers that NASA got her husband stuck in space on purpose, so she and dying Dad-in-law—who knows where a lot of Pentagon bodies are buried—decide to take on the military-industrial complex and get him back down to Earth. No need to guess how it all comes out. I've only seen the trailer. Here in Ithaca, we like to joke that we're still waiting for *Godfather II*.

At any rate, Darcie Schroyer and her people, always aiming for better roles, land her the cover of *Parade*, and in the interview, she's asked, "What is your favorite meal?" And I quote: "A family friend, Cary Dunkler, runs this little bakery, Clever Hans, where I'm from. When I'm ready to break the bank, calorie-wise, there's nothing I crave more than a big slice of his crustless leek quiche, topped off with one of his signature mint-chocolate brownies. *(She sighs)* Heaven on earth."

People believe what they read in the papers. Never mind that the crustless quiche is my sister Judy's invention and that Clever Hans had been selling carloads of mint-chocolate brownies long before I first apprenticed there in 1981. My "signature" is an inherited recipe I have never monkeyed with.

That was Sunday. When I reached the bakery at four a.m. on Monday to begin the first rise, there were eight messages on my answering machine. More came throughout the day—by noon, I was having my associate, Reena, take down names and phone numbers. Some, from friends, were simple congratulations. Eleven were from restaurants as far off as Rochester and Albany to see whether I shipped product. *Yankee, Southern Living, Redbook,* and *The Reader's Digest* wanted to publish the recipes, but only *Redbook* mentioned compensation. What I regarded as crank calls Edgar labeled *propositions* when I got home in the late afternoon. The most interesting was from The Cellar @ Macy's department store. They were offering to pay me to come down to New York and make "Darcie's favorites" in their test kitchen. If they liked the results, we could discuss an exclusive licensing deal.

After the nightly news, Ed and I began arguing about the offer, one not unknown in its theme and variations. He thought Macy's Cellar was an opportunity, while I dismissed it as a time-waster. He talked big picture: spreading my wings, realizing my gifts, finding my fullest self, and I countered with minutiae: I didn't have time to spare, I had never liked New York, who would run the bakery? Then, pausing between a lateral and a canine on my floss, I reminded him that I was his partner, not one of his frightened IC seniors facing post-college life, and he said to me, "You *are* frightened."

He had never said that in our nearly five years together. He was on the other side of the bathroom door, in his ratty lavender *Christopher Street* T-shirt, waiting in his night chair for me to lift him into bed.

I yanked at the floss. "What?"

"You *are* frightened, Cary. Fear runs your life."

"That's nuts. You're nuts."

I wet and loaded my toothbrush. I'd had my share of downs, but frightened people don't own their own businesses by the time they're thirty. Or commit romantically to paraplegics. Frightened people become drunks or drug addicts or live in their parents' basement rec rooms; they work in call centers or clean houses or busk for quarters on the Commons. I was happy with my life. I made a good living doing something I loved in a town I loved; people liked what I baked; I shared my life with an amazing man; we had a busy social calendar and five years left on our mortgage; and now I was even able to try my hand at child-rearing by helping Judy raise Dan-o, the toddler she'd brought home with her from Uganda last year.

For Edgar to claim that fear underwrote my life could only mean he wasn't satisfied with me in some undisclosed way. I rinsed and spat and, facing the mirror, called out, "Why are you with me then if you think fear runs my life?"

Saying something along these lines usually cued an eventual round of post-fight sex, but something was really riling Ed. "Cut the shit, Cary."

"*What?*"

He sighed deeply. "I hate this."

With my big toe, I flipped the night light next to the toilet—an owl. Our bladders were too young and elastic to require nocturnal trips, but I can't resist an owl *tchotchke*. Edgar is the Owl. I am the Fox. (This, according to Grace, the zonked-out tarot and totem lady at the Farmer's Market.)

"Define *this*," I said.

"*This* is whenever I make the slightest negative observation and you overreact and turn it into a referendum on my commitment to you. 'I don't like how you are.'"

"That's not what I said."

"Grow up, for God's sake."

"I'd hardly call your 'negative observation' 'slight.'"

"Fine," he snapped. "Call it for what it is."

I had begun my crouch to prep his lift, but Ed swatted my arm away. I saw Hector's eyes glow under the bed. He was waiting for us to settle in, then he'd jump up and sleep on a vertical, his head between ours, as if to remind me that Edgar had belonged to him first. It's struck me more than once that the old tabby enjoys our scraps.

I will admit I am conflict-averse—I mean, really, who isn't—so while I knew somewhat what Ed meant, I didn't know what to say. Grow up to what, to be what, to do what, to be who? I was grown. The one therapist I'd seen, in a catatonic state after my brother Dave's death, said in our single session that my fight or flight response was all flight and no fight. That made sense, as did her mini-lecture about survivor's guilt, but I had to cut things short when we discussed my mysterious birth. Whenever I used the past tense to say, "I *was* a foundling," she'd counter with the present tense, "You *are* a foundling, Cary." I told her to stop saying that, and she asked me why; so, rather than fight, I fled.

I'm kidding. Basically, I ran down the clock, thanked her for her interest, and said that the appointment had been instructive. Her parting shot, said with a cutting tilt of her head, was that, in my case, there was a crucial difference between the past and the present tense.

I didn't, and I don't, like being a case of anything. Anymore than Edgar enjoys being an inspirational, A-list paraplegic. I don't tell him that, of course. That might lead to Armageddon. He's turned down a book *proposition* or two since we've been together, saying he wants to be known for his work, not for his life story.

"Let me put you to bed, honey," I said. "I'm beat."

"If you return the Macy's call."

"I think it's a dumb idea."

"Maybe so, but it's your take."

"It is not my take," I replied automatically.

It was, though. It was my turn to do something I didn't want to do. Early on, Ed and I had put this reciprocating institution in place. If we couldn't agree on something, we'd alternate taking one for the team of us. "Taking" covered big things—purchasing life insurance—and little—having a meal out with Darcie's mother, Kristy. There was no discussion allowed over the relative magnitude of any request. If one of us decided that the issue on the table was a take, then the other had to take the take. Edgar's last take was going with me to see *Beauty and the Beast* at Pyramid Mall. He hates all things Disney. I cried three times.

He shot me his "that's enough nonsense" look, and I laughed and agreed that yes, it was my take. I slid my arms behind his knees and put us to bed in the December cold. Drifting off, I found and held his hand under the covers. "Promise me we're not in trouble," I murmured, not sure whether I wanted him to hear the question, but he was already out. Edgar Shinner sleeps the sleep of the just, while I toss, turn, fret, writhe with regrets, and generally beat all the dead horses of the day until they've turned into glue. Because Edgar is the acme of human decency, I predict for him a peaceful death in his sleep. Dave's death was gruesome, going the same way as his birth parents, a car accident. Wayne Schroyer, Darcie's reptile of a father, had a crazy death last summer; he aspirated a hazelnut on a whale-watching boat in Catalina, coughed himself overboard, and drowned. Just desserts thought some at the time. I wouldn't go that far, but it was typical of Wayne to insist to the ticket takers that he could swim rather than wear a girly life preserver. If I'm still alive and in Ed's picture, and he doesn't choose cremation, I'll have him buried in his academic robes, commencement being his favorite day of the year. I'll be cremated.

I bussed to New York the day before my Macy's meeting and stayed with Robin Tascher in Murray Hill. We had been aimless underachievers in our teens, she more so because her father was a German prof at Cornell with big expectations for his only child. Robin had dropped out of college and had been biding her time driving Klaus and Bettina Tascher nuts by doing nothing more constructive than graveyard shifts at Meyer's Smoke Shop—their extensive dirty magazine selection brought in skeeves she liked to fuck in the stock room—when she got her wake-up call: a cauliflower patch of genital warts that had to be burned off. Within six months, Robin, who always had great style, was at FIT studying fashion photography. Once out of school, she morphed over time into an industrial designer. Married, divorced, no kids, she now specialized in food packaging and, big surprise, was even more excited about the Macy's Cellar proposition than Edgar was.

"The price of admission," she said at the door, with a kiss to both cheeks, "is hiring me to do your look. I have tons of ideas."

I'd never been on Robin's turf. During her post-Ithaca decade, I'd seen her only on parental visitations. She wouldn't plan ahead; she'd just turn up at Clever Hans with a bottle of Riesling, expecting me to drop what I was doing and lunch there, outside if it were nice.

"I'm big as a house, Cary."

There had never been a time when Robin didn't announce this, with a weird gleeful undertone, in the first two minutes of any meet-up, the consequence of having a Jewish mother built like a whippet. Of course, I used to have an arsenal of comebacks—"Ten more pounds and you could apply for statehood," shit like that—but now, dressed head to foot in New York black, she was, yes, plumper, but by no means fat.

"I think you look great." I dangled my box of pastries by its string, and she swiftly relieved me of it. "Hot Skunk '79," I added. Robin had been the most exotic girl in our class at Ithaca High. Her pleather short shorts and sequined mini-dress and fishnet stockings stood out in a sea of Laura Ashley prints. She wore bangs and beauty marks, black brassieres under white shirts, crossed her sevens, and had a filthy mouth, which was why I fell for her in woodshop sophomore year, where she was the only girl in class. I'd built a shoeshine kit, which disappeared into the Gabelson basement shortly after its unveiling as a Christmas present for my foster father, Hugh. Robin made a cool cherry wood jewelry box with three secret compartments, cannily anticipating a need for drug stashes in her future.

"You too, dearie dear. You've finally grown into your nose."

"At last, an answer to prayer," I replied. My disproportionate nose, and how to work around it, was another keepsake of our youth. We'd joke that my birth mother was Armenian, and my father, a dromedary in the Foreign Legion.

"I'm not kidding, Cary."

"Clean living?" I offered.

The tiny face she made reminded me that I suspect Robin thinks I lead too respectable a life.

"How *is* Edgar?" she answered on cue. It's sad that they only tolerate one another. Robin is suspicious of educators, and Ed doesn't like to spend time with "less than genuine" people. Had Robin been upstate in 1987, I know she would have tried to keep us from falling in love. The man she married I met just once, at their garden nuptials, an affair so hoity-toity she didn't hire me to do her cake. And now she wanted *my* business.

"Ed's good. He's stoked about Macy's."

"And you aren't." I shrugged. "You're such a cluck," she said, using a favorite disparagement from days of yore. She'd call me "Cluck," and I'd call her "Hef," short for "heifer."

We dropped the subject in favor of gossip, picture albums, wardrobe and accessory pruning, etc., but some hours later, while we were consolidating Chinese take-out boxes, she said that Dave, were he alive, would also be stoked about Macy's.

I nodded, my eyes stinging, and ducked into her living area. Two years on, and I still had never cried over Dave's death. I figure if I start, I might never stop. I guessed the trigger tonight was Manhattan, his domain. He had moved here with Gavin Steeg, the former Artistic Director of the Hangar Theatre, the August he graduated college. It had been a rocky summer for me, and for us as brothers, so I had ignored his phone messages to visit him until that December. Four months was the longest span of time we'd ever gone without speaking or seeing each other.

Rather than head from the Port Authority to Gavin's apartment on Morton Street and retrieve the key taped under the mailbox in their vestibule, I walked east in the holiday bustle to the ice rink at Rockefeller Center, where Dave was working as a guard. Spotting him by his Big Red ski hat, I watched him weave several circuits through a crowd of tentative skaters. It hardly seemed fair that in addition to being blond and masculine and handsome, Phi Beta Kappa *summa cum laude,* he was also a terrific winter athlete, who had only dropped hockey at Cornell his junior year when it became too hard to manage practices around his double major. Former Olympic hopeful (and Ithaca undertaker) J.M. Dondher, who coached him privately through his teens, said that Dave had been his most promising talent ever.

"Dave," I called out, adding "Prescott Bailey" in a split-second in case the rink was filled with Davids. He spun in a half-turn, and the way his face lit up to see me hit me in the knees first, then the stomach, then I was out of breath. If I'd had a hat on, I'd have pitched it in the air, Mary Tyler Moore style.

I can't gauge how unusual the tightness of our bond was because I don't know many brother pairs. But, from observation, I do know that Edgar and his brother, Mark Shinner, considered very close by their family because of Ed's accident, don't create the kind of happiness in each other that Dave and I once did. Maybe one day I'll learn how much of me went into the ground with him.

With the subject broached, Robin kept at it. Dave would have wanted me to succeed; to the end of his life, whenever they got together, the two of them would scheme how to get me to New York and live a larger life like theirs.

"You and Dave—*here?*"

That they would, could, and did see each other, independent of me, was instantly upsetting. It was like a dinosaur pushing a stroller, or George Washington dating Lily Tomlin, or—what I'm saying is that their personal overlap didn't compute.

"Not in the apartment."

"Where then?"

Robin had begun dragging her knockoff Noguchi coffee table, her latest "bougie achievement," toward the wall. I took the cue and started pulling and stacking the cushions from the foldout couch.

"On shoots."

"Photo shoots?"

"Sargento is an Ogilvy client. Dave and I worked together on the rollout of cheese sticks. There was one whole year when we saw each other twice a month—presentations, shoots, lunches. He was really great at what he did."

Neither of them had ever mentioned it to me. That I was instantly jealous of their time together made me feel like Robin's Cluck of Yore. I heaved up the bar handle and, yanking the mattress frame out of the sofa, heard something rip in the workings.

Robin kept on. "Every last man and woman on Madison Avenue put on lipstick when they heard Dave Bailey was going to be on set."

"He was a handsome dude," I said.

My neutral tone made her hoot. "*Handsome dude?* How about King of Man and Ladysplash?"

I scoffed. "That's not news, Robin. I think I tore your top sheet."

We examined the rip. I promised to repair it in the morning if she could find her sewing kit. I would also launder the sheets and wipe down her refrigerator, which was a horror show. Robin, a slob, couldn't even wash a dish back in the day.

Robin circled back again. "He was always hot, even in middle school, but watching him in charge of a shoot was a turn-on. He made the Sargento string cheese team feel like they were crushing the Axis."

She headed to a closet. That she hadn't dropped the subject was making me nervous. When we were kids, Robin got a kick out of shocking me, and she was definitely leading up to something.

She came back with two pillows, cases, and a shock. Dave Bailey was an ad biz slut so legendary that she would warn her interns and young male staffers to be on their guard against unwanted attentions. On the other hand, if such attentions weren't unwelcome, she made them accept two rules: 1) safe sex, and 2) not on company time or property—there was a famous story of a Dave Bailey three-way in the Ogilvy and Mather library.

I focused on sleeving the pillows. I'd gone white as a ghost or red as a beet, the former probably, because I was shivering.

"What? What, Cary? What did I say?"

She was smiling. To my peril, I had forgotten her malicious streak. She knew that this was all news to me. A more rational person would have asked her why she thought I needed to hear these things or would have given her a genuine answer that would have led to a genuine conversation. I fled.

"Nothing," I replied. "I'm just—it's cold."

She didn't push further. She didn't need to.

⊢———•——⊣

I churned a gigantic vat of glue that night. Robin had all but called Dave a sex addict. Had I ever suspected this? Had we never talked about sex? Why had we never talked about sex? Do siblings talk about sex? Why was *I* not a sex addict? Had sex changed for Dave in New York? Had Gavin known? Had Gavin approved? Did he and Gavin have an open relationship? Had AIDS unleashed something in him? Had he been safe? Had he been infected when he died? Had he had a death wish?

The next day I made five crustless quiches and four dozen brownies in a fog. This was not, technically, a problem since my hands had made thousands of both while my mind was elsewhere. The Macy's test kitchen, more chem lab than the Julia Child show on PBS, held every grade of flour and kind of sugar, every size of egg, every shade of butter, every variant of Gruyère, mint leaves, mint dust, mint extract, mint oil, *crème de menthe*, and chocolate— chip, syrup, bar, powder—as cheap as Hershey's and as pricey as the Belgian brands whose names I can't pronounce. The chocolate shelf in the Cellar larder held everything but carob, which has a small but passionate following in the People's Republic of Ithaca. I don't use carob at Clever Hans because I don't make food I wouldn't eat myself.

I wasn't accustomed to baking for jurors taking notes like med students watching a surgery. I had two assistants, but I didn't use them, except to have one turn on a sink faucet too state-of-the-art for me to decode. The clinicians held their questions—there were dozens—until I'd set the pans in the oven and finished my brownie topping.

Edgar often referred to the bi-monthly Dean Roundtables at Ithaca College as "Being nibbled to death by ducks." I now knew what he meant. "Why sift the flour for the quiche and not for the brownies?" "Why did you fan the leeks before you sliced them?" "You grated, rather than minced the shallots, why?" Why grate the Emmenthaler, but slice the Gruyère?" "Was that Parmagiano-Reggiano or Pecorino?" "Was that a typical pre-heat?" "An icing *and* a glaze?" "Have you ever substituted chocolate chips?" "If in season, do you use fresh mint?" "Why so few eggs?" "Why glass? "Why copper?" "Why the gravy whisk?" "Why a water bath?" "Why why why why why?"

Given their accusatory tone, and given that most of my answers were shrugs, or "I don't know, really," or "It tastes better this way," I grew impatient, then downright exasperated. Tired of being sent to the dunce's corner, I finally said, "Look, you invited me here. Some of you must know what it means to cook. You—I—do it by feel."

I caught a sympathetic side-eye from an assistant, but there wasn't a sound from the experts. Once again, I'd done something my way and blown it, and suddenly, hard to believe, I wanted the Macy's gig more than anything I'd ever gone after in my entire life. For me and for my believers: Dave and Judy and Edgar, and even Robin, and Hugh and Mary Gabelson, whose years of care I paid back by avoiding them on the streets of Ithaca if I saw them with enough time to duck away.

Fortunately, the brownies and the quiches came out of the oven as their ideal selves. Meaning that Oscar hopeful Darcie Schroyer had good taste and that Macy's and I would be in touch. I signed a release form, unaware they had filmed my demonstration. "You know where to find me," I said, shaking the hand of the Executive Chef, a stout clubwoman-type with hair like a hat. On my hasty exit, I bought a package of high-end shortbread for little Dan-o, forgetting that I was a professional baker.

|◆————————◆—————————◆|

We agreed I should be less defensive at my "callback." Edgar, divining that I'd had a poor sleepover reunion with Robin, convinced me to get a hotel room out of Macy's. If they wanted me, they'd have to pay. I wasn't ready to share with Ed what I had learned about Dave. I don't want him to think ill of the dead, especially when I couldn't decide myself about my brother's behavior. Dave was always first and always best; why shouldn't sex at every bend in the road have been part of his eminent domain? Edgar, though, hates cheaters. Neil, his psychiatrist boyfriend prior to me, had been a serial cheater. A day doesn't go by, Ed says, that he doesn't hope to see Neil lying on the Commons with a tin cup and open, running sores. This vengeful streak doesn't square with his life as all-caring Dean of Students, but he maintains that a) gimps aren't saints and b) enemies keep you honest.

If Edgar can be vengeful to a fault, I am righteous to a fault. The only "cheating" period in my life was the summer of 1980 when I was in *Damn Yankees* at the Hangar and having sex with a playwright and an actor. "Two-timing" better describes the situation, and no one got hurt but me.

Like all of the men in my life, Ed had had to make the first move. I met him at a birthday dinner party he threw one March for his brother Mark. Both Shinners swear it wasn't a set-up. Mark and I go back a whole decade, to early, happier Kristy Schroyer days. Mark also dated Judy for a meandering stretch, but Uganda won out. At any rate, the townie part of Ithaca's population is very interconnected. Edgar knew I ran Clever Hans, and I knew he was the famous IC Wheelchair Dean. Somehow we had never intersected. I was hand-washing his crystal after most of the dinner guests had gone—lest you think I perform household chores for any host who asks, I'd been given his direct permission to do so—when Edgar came up behind me at the sink, girdled my hips with his hands, pulled me into his chair, and pressed the side of his face against the middle of my back. All I need to say is that the attraction was intense, mutual, and I didn't drop a goblet. If blind people have better hearing, and the deaf compensate by developing greater visual acuity, then people with spinal cord injuries develop heightened tactile response in less traditionally erogenous zones. Edgar has taught me a lot about the neck, eyelids, temples, clavicles, elbows, shoulders—his and my own. He has very, very strong arms.

After five months of dating, I outfitted my house with ramps and grips, and he moved in. There is no secret to our fit. We were a lucky find; since then we've been smart enough to each put the other first. As a boy, I was stuck on Noah's Ark. I drew and colored the same Noah's Ark picture hundreds of times. Perspective-wise, post-boarding was an easier image for me to draw than marching the animals up the gangway two-by-two. My ark, positioned horizontally, had matching heads poking out of a double row of portholes. Being part of a pair, safely tucked into the hold with all the other pairs, was a special secret for me. Dave was my match, of course. Our faces smiled through a porthole below the giraffes and between the bears and the llamas.

If possessed to draw an ark today, I would put Edgar and me in a porthole, and Gavin and Dave next to us. If mistakenly assuming that they had worked the "forsaking all others" angle the way we did makes me naïve, so be it. (I'll build an ark for Dan-o when he gets old enough not to swallow small, carved objects.)

For my return to Macy's, the mint brownie ingredients I'd used the first time were already measured and set out on the counter. There was the same pair of assistants, plus Brad Klew, an associate chef who would duplicate my moves at the next cooking station. I had to laugh when he told me that my crustless quiche was, once they'd run a nutritional analysis, a non-starter for ambitious, health-conscious New Yorkers. Hadn't Darcie Schroyer said as much in *Parade* magazine?

"There goes half my fortune," I said.

"It was scrumptious," said Brad. "But guess the calorie count in a four-inch wedge?"

"I'm thinking twelve, thirteen hundred?"

"Thirteen eighty."

"Imagine if I still made it with slab bacon."

The pressure was off me this time. Brad Klew was a rare bird: a chef with an MBA. His shadowing me on the brownies—we made six separate batches before we called it quits—was a collaborative discussion about alternative (read cheaper) ingredients and streamlining the baking process, wherever possible, for potential mass production. We achieved consensus (Edgar's term for "agree") on several price versus quality trade-offs. My Cellar debut was looking more likely.

We scarfed down a quick steak dinner, and then Brad walked me to the Iroquois Hotel on 44th. I passed on his offers of a nightcap at the Yale Club and the Wigwam Bar. I'd said good night and pushed the up button at the elevator bank when he asked me whether he could come to my room.

"Do you need to use the phone?" I answered. I was that dumb.

No, he did not. His need would take longer than a phone call.

"How old are you?" was all I could think to say in my embarrassment. I examined his face for the first time. Black Irish, thin-lipped, with a heavy five o'clock shadow. A massive brow, deep-set eyes. A chin dimple. A focused look of seduction.

"Twenty-six."

"And as bold as brass," I said, channeling a Mary Gabelson term.

"Is that a yes?"

"I am in a serious long-term relationship, Brad." When that didn't send him scampering, I added, "It's been almost five years now."

"I don't see a ring."

"There isn't a ring. We're monogamous, in any case."

"Okay." He smiled—nothing ventured, nothing gained. "The best ones are always taken."

"Good night." I stepped into the elevator, which had arrived in the nick of time. Maybe Edgar and I ought to look into getting rings.

"I'll call you," he said to the closing doors.

I would have plenty to mull over when I reached room 611, but the first order of business would be two rounds of furious sexual release.

┡━━━━━━┿━━━━━━┩

Barriers I hadn't known I'd put into place swiftly fell. Plain jerking off thinking about Brad led to more treasonous visualizations of Brad during sex with Edgar and then to flat out adulterous phone sex with Brad every other early morning at Clever Hans before Reena showed up with coffees and my breakfast sandwich. I was fourteen again, thinking with my dick: checking crotches (and hands, noses, feet, asses, and ears) wherever I went, imagining sex with suppliers, customers, old friends, television anchormen, musicians on the Commons, college kids, ancient, crab-walking hippies. I noticed glory holes in public restrooms for the first time in years, noticed that the gay porn selection at Meyer's Smoke Shop had diversified in the last decade to include Bears, Chicks with Dicks, Asian men, Latin men, Hot Black Daddies, noticed how much more visible and militant the young queers now were. Without question, the throwback to my early adolescence was shot through with adult guilt pangs that made me feel rotten to the core.

The barrier not to be breached was touching Brad. I'd warned him so on the phone before I came down for a third Macy's visit that took place in a conference room filled with suits. The kitchen had made my brownies without me. There was a batch for us and a batch for a room of tasters on the other side of a one-way mirror. We were there to listen to their reactions, elicited by a cadre of marketers who first asked specific questions about taste, crumb, mouthfeel, and the like, and then posed more metaphorical questions—What does this brownie make you feel like? What would be the ideal dinner menu to precede this brownie as dessert? What month/foreign country/movie star/rock band/holiday is this brownie? (Given the green frosting, Irish-related and springtime answers predominated.)

195

I might have collapsed with laughter on "What animal is this brownie?" except I remembered that my scientifically trained brother had set up experiments like these for his impressive living. Also, Brad Klew, three seats away, perpendicular to me, his eyes fixed on mine, was making a mess of my undershorts. To ease that pressure, I began casing the table for a third party to join us. Why not reenact Dave Bailey's legendary Ogilvy threesome? That's when it hit me that the temptation of Brad Klew had forced me into Dave's shoes. If Robin could be trusted, Dave had cased every room he did business in just this way. Did I miss him so much that I wanted to be him? Scarier thought: had I always wanted to be Dave instead of me? Until sixth grade, when he'd left us to go live with Leigh Bailey, we pretended that we were fraternal twins. But was that actually completely true? Maybe I was misremembering. Dave hadn't drawn cozy Noah's Ark pictures. He had chalked large-scale maps of the solar system all over the basement walls and picked a new favorite planet every month; he'd drawn rocket ships and space stations with himself in solo command.

I felt half like hauling Brad Klew onto the conference table and fucking his brains out and half like crawling under the table to puke my guts out. In either case, something needed to come out.

The closest we got to touching on that trip was when Brad, hailing a cab at the corner of 35th and Broadway—a freezing rain and no umbrella kept me from footing it to the Port Authority—pushed me by the shoulder into the back seat. What that briefest of sensations did to me felt more like cheating than phone sex. Holding on to the shoulder for most of the bus ride, I felt like I was going to explode.

◆————◆————◆

Though in a very bad way—how do you tell a man in a wheelchair that you're thinking of leaving him?—I covered to the best of my ability. I'm a moody person, so Edgar, always super-busy at school, didn't pry. Plus, we were now having sex four times a week, and who questions that kind of development? I couldn't see any way out of the dilemma, except to leave Edgar with no explanation. Or I could refuse Brad's calls. Except that not only was I living for his calls, but I also wanted that contract with Macy's Cellar. I assumed Brad didn't have the pay grade to imply that I couldn't have one without the other, but when you're in flight mode, your thinking tends to the simplistic.

Rufus Levinson provided some help. The name suggests a shrink, but Rufus was the new Artistic Director of the Hangar Theatre. Edgar, a trustee, had been on the search committee that selected Rufus, finally, over Hannah

Habecker, a whip-smart talent whose production of Virginia Woolf's *The Waves* had put the Hangar on the map last winter when she got to remount the production Off-Broadway. You could say that Darcie Schroyer and *The Waves* were the two principal exports of Gavin Steeg's regime.

Anyway, it was early March, and Rufus Levinson was in town, glad-handing donors and subscribers and auditioning locals for his first season. Wanting to meet with his vendors, he called me in for a tasting. In all the years I'd supplied the theater with pre-show and intermission treats, Gavin had never once asked about the product. Ithaca was soon to learn that Rufus Levinson never let a detail go by that he didn't need to approve and/or improve.

If I thought that just because Edgar was a trustee and his brother Mark was Rufus' Managing Director Clever Hans would get a special dispensation, I was wrong. (I found out later that Rufus had sampled my competitor's wares all over town. Smart sonovabitch, I thought.) He'd done his research in other ways too. I set down my bag to shake his hand, and he greeted me with, "I've been dying to meet Edgar's better half. How close are you to booking Macy's?"

"It's looking pretty good," I mumbled, flashing on Brad's five o'clock shadow.

"Fantastic! If you need help with the contract, I know good people in the city."

Great, I thought. Legalese, one more thing to make glue with. Fuck Darcie Schroyer and her big, sentimental trap. Why did I want the gig? Did I really care if tourists from Idaho and Japan ate my brownies?

I didn't have to say much. Pale and handsome, with intense eyes and a sly, crooked smile, Rufus Levinson shot off sparks in several directions every moment. The office was too small for his energy. I could see Doris Littauer, the Hangar's ancient Know-and-Do-it-All, beaming at her typewriter. Rufus attacked the pastries with a discerning palate. He detected, for example, the pinch of cloves I put in my Linzer Squares. The mint brownie, he declared, "was a poem." At my blank look, he said that that was a line from one of his favorite movies, *The Lady Eve,* did I know it, and did I think it would make a good musical, he was trying to secure the rights, but the Sturges estate was tighter than the Kurt Weill Foundation and the Rodgers & Hammerstein Organization combined, he was just sick about it?

Ed had told me that the Board hired, as boards often do, what it already knew. Like Gavin Steeg, Rufus Levinson was a gay Jew with a New York sensibility and more than a touch of the huckster in him. Hannah Habecker, on the other hand, was a laid-back California dreamer with an arty streak a mile wide. Clichéd thinking, Ed conceded, but that's how consensus gets made.

"Your work is incredible," Rufus concluded, eyeing the empty box, capturing some final crumbs from the desk with his thumbs. I don't know how he stayed so skinny.

I shrugged. "It's just baking."

"You are an artist, Mr. Dunkler." I heard Doris chuckle. He snapped his fingers suddenly. "Do you do Italian? Desserts, I mean."

"If you mean cookies, no. There's no market for them in Ithaca."

"No, I mean things like cannoli, tiramìsu."

"Tiramìsu? I've heard of that."

His eyes lit up. "It's Italian for 'pick me up.' Oh my god, sponge cake, mascarpone cream, espresso, ladyfingers, cocoa. It's completely colonized Manhattan. You won't believe how good it tastes—*da morire!*"

On the spot, Rufus had gotten the idea for me to create a dessert for every Hangar show. He was opening the season with *A View from the Bridge*, an Arthur Miller play set in an Italian neighborhood in Brooklyn. He was going to stage it like a Greek tragedy, with columns, almost no furniture, and a gigantic chorus of "denizens" who would watch the action unfold. Ideally, he wanted all of the denizens to be Ithacans who had never been to the Hangar before.

"A boost for subscriptions and great PR," said Doris, clearly on the same page.

"I've done cannoli for weddings," I said, speaking thoughtfully, as an artist might. The guy was inspiring. "And I can follow any recipe you throw my way. Lead me to one for tiramìsu, and I'll make it for you."

My "brother-in-law," Mark, came in at that point. He'd been out selling ads for the program. We threw out dessert ideas for the rest of the season, Doris taking notes. *Dames at Sea*, a spoof of thirties movie musicals, was the toughie since Depression-era mock apple pie or prune whip wouldn't cut it with the patrons. When that discussion trailed off, Rufus asked Mark whether his wife, Isa, was auditioning for *A View from the Bridge*, could she come in the following day at Lincoln Hall on the Cornell campus?

Mark's wide-eyed look matched the one I'd given when Rufus had asked me whether I had booked Macy's Cellar.

"She's too young for Beatrice, but she's got the right look, and I've heard she can act. I also hear her on the radio. She's got a great voice."

"Except she doesn't act anymore," said Mark.

Rufus laughed. "That's what she tells you, Mark, but actors never stop acting."

"Really?" Mark's dumbfounded tone set Doris laughing.

"Call her and ask—she has to know Beatrice is a great part." Rufus turned to me. "When I get an idea, my policy is to call right away."

"She's on the air now," said Mark.

"Leave her a message then. I can do it, if that makes it sound more official. It isn't nepotism, Mark. I need a Beatrice."

Mark picked up the phone, but then, shifting from foot to foot to foot to foot, he seemed to forget the receiver in his hand. "I—we're—well—." His face had grown real red real fast.

"What's wrong?"

"I—shit, I'm not supposed to say yet."

"Say what?" insisted Rufus.

He looked stricken. "We…Isa could be pregnant. *We* could be pregnant. Please don't tell her I told you. Don't tell anyone. We'll know for sure in two more weeks."

Doris took the receiver from Mark's hand and gently pushed him into his chair.

"Mazel tov!" shouted Rufus. "I mean, fuck me and Arthur Miller, bad news for us, but all congratulations to you and yours. This is so fantastic. You want this child, am I right?"

Mark nodded. "Isa jokes that she wants nine kids, wants to raise her own baseball team, she says. But…"

"But what?" Rufus, Doris, and I practically screamed this in chorus. Then we leaned in.

"It's just. I'm going to be a very old father." He dabbed his eyes. "I'm scared."

"Scared of?" asked Rufus.

"Scared of it, scared of it all. I'm not—" Mark balled his fists and dropped his chin to his chest. I'd never noticed how the shape of his crown was a match for Edgar's. What was I going to do about Edgar? Stay? Go? Tell the truth and get kicked out?

"Does Isa know you're scared?" asked Rufus.

"No."

"Why not?"

By this point, Rufus was kneeling in front of Mark's chair and had taken his hands in his own. The cynic might say it looked stagey, but like the best theater, it was the opposite of fake.

"I'm afraid to tell her." Mark was whispering now.

"Do you think she senses that?"

"She, uh, she might."

In the dramatic pause that Mark and Rufus held in their hands, I could hear the wall clock behind me. A truck rumbled down Cayuga, then stopped in front of the Mall. Doris adjusted the gigantic white patent leather belt over her brown wool dress. A shifting light caught the grease spot my cinnamon twist had left on the desk blotter and Rufus's silver and turquoise fountain pen.

"Well," said Rufus, breaking the silence. "I think Isa does know you're scared, and I think it would be the best thing if you told her so yourself."

Mark's chest had been jerking with his effort to take deeper breaths, but then something broke inside. He looked up, eyes glistening, and stood.

"And like right now, Mark. Buy flowers and go to WTKO and wait outside her booth. Tell her what's in your heart. Then, on your way home, buy a copy of *Carousel*—the original Broadway cast with John Raitt, not the soundtrack with Gordon McCrae—and listen to "Soliloquy" and learn what *not* to do you're expecting a first child."

Rufus gave Mark a huge hug, lengthier than I knew Mark liked—Artistic Directors were huggers. I would be happy to report to Edgar that the Hangar was in good hands. Mark left on his mission, and Rufus Levenson, freelance shrink, turned to me. My heart was full too, but my flight out of the Hangar office was warp speed, whatever that really means.

⊢——————•——————⊣

I did try. Two mornings in a row, I ignored Brad's call, telling myself I had the grit to never pick up again *and* never tell Edgar about it, but deep down, I knew that a sin of omission this huge was not in my character. No matter what Dear Abby or Ann Landers or Dr. Joyce Brothers might advise, and I had been scouring their columns for weeks, I had damaged our relationship, and the gash would never fade or disappear.

"Why are you doing this to me?" I yelled at Brad on the third morning, *after* my orgasm. "I am a country mouse."

"I thought you liked this, Cary."

"I do like this. I like this too much," I said, trying to fling the semen off my hand toward the wall. "Fuck."

"Fuck?"

"Just fuck, Brad." I'd missed the wall and hit the side of a mixing bowl. Active yeast and my seed—mark it with a 'B' for baby and me. What a Frankenstein's Monster I had been baking ever since taking the escalator down into the hell of Macy's Cellar.

"When *are* we going to 'just fuck Brad?'"

"Shut up!" I snapped. I zipped up my fly and spread my back against the oven for some warmth and some spine. March is a bitch of a month in the Finger Lakes. "Why don't you find yourself a boyfriend and leave me alone?" I pleaded.

"Who says I don't have one?"

"You say."

"I never said that, Cary."

"You—. You—. *What?*"

"Who says I don't have a boyfriend named Jeremy Heller asleep in our bed in the next room who gets up an hour later than I do because he doesn't go to the gym and because he is senior management and doesn't need to hustle the way I do?"

"Because...."

"Because what?" Brad sounded amused. After a bit of silence, he sighed and said, "Grow up, Cary."

Whether Brad was lying to me or not about a Jeremy Heller in the next room, there was now one thing he and Edgar could agree on—my lack of maturity. So, add that complication to my low-level, but steadily climbing frenzy. Two days later, the first thing out of my mouth to my sister was, "Do you believe in monogamy?"

Judy and I were on the Cornell Arts Quad, waiting for the dragon's annual emergence from Sibley Hall. I don't myself deliver to IC or Cornell anymore, but I make an exception for Dragon Day. I wanted little Dan-o to experience the madness, though not on tabs of acid the way Robin and I used to. Dan-o stood between his mother and me, on a slushy asphalt path, a perfectly serene three-year-old in a yellow parka that made his black skin seem even darker. I had to remind myself that cold and snow wouldn't faze him. He probably had no memories of his homeland.

"Africans don't believe in it," Judy answered. "Certainly not the men, so like a lot of cherished First World ideas, monogamy was probably invented by the Germans as a sick joke for the rest of us poor slobs."

Not the answer I needed, but East Africa had radicalized Judy Gabelson. The Ugandan government had thrown her out for her refusal to cease her subversive activities. She wasn't a spy, like Dave and Ed and I used to speculate. Her case was worse. Judy was a feminist, whose gumption to question Uganda's astronomically disastrous birth rate had led her to open a space in Kampala for women to simply *discuss* rational family planning. They'd burned her out twice. In the end, they revoked her visa, and an eight-car police escort drove her, with a siren serenade, to Entebbe Airport. Getting Daniel out with her involved high-level blackmail, though she wouldn't reveal where she'd gotten the gobs of cash or whether the bureaucrats she'd blackmailed were American or Ugandan. Both, probably. The political corruption over there was beyond comprehension. She dreamed of returning to Africa and continuing to subvert the patriarchy, one woman at a time, but for now, she worked in the Cornell system and kept her "Book Drive for the Bush" non-profit going as best she could.

"But do *you* believe in monogamy?"

Judy rolled her eyes. "Look at my hair, what does that tell you?"

She wore a thick braid down the center of her back. I realized I hadn't seen her hair loose since she'd returned to the States.

"I can't say I know what your braid is telling me."

"This is the braid of a seriously post-sexual, humanitarian off-layer. Today's too cold for my sandals and camisole, but they're other essential parts of the international aid worker uniform."

"Post-sexual?"

"More or less, Cary. I don't go out looking for it. And don't bug me about it."

Suddenly there was a great clatter of drums and trashcan lids. About one hundred students came howling down the path between Sibley and Lincoln Halls. Many were costumed as red devils or green goblins, with makeup and swords to match.

"Up!" said Dan-o. "Up!"

Whether he was frightened, or wanted a better look, I couldn't say. I picked him up and settled him on my shoulders. Though he tested as very bright, Dan-o had delayed speech issues. The chief reason Judy worked for Cornell was for the opportunity to enroll Dan-o in the kindergarten at the Family Life Development Center in the Human Ecology School, the same place where Dave and I had landed without parents in 1964. Talk about full circle, especially when you consider that Daniel had been, like me, a foundling, literally rescued from shit as a newborn delivered, or tossed, into a pit latrine. Judy, volunteering her Sundays to the central city orphanage, had monitored months of Dan-o's development before making her selection. Unlike Hugh and Mary, who'd made a snap decision with Dave and me.

"Look, Dan-o, there it is!" I pointed to the dragon rounding the path. "Can you say 'dragon?'"

"Drrgah. Drrgah."

"Dragon," said Judy.

"Drig-gah." He was trying.

This year the first-year architecture students had built an upright, Godzilla-style creature (with wings and arms) instead of the easier and more traditional, undulating Chinese-style dragons held up by students with poles I'd seen most years. This dragon stood maybe forty feet high on a rolling platform and had yellow eyes with red pupils. The scale pattern on its torso and wings was gold, black, and hot pink. The verticality slowed its gait, but the students had compensated for its lack of speed with an internal screech mechanism that regulated jets of smoke through its red and yellow-rimmed nostrils and made Dan-o giggle. I suspect the designers had rigged the nose with dual fire extinguishers.

"Why do you like this so much?" asked Judy. "They're just going to burn it up."

"Tradition," I said. I'd learned at a tender age, maybe it was the year after Dave left the Gabelsons, that watching the bonfire at the end of Dragon Day made me unbearably sad. I'm pretty sure it was the first bonding moment I'd had with Robin Tascher. We had caught each other wiping our eyes, and didn't bother bullshitting about ash, cinders, smoke, etc. And let's not forget Puff being abandoned by Jackie Paper. Some years, depending on my mood, I would cut out long before they lit the fire.

"It's very African," she said. "I'll give it that."

We watched a bit. Several topless female revelers had painted their breasts green. A cartwheel competition turned into a gleeful mud fight. A sound system, hauled out of Sibley, started playing the Dead, so the stoned freestyling began in earnest.

"Are you having fun, Dan-o?" asked his mother in a way that meant she'd had enough of Dragon Day.

To counteract the cold, which Judy hated, I brought up something she liked. "Hey, sis. They need an MD for *Dames at Sea* this summer. The new Artistic Director is really cool."

She laughed. "Rufus Levinson already asked me. Laid it on pretty thick, I have to say."

"Well?"

"I don't have the time, Cary," she said. "It would be like you joining the chorus this summer, ten years after *Damn Yankees*."

"Don't think he didn't ask," I said. "Lucky for us all, there is no chorus in *Dames at Sea*."

We could both laugh at that. *Damn Yankees,* the last show I ever did, had been a confidence builder when I hadn't known I needed one.

A goblin came up out of nowhere, shook a trident in Dan-o's face, then darted away before I could shoo him off. Dan-o's oddly delayed reaction to the threat was a weird bleat, so I handed him to his mother.

"He's very calm," I said.

"He's seen a lot in his short life. He takes everything in, even if he can't verbalize what he sees yet. It's okay, small man; Mommy promises we'll get you inside very soon."

"We can have cocoa at the Temple of Zeus, Dan-o," I said. "Would you like that?" He nodded soberly. No goblin could rattle his cage for long.

We turned toward Goldwin Smith Hall. There was a bizarrely feathered dragon's head on the bronze statue of Andrew Dickson White, who had founded the Architecture School in 1871, the first in America.

"Sis?"

"Yes?"

"Did you know that Dave slept around? Like a lot?"

Judy stopped a second; her eyes narrowed. "Why do you ask?"

That was all the answer I needed, but for once, instead of pursuing a more pleasant topic, I asked more questions. She knew that Dave had had an ongoing affair in his teens with his skating coach, J.M. Dondher. He'd quit Cornell hockey to keep a jealous J.M. from outing him on campus. He'd also been notorious with the chorus boys on his summer trips up to see Gavin. She had caught him twice post-show in the men's dressing room under the stage right vom. They never discussed it; it wasn't her business, except once Dave said to her—

"Oh, look, Dan-o," she interrupted herself. "Here we are. See all the big white statues. Those are gods."

"Gozz," he said, pointing.

"That's right, small man."

We had reached the portal to the Temple of Zeus, a Bohemian café that went through ten dozen chocolate mint brownies a week when Cornell was in session. No matter how much care they put into them, the Macy's Cellar version would never taste as good as mine. Heading down the marble steps, I set Judy back on track.

"Said *what*?"

"Said what what?"

"What did Dave say that time you caught him in the right vom?"

Judy pressed her lips together and turned to me. Grabbing the knob to the glass and iron fretwork door, I held her gaze. It wasn't going to open until she told me.

"He said, 'Don't tell Cary.'"

"*What*? Why?"

She and Dan-o swept into the crowded café. The heat of dozens of students in winter coats, and their amped-up noise added to my nausea.

Sweaty, short of breath, I felt far worse than I had at Robin's reveal in Manhattan. Dave was about to reveal a secret he wouldn't tell me in life.

"What can I do you for?" asked the student server.

My ears rang as I took Judy's order and pointed them toward a table. Then I sleepwalked through the motions of purchasing our snack. The cocoa mugs shook in my hands as I set them down in front of Judy, who then went back for the desserts.

When she returned, my gravity set off her nervous system; her fingers made a botch of unpeeling the fluted wrapper from Dan-o's dragon cupcake.

"Why didn't Dave want me to know these things?"

Afraid to look at me, she talked to her lemon bar. "You were always more fragile than Dave. Things could really upset you, remember? That's why Hugh and Mary were set on having you. They saw that you needed more care and attention. You only mellowed in your teens, Cary. Remember?"

This struck like a thunderbolt direct to the skull, hurled by Zeus, from his throne twenty feet away. The "Buy One, Get One Free Orphan Deal." What we had laughed about when all three of us were still alive wasn't a joke now. I pressed my arms to my side to stop the shivers and to blot the sweat I felt pearling down my flanks.

"No, Judy, that's not true," I replied, careful with my words. "Hugh and Mary picked Dave first, and then you picked me, because you felt sorry for me."

"No." She made a move for my hand, but I refused it. "No, Cary. Mom and Dad had picked you, but then I said that we had to take you both."

"That's just not true, Judy."

The challenge to her version of events was enough of an irritant that she could meet my face. "I was in junior high school, Cary, and more than capable of following an adult conversation. I had been listening to the social workers and the psychologists while we watched you on the other side of a one-way mirror. You and Dave were sharing your toys, your blocks or whatever, and my ears pricked up when a nurse—"

"There couldn't have been any nurses in the room," I said.

"Well fuck me, Cary, *I* thought she was a nurse—"

"Okay, okay."

"Whatever the woman was, she used a term that has always stuck with me."

I couldn't make a sound. My tongue felt sheared off; I flapped my fingers to get her to name the term.

"It was 'failure to thrive.' She said, 'failure to thrive.' I've since learned that failure to thrive, medically speaking, has to do with weight loss in infants, but in your cases, they were using it metaphorically. Taking just one of you in would harm both of you."

"But...but..." Now I could just manage a whisper. "But I always thought...."

She leaned in and grabbed my hand. "I know. You always thought they wanted Dave more than they wanted you."

I felt even sicker. Now shy of *her* gaze, I looked at Dan-o, calmly painting his chin with green frosting, and listened to her say that their choosing Dave first was something I had needed to make up in my own head, a fantasy likely reinforced after Leigh Bailey took him away. I, Cary Dunkler, had been, in fact, the chosen one, if that was any help for me to know.

"Really?" I said, needing to hear it one more time.

"Really and truly."

"You were there."

"I was there, Cary."

Tears had been building in me for weeks, months, years. When I hadn't wept after Dave's death, I thought perhaps I couldn't cry. It took a moment to realize why my cheeks were wet, and hot, and why I was choking.

"Did Dave know?"

"He never asked," said Judy.

Of course not. He had just *assumed* first position. That was my brother Dave. When I had settled a bit, I said, through wet fingers and a headful of snot, "You know what else I made up?"

"Tell me." My crying had set her off. I hesitated. She squeezed my hand. "Please, please tell me."

I yanked out the thunderbolt—no, I yanked out the tiny speck of sand that had grown over time inside the shell of my hurt to the size of a cannonball. I yanked out my birthright and confessed everything.

"I made up the fantasy that my real mother is still working at Martha Van Rensselaer Hall. And she thinks about me every single day, regretting her decision." And then, for the final scrap of my confession, I lowered my head even further; I'd have put it through the table if possible. "And one day, she is going to come looking for me."

Now we both were crying, for all of our losses, while Dan-o painted on. Students nearby began clearing out or switching tables. Finally, the manager, Craig, came over with some napkins. We'd known each other for years.

"Cary? Are you okay? What's wrong?"

Craig probably thought I'd tested positive. Or had lost my whole family in a plane crash.

"They're going to burn the dragon," was all I could manage to say.

"Drrg-in," said Dan-o and clapped his hands.

————

We work with our wounds until they don't serve us anymore. I had not, in fact, lost my whole family in a plane crash, only Dave, and it was time to let him go. After Judy and I had dried up, or dried out, and Dan-o had been wiped down, I found I couldn't wait to get home to my Edgar, couldn't wait to tell him everything, couldn't wait to discover whether he would kick me out or take the take and keep me on. I was so frantic I screeched the tires on the turn into the driveway. I bolted up the walkway. Inside the door, I heard a Haydn symphony; I was fairly sure it was Haydn, and not Mozart, emanating from the den. (Hadyn is more rational, Edgar likes to say.) Ed wasn't dead. He was in there, sitting in front of his bookcase with two fingers of rye, waiting for our evening to begin. On the first landing of the front stairs, Hector had assumed the Sphinx pose. There would be a battle royal for kitty to referee before the three of us would be able to get our rest. A manila envelope from Macy's, large enough to hold a contract in triplicate for me to sign, or not, was lying on the piecrust candle stand in the hallway, next to our bowl of keys.

Acknowledgments

In addition to my dedicatees, Bob Moss and Kennie Pressman, I owe a debt to the following theater artists who, over the course of forty years, became my teachers, directors, scene partners, mentors, colleagues, and collaborators: Ross Haarstad, Lisa Peterson, Catherine Weidner, Michael Krass, Gordon Rogoff, Michael Mayer, Margaret Hunt, Des McAnuff, Stan Wojewodski, Jr., Eric Overmyer, Irene Lewis, Judy Dennis, Jim O'Quinn, Catherine Sheehy, Jill Rachel Morris, Susan Birkenhead, Charlotte Stoudt, Lillian Groag, David Schweizer, Kathy Shapiro, Mark Bly, and Danny Scheie, as well as the late David Bucknam, Richard Gilman, Leon Katz, Robert Blacker, Peter Culman, Margo Lion, Marion McClinton, Mark Rucker, and Tim Vasen.

I leaned on Cornell '82 classmates Deborah Geis, Ed Ku, David Weiß, Sam Wolfe, and Carla Zackson for all things Ithacan.

I give thanks once more to Baltimoreans Betsy Boyd, Elisabeth Dahl, Jane Delury, Kathy Flann, Christine Grillo, Elizabeth Hazen, and Marion Winik for their friendship and their narrative input.

Residencies at MacDowell and the Virginia Center for the Creative Arts were essential to the writing process. I am grateful to Richard Peabody for publishing Part One as "Shift Work" in *Gargoyle 64*.

A special shout-out to Gregg Shapiro for introducing me to Ian Henzel and Rattling Good Yarns Press. Ian's editorial lapidary was priceless. Among his many other gifts, he disabused me of the conviction that I had mastered comma usage. I feel equally blessed that Rhona Bitner permitted us to use one of her photographs, from her series, titled *Stage*, for my cover image.

Steering me through the best and the worst of times, onstage and off, is my husband, Steve Bolton.

About the Author
James Magruder

James Magruder is a fiction writer, playwright, and translator. His stories have appeared in *The Gettysburg Review, New England Review, The Idaho Review, Subtropics, StoryQuarterly, Arts & Letters, Third Coast, Prairie Schooner, Bloom, The Normal School, The Hopkins Review, Gargoyle,* **New Stories from the Midwest**, and elsewhere. He has published three books of fiction: **Sugarless**, a finalist for a Lambda Literary Award; the linked story collection, **Let Me See It**; and **Love Slaves of Helen Hadley Hall**.

His work for the stage includes the books for two Broadway musicals, **Triumph of Love** and **Head Over Heels**. His translations of Dickens, Marivaux, Molière, Dancourt, Lesage, Labiche, Gozzi, Giraudoux, and Hofmannsthal have been seen on stages across the country and in Germany and Japan. His **Three French Comedies** (Yale University Press) was named an "Outstanding Literary Translation" by the American Literary Translators Association (ALTA). Current projects include a commissioned chronicle of the first fifty years of Yale Repertory Theatre, titled **Serving the Play**.

He is a five-time MacDowell Fellow and a six-time recipient of an Individual Artist Award from the Maryland State Arts Council. His writing has also been supported by the Virginia Center for the Creative Arts, the Hermitage, the New Harmony Project, the Ucross Foundation, the Blue Mountain Center, the Jerome Foundation, the Albee Colony, the Kenyon Playwrights Conference, and the 2010 Sewanee Writers' Conference, where he was a Walter E. Dakin Fellow in Fiction. He has made Baltimore his home for almost thirty years and currently teaches dramaturgy at Swarthmore College.

CPSIA information can be obtained
at www.ICGtesting.com
Printed in the USA
LVHW031648061221
705420LV00004B/530